PLUM & JAGGERS

SUSAN RICHARDS SHREVE

PLUM & JAGGERS

FARRAR, STRAUS AND GIROUX

NEW YORK

Farrar, Straus and Giroux
19 Union Square West, New York 10003

Copyright © 2000 by Susan Richards Shreve
Distributed in Canada by Douglas & McIntyre Ltd.
Printed in the United States of America
Designed by Abby Kagan
First edition, 2000

Library of Congress Cataloging-in-Publication Data
Shreve, Susan Richards.
    Plum & jaggers : a novel / Susan Richards Shreve. — 1st ed.
        p.   cm.
    ISBN 0-374-23462-0 (alk. paper)
        I. Title: Plum and jaggers.   II. Title.
PS3569.H74 P58 2000
813'.54—dc21   99-047619

THIS BOOK IS FOR

PO,

ELIZABETH,

RUSSELL,

CALEB,

KATE,

AND ON AND ON

ALWAYS FOR

TIMOTHY

I

1

SAM MCWILLIAMS WAS THE ONLY MEMBER of Plum
& Jaggers who remembered the afternoon of June 11
when the first two cars of the Espresso from Milan to
Rome exploded, killing everyone on board except for a four-year-old
French boy and a conductor. Sam remembered exactly. He was seven
years old, eight in November. Julia was too young for memory, sleeping in Sam's arms, where their mother had put her when she left.

"You take Julia, shoofly, and I'll go help your father get lunch."

"I would like tea," Charlotte said, looking up from her book. "And
four cookies."

"I'd like a chocolate milk shake," Oliver had said.

"There are no chocolate milk shakes in Italy," their father said.

"I want one anyway," Oliver said pleasantly.

"Then I'll bring one," their father said.

Had he returned with a late lunch, he might have brought tea
instead, or milk, or mineral water.

"Here's your chocolate milk shake, Oliver," he would have said.

THE EXPLOSION blew the door off the car where the McWilliams
children were sitting, waking Julia, who screamed so long without a
breath that Sam was afraid the air had gone out of her for good. Char-

lotte fell immediately asleep, a habit she would retain in emergencies for the rest of her life, and Oliver turned upside down and crawled under the seat, staying there until a woman seated across from them pulled him out, hurrying the McWilliamses to safety outside the burning train before the rescue team swarmed into the remaining cars and got out those passengers who had not already fled.

The weather had been cool for June, a soft, pale, constant sun, not bright enough to warm the small corner of the globe where the McWilliams family were traveling "into history," as James McWilliams had told his children.

"We're taking a trip into history, gang," he had said when they got on the train to Rome. "We've got to find out what happened before we arrived in this marvelous place."

James talked that way, in grand terms, connecting them personally to the world in all its past configurations, as if their voyage were maiden, like Lindbergh's across the Atlantic, an international event.

The McWilliamses were traveling from Kibbutz Gatz near Ashkelon, where for two years they had worked in the kitchen, in the fields, in the health clinic, for "the joy of it," as Lucy McWilliams had said. For the joy of it. Going by bus to Jerusalem, to Tel Aviv, over land and sea to Athens and then north to Milan, where they stopped for a few hours between trains just to see Leonardo's *Last Supper*, the faded fresco flaking tempera off the one remaining wall of the monastery refectory of Santa Maria delle Grazie, destroyed by a bomb during the German occupation in 1943.

"When the walls of the refectory crumpled, this painting survived," James told his children, reading from the dog-eared guidebook Lucy carried in her backpack, his voice memorable for the fullness of emotion, the pleasure he had in detail, the sound of it lifting their lives out of the ordinary.

"I can't see the picture," Charlotte had whispered to Sam.

"Don't worry," Sam had said. "There's nothing to see. It's only Jesus standing up."

———

YEARS LATER, remembering June 11 as if the events of that day were in the process of happening again and again, Sam thought of his parents, sitting in the dark remains of the refectory, their children locked between them, their eyes squinting in the dim light to focus on the fresco. They must have believed in *The Last Supper*, its survival a kind of personal sign of their own invincibility.

THE YEAR WAS 1974, the summer Richard Nixon resigned, the year Karen Silkwood died in a mysterious car accident after charging her employer Kerr McGee's plutonium-producing plant with atomic safety hazards, the year the small terrorist Symbionese Liberation Army kidnapped Patty Hearst.

But the McWilliamses were citizens of the world, their lives unaffected by events in America. They were optimistic travelers with plans to fill the map of the globe with red dots and lines connecting all the places they had been and worked and lived.

Not without risk. They had been in Munich in Black September, 1972, when Palestinian terrorists attacked Israeli athletes at the Olympics, taking nine hostages and killing two. They had been in Botswana, working with the American Red Cross, and were among the white people to shelter the Zimbabwe People's Union forces when they began cross-border guerrilla attacks from bases in neighboring countries. And they had been traveling in the Middle East when the Six Day War broke out in June 1967 and Israeli forces waged an air and ground attack on Egypt. They believed that they understood danger and could protect themselves from it.

James McWilliams had been born in Edinburgh in 1939, the youngest son of elderly parents, both dead by the time he was eighteen, when he moved to the United States to attend the Rhode Island School of Design. He was a landscape painter whose interest was shorelines—strange drawings of accurate, almost microscopic detail, close-ups of the point at which the sea meets the shore, of rivers and oceans and creeks and lakes, of the fluid, changeable line where the land gives way to water.

When he met Lucy Lucas, she was in her senior year at Pembroke College, with plans to attend Georgetown University Medical School in the fall. But she changed her mind and they married in June 1961, the week after she graduated from Pembroke, her medical career abandoned as she followed James to India, where he'd been selected as a member of the first class of Peace Corps volunteers. In India, they settled in Bombay, Lucy working with a group of Indian women to encourage birth control, while James built latrines in a village north of the city.

Their lives in those years were similar to those of the first veterans of the army for peace, who had endured tenures in the desolate villages of Africa or India or Latin America. They were travelers. After Bombay, they became teachers, moving to Botswana, then Cairo, Athens, Jerusalem, and Ashkelon. In the early sixties, travel was cheap and safe. Young Americans like the McWilliamses had a feeling of invulnerability, of certainty and hope. With their expanding troop—Samuel was born in 1966, Charlotte in 1968, Oliver in 1970, and Julia in 1973—they could do anything, go anywhere, chiefs of their own small tribe.

THEY GOT ON THE TRAIN in Milan at noon. Sam remembered the hour because his father wanted to get to Rome in time to show his children the Forum at dusk, to be there that June night because the moon would be full.

And so, late for the noon train, they ran through the wide marble hall of the Stazione Centrale, through the crowds of Italians milling around the kiosks, hurrying to their trains, chattering in their noisy, argumentative way.

Sam gripped Oliver's hand, Oliver squealing with the excitement of the run, Charlotte, sweet serious Charlotte, her spectacles filling her tiny face, complaining, "Not so fast, Mama, not so fast for me," and Julia flopping in the carrier on her mother's back.

"Let's fly," James called behind him.

"We are flying," Sam said, bringing up the rear.

He saw his father, flushed, his black hair in all directions, leap on the stairs of the train, put out his hand to Lucy, pulling her onto the step with him, kissing her cheek in his expansive way, kissing Julia's head. He picked Charlotte up in his arms and reached out for Sam.

"Wait for my boys, conductor," he called to no one in particular, no one who spoke English; only his boys could understand, only Sam and Oliver, reaching out their hands to their father, landing on the step just as the Espresso to Rome pulled out.

ON THE TRAIN, the McWilliams family sat three across, facing each other, Sam next to his father. The noon sun washed the landscape white, light separated from light; the scattered villages streaking by the window didn't seem real.

Across the aisle from them, a woman alone, dressed in a heavy coat and woolen hat, too warm for a cool June, her hands folded in her lap, stared at Sam unapologetically. She wasn't old, her hair still ink black and full, but there was something in her bearing that seemed old, and Sam didn't like her looking at him.

"She's not looking at you, son," his father said.

"She is," Sam said.

"She can't see you," his father said. "She can't see."

"Then why is she staring?" Sam asked.

"She's following her ears," his father said. "That's what you do if you can't see."

THEY MUST HAVE BEEN SLEEPING, waking shortly before the train arrived at the station in Orvieto, and then Oliver wanted lunch.

"Now," he said. "Maybe now."

Charlotte looked up from her book.

"I'm hungry also," she said. "We stayed so long at that supper painting, I got starved."

Charlotte was unworldly by temperament, and shy. She had learned to read early and could read anything, even books in Italian, as pleased by the music of language as by the sense of it, sounding out the words although she didn't understand their meaning.

She was the only one of them who'd picked up the languages in the places where they'd been. Although she wasn't a talker, her ear for sound was so exact she couldn't help herself.

"How come you can't speak Hebrew?" she had asked her mother as they were packing to leave the kibbutz.

"I don't know, darling," Lucy had said. "I suppose I'm too American."

"But how can you be if we never live in America?" Sam had asked.

"Someday we'll live there." Lucy laughed. "When we're enough filled up with the world to go home."

Like Charlotte, Lucy Lucas had been bookish as a child, and literal-minded, with a kind of luminous optimism that drew people to her. She was the only child of adoring but abstracted parents, growing up with an unreasonable confidence in her own good fortune, an experience of life which came from reading. At twenty, when she met James McWilliams at a coffee house in Providence, she was still surprisingly childlike, but restless, urgent for something to happen, ready to fall in love.

"I DON'T THINK OF AMERICA AS HOME," Charlotte had said. "I think of us as home."

"Exactly," her father agreed.

James was a natural convert, suited by temperament to the bold irreverence and high spirits of his adopted country, taking on American manners and expressions as his own. He spoke no languages except English, but in his travels, he tried speaking everything, slogging enthusiastically through the syllables, heavy-footed but cheerful. People clapped him on the shoulder as he tried out "Hello, how are you? Two beers, please," in Turkish or Egyptian or Greek.

———

SAM DIDN'T WANT LUNCH. He felt a strange uneasiness that afternoon, or at least that's the way he remembered it.

"Nothing for me," he said, looking out the window.

In the distance, like a faded watercolor, washed in light, he saw a town appear on a hill or hanging from the sky, maybe a village, maybe a small city, he couldn't tell.

"We'll be right back with lunch," their father said.

And then they were gone—James and Lucy McWilliams— through the door of their second-class car on their way to the café two cars down.

FOR A LONG TIME Sam sat above the wreckage on a hillside, milling with people, a strange acrid smell floating by on the light puffs of wind.

He didn't look. He sat on the ground where the police had taken him, sat very straight, Julia on his lap, her damp face burrowed in his neck, Charlotte beside him. She had lost her glasses in the confusion and kept her eyes closed. Oliver sat behind, his arms wrapped around Sam's waist, his face pressed into his brother's shirt, so he didn't have to see the smoldering train.

No one in the crowd seemed to be speaking. Not the Italian people from the village filling the hill below them, nor the police, nor the medical technicians, nor the firemen, who moved quickly but in surprising silence. There was no sound at all from the cars of the train to Rome.

At one point, a very young policeman knelt down and took Sam's hand.

"Passaporto?" he asked.

Sam shook his head.

"Mama?" the policeman asked. "Papa?"

"Questi bambini non hanno il passaporto," he said, standing up.

Charlotte couldn't speak Italian, but she said something in Hebrew which the policeman didn't understand. He motioned for another policeman.

"Niente passaporto," he said to the other officer, lifting his hands in a gesture of bewilderment.

"Niente passaporto?" The other officer shook his head.

LATER, medics ran up the hill with their canvas bags of supplies and took the children's pulses, holding their wrists, checking their watches.

"Am I going to die?" Charlotte asked in a flat, matter-of-fact voice.

"Die?" the nurse asked.

"Americani?" the other asked.

"Yes," Charlotte said. "American."

The nurse turned toward the medics just below, breaking the silence with her high-pitched voice.

"Americani," she called, pointing at the children. "Bambini americani."

And the circle of space around the McWilliams children seemed to expand, isolating them to a small unoccupied territory on the hill overlooking the train, the valley of silent confusion below them. In waking nightmares, that is the way Sam would remember it.

Years later, grown up, he saw a picture of children from Sarajevo. They sat, three of them about the same age, one girl, two boys, on a cement piling, bodies stiff, eyes wide with terror and something else, something ancient, like defeat. And suddenly Sam saw the four of them on a hillside near Orvieto, the McWilliams children, locked together like the shapes of a twisted trick puzzle, inextricable, bone-still, their eyes fixed on death.

A WOMAN the size of a plump child came running and took Sam by the hand.

"You come home with me," she said.

"No, I can't," Sam said. His legs didn't hold, folding to the ground beneath him.

"Daniele!" she called. "Daniele Danesi; aiuto!"

A man had rushed toward him, lifting Sam in his arms, holding his head against his large chest so Sam didn't have to look at the wreckage as they passed by it.

"I am Daniele, the father," he said.

The small, plump woman picked Julia up, held the baby like laundry over her shoulder.

Someone, an older child, or maybe two of them, took Charlotte and Oliver. Sam could hear them babbling, could hear Charlotte's soft voice saying, "I don't want to leave here."

"Me, too," Oliver said.

"We are going only a little way," one of the children said.

"I am Susanna. Mamma," the small woman said, breathless with the weight of Julia. "I take care."

THE HOUSE WAS SMALL and clean with a pale blue picture of the Virgin Mary on the wall and a wooden cross with Jesus, his head hanging, his arms outstretched, white walls and dark wooden furniture. The main room where the McWilliamses were taken was full of children, maybe six or seven of them, with black hair and soft hands, scrambling like puppies over the McWilliamses, patting them with their hands.

The mamma bounced Julia on the shelf of her belly, singing at full volume, filling the room with the sound of her voice, kissing the top of Julia's head, spinning her around the kitchen in a little dance, as if this were a perfectly normal afternoon.

A young boy called Gió sat next to Sam, pressed close, laying his small hand on Sam's arm. Anesthetized, Sam watched his family, held them in his vision so they wouldn't disappear.

Sam's hands and feet were numb and weighted, and he'd lost a sense of time, the day permanently locked in the moment when the café car of the train to Rome had exploded.

But sometime during the day, while he was sitting on the couch with Gió, where he stayed for a long time, his legs outstretched, his arms too heavy to lift, the afternoon gave way to a darkness which fell through the slender windows in strips of silver across his lap and Sam had a sudden fear of night, of the blackness coming on.

AT DUSK, the candles were lit on the wooden table set with mustard-yellow plates and tiny glasses, bottles of red wine and water, the room musty with the wet smells of fresh basil and thyme.

"I'm not very hungry," Charlotte said.

The mamma picked her up, tore a little piece of bread off the large loaf in the center of the table, and put it in her mouth.

"Mangia, mangia," she said, and sat Charlotte down at the long table between Daniele and Gió.

The McWilliamses couldn't eat the pasta with rich red sauce; the small house was thick with the sharp tomato smell of it, the dank odor of oregano. But they were given a thimbleful of red wine and Sam had a second cup. And then a third, until his head was woozy.

Sam must have fallen asleep.

Sometime in the middle of the night, he woke up to the sound of screaming so high-pitched it made his head hurt, and he sat up to see if it was Charlotte he heard, lying beside him with her eyes wide open.

"It's not me," she said.

He heard the rushing of footsteps then, saw the faces of the Danesi children in the bright pure light of a full moon, leaning over him, their hands on his shoulders, on his head, taking his hands, and he knew from the expression of alarm on their faces that he was the one screaming.

At first Susanna held him, but he couldn't seem to stop, one scream after the other bursting out of him like gunshot coming from his stomach. And then he was aware of lying down, aware of Susanna on top of him, stretched the length of his body so he couldn't move. He felt her warm breath on his neck, the weight of her on top of him, marking the edges so his insides didn't seep away, spill out onto the mattress, evaporate.

Finally, he stopped.

"YOU SCREAMED in your sleep," Charlotte said.

"I know."

"It made me scared," Oliver said. "I thought you were going to die."

"Well, I didn't," Sam said.

"I can tell you didn't," Oliver said, putting his head on Charlotte's shoulder. "I'm not stupid."

GIÓ CAME INTO THE McWILLIAMSES' ROOM early in the morning and stood at the end of the bed.

"A man wants you," he said to Sam. He pointed to the kitchen.

"Me?" Sam asked, sitting up in bed.

Gió spread his hand across the bed. "All children," he said, pleased with his English. "One, two, three, four children. Listen."

Sam listened.

The man was speaking in Italian, but Sam heard him say his own name, "McWilliams," heard it twice. The second time the man said, "Samuel McWilliams."

"Pretend to be asleep," he said to Charlotte and Oliver, closing his eyes, trying to breathe very little, to pass unnoticed by this man who had come to this house knowing his name.

Gió said that the man in the kitchen had come for them.

"We don't know any man in Italy," Sam said.

"He is American," Gió said.

"We won't go anyplace with a stranger," Sam said. "It's our rule."

"You don't have to go. Mamma told the man you cannot go until you have a bath."

"Will the man go away then?" Charlotte asked.

"He says he waits," Gió said.

Even Julia took a bath, all four of them in the warm, sudsy water up to their chins, their heads scrubbed with Susanna's strong hands. She had them stand in the middle of the tub and poured clear water over them, one pail after the next, and Sam wished they could stand there forever with her singing and the warm water falling over them, together in the bath in a small room with a blue Virgin Mary on the wall, in a cottage in Italy.

THE MAN, Mr. Blake—he called himself Mr.—was very tall and thin, with a blond mustache and fuzzy soft blond hair like a girl's. As representative of the American consulate, he had come to take them to Florence.

"Your grandfather is coming," he said cheerfully, as if they had simply been on an overnight with strangers.

"I won't go with you," Charlotte said.

"We have to go," Sam said. "We have to meet Grandfather."

THE DANESI CHILDREN gathered solemnly at the door to the cottage and watched as their mother walked with the McWilliamses along the path to the car.

Sam walked first and alone, walking into the sun so the car appeared as a splash of glittering aluminum foil and Sam had to narrow his eyes to reduce the sun's assault. Behind him, Sam could feel their presence, Charlotte walked alone and Susanna carried Julia, holding Oliver's hand. At the car he stood aside while Charlotte climbed into the backseat, taking Julia in her arms, and Oliver scrambled after them.

Just as Sam was getting in, Susanna snapped the stem of a purple wildflower and put the flower in the pocket of his shorts.

"Goodbye, goodbye." She kissed his hand.

SITTING IN THE BACKSEAT of Mr. Blake's long American car, Sam noticed that Gió had gone on ahead to the end of the dirt road to see them leave. He stood in a bright circle of sun, in a field of yellow wildflowers, nearly as high as he was, his arms folded across his chest. As the car drove past, he covered his eyes with both hands so Sam couldn't see his face.

THEIR GRANDFATHER HAD COME to Italy alone. Their grandmother didn't fly.

William Lucas was sixty that year, a tall, white-haired, dignified man. He was an artist of sorts, drawing birds and parts of the body, usually diseased parts for medical journals. A quiet, formal man, not given to expressions of emotion, surely not grief.

At the airport in Florence, Charlotte announced that she wasn't going to leave Italy.

"I don't fly," she said to her grandfather.

"I don't fly either," Oliver said.

"But we flew from Greece," Sam had said to her.

"I wasn't on the plane from Greece," Charlotte said.

They were all on the plane, of course. Israel to Athens by ship and bus and car, and then from Athens by plane to Milan to see *The Last Supper* before they traveled south.

But Sam didn't argue.

THEIR GRANDFATHER HAD SAT, his legs crossed neatly, the *International Herald Tribune* with the news about the terrorist bombing of the train folded on his lap. He checked his watch.

"They should call our flight in fifteen minutes," he said, as if he had missed hearing Charlotte's announcement.

The McWilliamses didn't know their grandfather well. The year Sam was three, Charlotte almost two, their parents had gotten teaching jobs in Athens, where they'd stayed two years; Oliver was born there.

And then they'd gone to teach in Jerusalem and then to work on the kibbutz. They had returned to Grand Rapids for a month in the middle of these years, and Sam had felt warmly about that visit—especially the evenings on his grandparents' front porch, the aunts and uncles and cousins chattering the silver night away, capturing lightning bugs in glass jars sticky with Popsicle juice.

But just before they left for Tel Aviv, there was a rare argument between his soft-tempered grandmother, who started the fight, and his mother.

"I don't know why you have to go to Jerusalem, Lucy," she'd said to his mother. "You aren't Jewish."

"It has nothing to do with being Jewish," Lucy said. "Many people go who aren't Jewish."

"I read in the paper about a bus which blew up, killing several people," his grandmother had said wearily. "You haven't given any thought to violence, I suppose."

"There's no safety anyplace," his father had said.

But James McWilliams—a tall, wiry, athletic man, black-haired, boyish, full of pleasure in his life—didn't act that way. He lived as if safety were everywhere he chose to walk.

"I don't know," his grandmother said. "I don't know at all."

"But they're going, darling," his grandfather said to his grandmother. "So we must wish them well."

ON THE PLANE to Tel Aviv, Sam had told his father he was afraid.

"There's nothing to be afraid about, Sam," his father had said. "This is an adventure, and then there'll be a new one and a new one. We're going to have a fine time."

The flight from Florence to Brussels left at 11:30 a.m., connecting in Brussells with a flight to New York.

Charlotte shook her head.

"I want to stay in this place," she said, as if it were a perfectly reasonable request, crazy that anyone should think otherwise.

"Me too," Oliver said.

Their grandfather, a man Sam would come to know as extraordinarily kind, took Charlotte's hand in his.

"We're not going to leave your parents in Italy," he said. "I've made arrangements for them to travel on the same plane."

Charlotte looked up at him.

"You're sure?" she asked.

"I'm sure," her grandfather said.

"Then I'll fly on this plane," Charlotte said decisively.

"Me too," Oliver said earnestly.

ON THE PLANE back to America, just as the tip of Nova Scotia came into view, Charlotte had looked up from her book.

"Sam?"

He'd been sitting with his eyes closed.

"Do you think we're going to die?" she asked.

He looked over at Oliver zipping his Matchbox cars across his belly.

"No," Sam said, giving the possibility a full measure of his consideration, weighing the odds, wishing to tell Charlotte the truth. "We're not going to die for a very long time."

AS THE PLANE DESCENDED along the coast of Massachusetts, across Connecticut, over the cluttered skyline of New York City, Sam McWilliams looked down the line of seats beyond the one where he was sitting: at Charlotte, reading her book; over the head of Julia, sleeping fitfully against her chest; at Oliver, clutching his shorts, unwilling to go to the lavatory for fear he'd fall through the airplane toilet into the sky.

"We'll stick together through thick and thin," his father used to say to them. "From now on forever," he'd add with his usual high-spirited drama as they went on trains and airplanes and buses and cars from Tel Aviv to Jerusalem to Cairo to Ankara to Istanbul to Athens to Milan.

And finally to Rome.

2

CHARLOTTE PUT HER BOOK DOWN and listened.

Downstairs, someone was knocking. She turned off the light beside her bed and looked out the window of their house on Morrison Street, but she couldn't see anything except a police car parked across the street without its lights.

The rented house where they had lived since they had arrived in Washington on Julia's fourth birthday was the only clapboard among a row of brick houses, white clapboard with plum-red shutters and a small front porch, an ordinary colonial built in the twenties, with four bedrooms and a study where their grandfather drew body parts, recently illustrations of diseased kidneys for a medical dictionary. There was a garage, a basement, an unfinished attic with pull-down stairs: 4616 Morrison Street, Northwest, Washington, D.C. The Lucas house, where the McWilliams children lived—remarkable in the neighborhood, as if it were a historical monument where children lived whose mother and father had been blown to smithereens in another country. Too much for ordinary children to comprehend.

"Four orphans live there," they'd whisper to one another as they passed the house, walking swiftly in case the condition were catching. "Their parents were bombed to death on a train," they'd say with a kind of dark pleasure. "That's the Lucas house, where the McWilliams children live," they'd say; a place of consequence.

THE REASON William Lucas gave for their move from the house on Sloan Street in Grand Rapids, where they had lived since James and Lucy were killed, was his work for the Smithsonian Institution. But he chose Washington for sentimental reasons, because it was the city where Lucy had been planning to move for medical school when James was accepted into the Peace Corps and she had followed him to Bombay. William liked to think that by moving to Washington, a place neither he nor Nicole, his wife—he called her Noli—knew, but would have known had Lucy gone to Georgetown Medical School, they could begin again, weave a different future for Lucy's children, take hold of that moment when her life hung in the balance—a small turn, an incidental choice, nothing permanent without the possibility for revision, nothing final, her future fixed like the butterfly, its glorious wingspread pinned to a stiff white board.

In fact, William Lucas's real work was no longer drawing birds or body parts or perfect skeletons but raising his daughter's children, a life, as he chose to live it, out of another time, small-town America at the turn of the last century, when the country was isolationist and provincial. He had no television, for he was unable to bear its invasive unreality. He read no newspapers or periodicals, only books written before the First World War: Dickens, Henry James, Trollope, Edith Wharton. And he listened to classical music on an old console radio which he'd bought with his first paycheck after he and Noli were married.

He wasn't fond of the swampy city of Washington, its anonymity of formal architecture and love affair with the daily news. He longed for the water landscape of northern Michigan.

But in 1977, when the Lucases told their friends about William's work with the Smithsonian, put their house up for sale and their fur-

niture in storage, and gave away the collected memories of forty
years of marriage, they had, as they saw it, no choice.

The real reason they had left Grand Rapids was Sam.

"WHO'S THAT?" Julia asked from the slender mat on which she
slept, keeping it under Charlotte's bed, sleeping there so she could
see the slats and mattress above her, although Charlotte would have
been perfectly happy for Julia to be in the bed with her, in the twin
four-poster pine bed, her mother's bed when she was young. It
pleased Charlotte to sleep where her mother had slept. Lucy
Lucas's bed. Charlotte loved to say her mother's name, Lucy Lucas,
over and over again, before she went to sleep.

She couldn't exactly remember her mother.

"Of course you do," Sam had said. "You were five. People can
remember a lot from when they're five."

Charlotte shook her head. "I really don't remember her," she said
reasonably, sensitive to her brother's temper. "I remember the smell
of her shoulder like paper whites when I leaned up against her, and
her long hair brushing my face, but I don't remember her."

"You have to," Sam said. "You just have to."

Charlotte tried, filling her room with pictures, keeping a few of
her mother's clothes, covered in soft tissue like holy garments, in the
bottom of her closet, reading the letters and stories and school
papers her grandmother kept in boxes in a closet in the hall. In case
of fire, Noli said, they could be rescued quickly.

She was quiet, almost preternaturally calm—drawing people to
wade above their ankles in the still water of her company. Especially
Sam.

THE PSYCHIATRIST to whom William Lucas had taken Sam when
they returned from Italy in June 1974, taken him immediately,
knowing there would be terrible problems festering, recommended
daily sessions.

"He has no defense system," the psychiatrist said. "Like any child of trauma, he needs to develop the normal ability to differentiate between crisis and ordinary daily life."

"I'm not sure about that," William Lucas had said. "Sam's all defense system. Sometimes he goes days without speaking."

"That's the beginning of trouble," the psychiatrist said. "He could get much worse. He might harm himself," he added in a tone of self-congratulatory warning.

"It's not true what he says," Noli Lucas told her husband, sitting in the kitchen after supper as they did: Oliver doing the crossword on the floor so the cat could sit on the newspaper beside him, Charlotte reading, Julia sleeping in her grandmother's lap, Sam doing his homework, so he claimed, but he never did homework, busy with his own observations—he had notebooks full of them—or lists he wrote carefully in black pen on unlined paper.

"We'll cancel the psychiatrist," Noli said. "He's making Sam worse."

Noli Lucas didn't leave the house. For a while after her daughter died, she didn't even leave her bedroom. She sat in the chair by the window overlooking the garden.

"I have a little agoraphobia," she explained to her grandchildren. " 'Agora' is a Greek word which means marketplace. You know Greece."

Yes, they agreed. They knew Greece. They'd been there as young children, so Greece must be in their blood.

" 'Phobia' means fear," Noli said.

"So you're afraid of the marketplace," Sam said.

"I think I am," Noli said. "I may be wrong."

Yet her world wasn't defined by the geometry of a rosy chintz bedroom or an ordinary colonial house, but by the wide expanse of a whimsical mind, childlike in its capacity to imagine full stories extending like soap operas from daily conversations. She kept in touch with people by telephone, by mail, engaging even strangers in their personal stories. Never her story. She was too mercurial for that. Just at the moment a person was on the brink of a secret from

Noli, she would mysteriously slip aside, hiding out in someone else's life.

She had been a great beauty, a "stopper," William Lucas said of her. When they met at the University of Michigan, she took his breath away. That beauty was the woman he still saw when he looked at her, although she had grown fat, with breasts that hung to her belly, a round, doughy face, with a pile of thick gray hair she often wore loose like a girl's.

Her grandchildren loved her. Beyond love, she belonged to them. A living mother who never left the house to do good works or visit friends or travel by plane to foreign places. She was in the kitchen when they left in the morning, a whisper of little steps around the room, and still there when they came home in the evening, the house warm with the smell of baking. If they should happen to arrive with friends from school, she would put out oatmeal cookies, disappearing into her bedroom, a secret grandmother invisible except to them.

WHEN CHARLOTTE WENT into the upstairs hall to see who was knocking, Oliver was already lying facedown on the stairs, his feet in the second-floor hall, his belly on the steps so he could see the front door where his grandfather was speaking to a policeman.

"What has happened?" Charlotte asked.

"Trouble," Oliver whispered.

"Who's in trouble?" Charlotte asked.

Noli stood with Oliver in the hall in the flannel nightgown she always wore, winter and summer, with eyelets and faded red hearts, her hair down, her hands folded under her chin, smelling of sweet perfume, gardenia, her very favorite. She loved scents.

"Sh-sh," she said to Oliver. "I can't hear what's happening."

William Lucas came to the bottom of the stairs.

"I wonder if you could get Sam for me, darling," he called. "Darling" was not a name he used. Nicola or Noli or Moosh, but not darling. In his broad, formal Midwestern accent, his low, melancholy voice, his dedication to the sound of a word, holding it, like a musical note, the name "darling" had the weight of social order, spoken for the benefit of the policeman. No trouble in this house, Officer, it said.

"I can't get Sam," Noli Lucas called back. "You must have forgotten. He's spending the night with the Alexanders."

"Can we reach him?" William walked halfway up the steps. "There's been some difficulty."

"No, I'm awfully sorry," she said in the vacant, faraway voice she saved for trouble. "The Alexanders have taken him someplace in West Virginia where there isn't a telephone."

Behind Charlotte, the door to the last bedroom opened, the one which overlooked the back garden, the alley, the garage where the McWilliams children had their private office.

Sam stood in the darkness just beyond the door.

HE WAS TALL for fourteen, angular, with high cheekbones, a handsome older face, full lips, dark hair—fair skin—high color from his Scottish father. He had a way about him, a kind of swagger, that didn't show so much in his movement as in the manner he assumed. A surprising confidence—"arrogance" was the word his teachers used at school. But the quality had more to do with a view of the world as a place where life is always fragile, where danger can be final.

When he first came back from Italy, he had developed enuresis.

"It could mean deep sleep from which he has trouble waking or depression," the psychiatrist said, "or it might anticipate nascent sexual problems."

He refused to go to the boys' room at the public elementary school in Grand Rapids. Occasionally he would come home from school with a large circle of pee on his corduroys, and some mornings he'd wake up swimming in urine.

"I DON'T UNDERSTAND why his peers don't make fun of him," the psychiatrist said.

"They're afraid of him," William Lucas said.

But it wasn't exactly fear they felt. It had more to do with a feeling of awe—a sense that Sam McWilliams, on whom age seemed to descend in decades rather than years, could see straight to the center of a person's heart and soul. He had no reason to accommodate other people, very little need for friends. His small family was sufficient.

OLIVER GOT UP from the stairs, tiptoed across the floor, and stood next to Sam.

"The policeman said you stole something," he said.

Sam folded his arms across his chest.

"What did you steal?" Oliver leaned against his brother.

"What did the policeman say I stole?" Sam asked.

"I couldn't understand him."

LATER, the McWilliamses sat around the kitchen table with their grandparents, Noli making raisin bread for breakfast. It was almost midnight. The lights were out and they sat in candlelight in case the patrol car was circling the block.

"If they're looking, they'll be able to see us in candlelight as well, Noli," William Lucas said.

"I don't think so, William," she said.

She asked Sam to get under the kitchen table just in case, since he was supposed to be in West Virginia. But he refused.

"Do you have an alibi?" Oliver asked Sam.

"I don't know what I'm supposed to have done," Sam said.

"According to the police officer, you took two lengths of metal pipe and a Coleman flashlight from Hechinger's Hardware this afternoon," William Lucas said.

"I see," Sam said.

"Maybe he needed it," Julia said.

"Grandfather means I stole it," Sam said reasonably. "Whether I needed it or not is unimportant."

"That's right, Sam," William said, his temper growing.

Noli was sprinkling raisins over the flat, damp dough.

"I wish you weren't making bread, Nicole. It's the middle of the night. You'll be up till morning."

"We needed bread," Noli said pleasantly.

"It's fine, Grandfather," Charlotte said when, in a gesture of despair, her grandfather had sunk his head in his hands. "We are out of bread for breakfast."

William Lucas was satisfied with small things, his work in particular, immensely patient with details. But sometimes in the last years, especially after the trouble with Sam in Michigan, he thought he could go crazy. A man of his age with such responsibility. Something could happen. An accidental slip of the mind, a heart attack, a stroke, a loss of memory of who he was in the world—a minor artist, noted for the exactitude of his drawings, a certain lyricism in his use of color. He was almost seventy. Too old, he thought, too literal-minded and simple to be the guardian of Samuel McWilliams. He wasn't up to it.

He folded his hands, speaking without emotion.

"The officer knows you took these things from Hechinger's because you were seen by a girl in your class. He didn't make it up, Sam. The girl identified you by name." He leaned across the kitchen table. "And then the officer asked me a question I ask you now, because I don't know the answer. Why would a boy need an industrial-size flashlight and two lengths of pipe?"

"I don't know," Oliver said, answering quickly for his brother. "Maybe Sam does."

Sam rested his chin in his hands and looked at his grandfather directly. He didn't want his grandfather to know why he had stolen, but he wasn't afraid of being caught. Caught he was, although for the sake of his family, he didn't intend to tell the truth exactly. He was more curious than nervous, wishing to know what had been going on around him at Hechinger's while he took the flashlight and pipe, who had been looking when he dropped them in the black nylon case he carried, a bag large enough for schoolbooks and other things.

"I didn't steal anything today," Sam said truthfully. "I wasn't at

Hechinger's. I was at the library after school, so you can tell the policeman that when he comes back."

"He's not allowed back," Noli said. "This is a private home and you're in West Virginia."

"What if they come up with evidence?" William Lucas asked. "What if the girl is willing to step forward?"

"I'll say it's a case of mistaken identity," Sam said. "I don't want you to worry, Grandfather. I don't want you to have a bad time with me."

He meant that truly. Sam had genuine sympathy for his grandfather, his substitute father, not a role William Lucas had by choice, and he had done it well, refusing to bend under the weight of duty, refusing old age.

"But if you were to have been at Hechinger's," William Lucas began, turning to Sam. "Or let's say any boy stealing a Coleman flashlight and two lengths of pipe—why that? Why those items, of all things?"

"To make a bomb shelter," Sam said. "That would be my guess."

SAM HAD BEEN BUILDING A BOMB SHELTER under the garage for almost a year, working steadily and in secret. When his family thought he was at school or at a friend's house or playing basketball on the blacktop at Lafayette Elementary, he was actually digging a hole under the floor of the garage which in time would become the size of a room, large enough for the six of them to occupy in relative safety for several weeks. He had read extensively about bomb shelters in books he found in the local library after Mr. dePaul, his seventh-grade history teacher, had described the one his parents had built in their back yard in the fifties during the Cold War.

"My father did it himself," Mr. dePaul told Sam. "It wasn't difficult. It just took a shovel and a very long time."

THE FIRST THING Sam took from Hechinger's was a shovel. It was an expensive shovel, almost $35.00, four feet long, with a slightly pointed blade. He hid it under his grandfather's long yellow rain slicker and walked out of the store unobserved.

In time, he had needed other things that were not available among his grandfather's limited supply of tools—pipe to create a retaining wall and rope and wooden rungs to make a rope ladder from the ground level in the garage to the underground room.

His plan was simple. He used a basic design from one of the books he found in the library—*Bomb Shelters for the Ordinary American Family*—a ten-foot-deep passageway into a nine by twelve by seven–foot room. By the time he was caught shoplifting, he had finished only the passageway, large enough for a grown man to climb down the rope ladder without getting stuck. In the plans, there was room for six cots, stacked like bunk beds, three across, a trunk for dried food and water, shelves for the boxes of his parents' letters, his father's paintings, their photographs, a few other personal possessions.

When he'd studied ancient Egypt in elementary school, Sam had been drawn to the Egyptian ceremony for the burial of their dead. He was particularly struck with the great care taken by the living, the gathering of treasured possessions, even beloved pets, to travel with the dead to another world, which seemed as agreeable, at least in concept, as the one they had left behind. He began to imagine the bomb shelter as a place of safety for all his family, living and dead.

The work was slow, days of shoveling, of carrying dirt from the expanding tunnel out the back door of the garage into the alley, distributing it in various back yards. He planned to be finished by spring, maybe late April or early May. Then he'd make a ceremony of it. Take his family into the garage, lift the wooden door he'd built to cover the hole, point his flashlight into the tunnel.

"There," he'd say, watching them climb down the rope ladder into the new room. "I've made a shelter for us."

CHARLOTTE LAY UNDER THE COVERS listening for the policeman to come back, listening to her grandmother padding around the kitchen in her soft slippers, making bread in the middle of the night.

"Charlotte?" Julia whispered from under the bed. "Do you think Sam stole?"

"I don't know," Charlotte said. "I haven't thought about it."

But she did know.

Out of the dream corner of her eye, she saw Sam walking up Nebraska Avenue from Alice Deal Junior High, a figure in faded jeans and black jacket, the nylon bag he carried everywhere slung over his shoulder, headed toward Wisconsin Avenue with a plan.

She saw him in Hechinger's Hardware, not bothering to notice if a girl from his ninth-grade class or a clerk or a manager was watching him unzip his bag and drop the pipes and flashlight in. And the girl, following him to Hechinger's with a group of other girls who had crushes on Sam, lurking behind the display cases, watching him from an aisle away, would be the one to turn him in. Such was the perversity of romance.

"A boy in my class has shoplifted," she would say to the manager. "His name is Sam McWilliams and he lives on Morrison Street."

But by then, Sam would have dropped underground with his booty, into the metro at Tenleytown.

"SAM?" His grandfather had followed him upstairs and was standing in the doorway to his room. "Why didn't you ask me for money if there was something you needed?"

"I should have," Sam said. "I'm very sorry, Grandfather." But he couldn't explain why it was that he didn't ask his grandfather to pay for a bomb shelter. The subject of his parents' deaths never came up with his grandparents. Instinctively the children knew that they could speak of James and Lucy living but they should avoid mentioning their deaths. The reason Sam hadn't asked his grandfather for money was kindness, or such was his thinking. A bomb shelter would suggest the bomb in Orvieto, and so he decided, without remorse, to take what he needed from Hechinger's, because he needed it very much. Sam's code of ethics—and he had one—was simple. He did what was necessary to protect his family. Stealing didn't figure as a breach of principle.

WILLIAM LUCAS SAT ON THE END OF HIS BED in his undershorts and slippers, staring across the room at nothing, at the table full of bottles of perfume, which Noli collected, and kaleidoscopes, which she also collected, and rings, at the mirror over the dresser, which reflected their heavy oak bed, dark as a casket in the mirror.

He listened.

Sam was leaning in the door talking to Oliver in that language they had together, a kind of gibberish. He heard Charlotte and Julia mumbling back and forth and Noli on the stairs bringing him hot milk, which he didn't want, never wanted, but she brought it anyway, insisting it would make him sleep.

"He didn't do it, William," Noli said, walking into the bedroom with his mug of hot milk. "I know you think he did, but it's not possible."

"Of course he did," William said. "He was seen."

"By an unreliable girl," Noli said, putting her soft, fleshy arm around her husband's shoulder, her cheek against his cheek. "Don't worry, William."

"I suppose if he's in jail, we'll have less to worry about," William said. "We'll know where he is."

"He's normal, William," Noli said. "Maybe he's more sensitive and suspicious than other fourteen-year-olds, but he's a perfectly normal boy, I promise."

WILLIAM LUCAS COULDN'T SLEEP. Every time he closed his eyes he heard the policeman stop in front of the house, and then he'd get up to look out the window at the black night. Once, he thought he heard someone in the kitchen and went to the head of the stairs, but it was only Noli.

"You don't seem to be sleeping," Noli said, padding into the bedroom after 3 a.m., smelling of hot bread.

"Bad dreams," he said.

She climbed into bed, pushed up against him, a shift in the blankets, a whiff of gardenia. She reached down and took his hand.

"I wish Sam didn't make lists," she said. "He's sitting up in bed doing one now. All these categories of this and that. It's not a family trait from my side. List making." She turned toward William, closing her eyes, lying on her side.

"Did you hear what Sam said about a bomb shelter?" William asked.

"No, I didn't," Noli said sleepily, and just in case William had plans to repeat the conversation, she added, "I don't want to talk tonight. Let's go to sleep quickly."

SAM SAT propped up in his bed, a long-necked lamp pulled half over his lap, shining in a yellow circle on a notebook page with a list of names he was recopying from old file cards scattered in piles on his bed.

Saul Frankel, age 37, and his son Amos, age 7. Killed October 13, 1977, in a bomb explosion at a grammar school in West Jerusalem.

Mavis O'Leary. Age 19. Killed on December 14, 1977, in Belfast in an explosion at the West End Public Library.

Marshall Felder. Age 47. Killed June 18, 1978, in the Rome International Airport in a bomb explosion.

Sara Ross. Age 7, daughter of Henry and Rebekkah Ross. Killed in the Rome International Airport.

From time to time, he listened for the policeman. Twice he thought he heard someone trying to get into the garage, which was kept locked, but when he got out of bed, turned off his light, and looked, no one was there, unless it was a raccoon he had heard scrambling in the garbage. In the front room, he could hear his grandfather tossing and turning, his grandmother speaking above a whisper. He heard her talking about his lists.

Sam collected stories of terrorists from newspapers and magazines, listing the names of victims and their families on file cards, smudged and dog-eared from reading over at night when he couldn't go to sleep.

He had started the collection one spring when he was ten and they were still living in Grand Rapids. In the afternoon, he used to go to Blazer's Drugstore to read the daily paper, since the bad news of the world wasn't permitted inside the Lucas house. He would settle on the floor beside the stacks of magazines, eating a Clark bar and reading. Charlotte would meet him after her dance class, picking up Oliver on the way, and they'd all walk home together.

ONE PARTICULAR AFTERNOON when he was ten—he had the date in his notebook—October 13, 1977—a news story caught his eye and took his breath away: front page, top of the fold.

American father and child die in school bombing in West Jerusalem.

According to the news story, the family was from Erie, Pennsylvania, working in Israel for two years. The father, a visiting professor of Jewish Studies at Hebrew University, was picking his son up at school, while the mother remained at their apartment in West Jerusalem with their baby girl. Saul and Rebecca Frankel and their children. Amos was seven, Sam's age on June 11, 1974. He tore the article out of the paper and stuffed it in his pocket.

When Charlotte arrived at the drugstore with her dance bag and library book and Oliver, Sam was sitting on the floor beside the stack of newspapers, looking off into the middle distance.

"I guess you're sick?" Charlotte said in that motherly way she had, placing her hand on his forehead.

"I'm fine," Sam replied. But when he stood up, his legs were weightless, cut off at the knee. "Maybe I am a little sick," he said.

"Don't throw up in the drugstore," Oliver said.

"I never throw up," Sam said.

The walk home was endless. He had the sense of moving through waist-high mud, of disassociation, as if his head, filled with helium, was floating just above his reach, as if he were passing into a war zone right there on Maple Street under a canopy of cherry trees in full bloom.

ONCE HOME, he went to his room, took out the newspaper article, his composition book, and wrote a letter.

Dear Rebecca Frankel,
I am writing to express my grief to you and your baby for the
terrible deaths of your husband and son, Amos. I read about you
in the Grand Rapids paper today after school. I want you to know
that on June 11, 1974, my brother and sisters and I were on our
way to Rome with our parents when the lunch car where our
parents were buying us lunch exploded.
So I understand how you feel.
> *Your friend,*
> *Samuel Lucas McWilliams. Age 10*

He called the Grand Rapids newspaper for the address of Rebecca Frankel, and they gave him an address for her mother in Erie, Pennsylvania, and he sent the letter to her.

IT WAS MONTHS before Sam heard back, and in the meantime, Matthew Gray, recovering at the hospital from a ruptured spleen, had made his accusations about Sam, and the Lucases were packing up to move to Washington.

The letter from Rebecca Frankel came in June, the day the Mayflower moving van arrived.

Dear Samuel,

Thank you for the kindness of your letter. My life will never be the same, of course, and neither will yours. An act of God is one thing. An act of man another, and leaves a person blacker in his heart than he ought to be to survive this world of changing seasons.

They have caught the two young men responsible for the bomb that killed my husband and son, and they will die for it. But that isn't sufficient.

In the mornings after I have tried to sleep with very little success, I go into my baby Miriam's room and she is lying on her back, thinking maybe, maybe not, and laughing, laughing, laughing, as if there is something on the ceiling entertaining her. It helps that I have this baby who thinks something is funny.

I go into the kitchen and warm her milk, make her oatmeal, add a little brown sugar, which she loves, lightened by the sound of laughter in the next room.

I have told you this story about Miriam in the hope that it will matter to you later as you grow up.

I send my best wishes to you and to your brother and your sisters.

Your friend,
Rebecca Frankel

Sam kept the letter with the news article. He didn't exactly understand what Rebecca Frankel had written about her laughing baby daughter, but he sensed the spirit in which it was said and the kindness of it. And he understood that what she had written about laughter was in particular addressed to him.

He didn't write her back, but her letter turned him to a different, secret task. He began to read every newspaper he could find, daily, in search of victims.

AFTER WILLIAM and Noli had fallen asleep and Sam had finished updating his terrorist file, he set the alarm for 5 a.m., slid the clock under his pillow so it wouldn't wake his grandparents, closed his notebook with the names of the dead, and turned out the light.

When the alarm rang just before dawn, he was already awake. Perhaps he had not even fallen asleep. He couldn't tell.

He dressed for school—which he had in mind to skip, one skip a week, he figured. He wore everything but his shoes, which he carried so no one could hear him. In the hall, he stood for a moment undecided whether to wake Charlotte or Oliver. But Oliver was already awake, lying on his stomach reading comics with a flashlight.

"I was waiting in case the police came back," Oliver whispered. "What are you doing up?"

"Get dressed and meet me in the office," Sam said.

"Now?" Oliver asked.

"Now," Sam said. "Before it gets light."

Sam had an eye for the look of things. The garage was done up, decorated, given the sense that someone, not a young boy certainly, had paid attention to the room. There were windows on three sides of the rectangular structure, built for the narrow cars of the twenties, two windows facing the house, one the alley, and a door which opened to the garden. Six of James McWilliams's paintings—rugged Scottish shorelines of his childhood, the water more black than blue, the land scrubby with low brush and large rocks down to the edge of the sea—were hung next to windows as if they had been conceived with windows in mind, so the changing light of day glanced across their surface, altering the rich color as the earth moved around the sun.

The room was sort of Middle Eastern, with bright, worn rugs and soft, muted Indian cloth covering the old furniture: a couch, an overstuffed chair, a large desk in the center made from an ancient door. Sam's office. It was the place where he wrote his lists and read his parents' letters home, which had been written during their travels, as recent as the week before they died.

In the afternoons, the McWilliams children worked in the office. Work is what they called it, and since Charlotte and Oliver did well in school and Julia well enough, their grandparents assumed that the work was schoolwork. It didn't matter. The place was theirs and it was entirely satisfactory for Noli and William to know that the children were out back, in view of the kitchen window, whatever they might be doing.

"WHAT'S GOING ON?" Oliver asked, slipping in the door to the office, where Sam was already busy in the corner of the room, working by the light of a candle, since it was still too dark outside to see.

"I'm making a bomb shelter," Sam said, reading the book of instructions by candlelight. Beside him the flashlight and lengths of pipe lay on the rug. "I wasn't going to tell you until it was finished."

Oliver folded his arms across his chest. He was small for his age and blond like his mother, ruddy-complexioned, long-legged, so he might grow, although the pediatrician had predicted a 5' 8" cap of height, quite a lot smaller than Sam. He and Sam fought about it, as if height were a matter within their control.

Noli called Oliver "Chief Deep Water," and at home, he was thoughtful and interior, similar in presence to Charlotte but with a turn of mind more philosophical, given to broad statements about mortality and life and God, whether His nature was benevolent or angry, whether He existed, whether He ate meals and slept at night and had conversations with other people in heaven. These pronouncements, uttered in a surprising bass voice, methodically and in full sentences, were funny and heartbreaking from a young boy with blond hair and bright cheeks. At home, he was the source of dinnertable laughter. School was another story. Gong, he was affectionately called, for his sonorous voice. He was popular, the first one picked when teams were chosen, president of the class, the spokesman, not too verbal or too intellectual or too sensitive to be a regular boy, right in the center of the pack. In fact, the pack itself. "Good" was written across his fifth-grade report card. Adaptable, Considerate, Responsible, Cooperative. The only hint of "Chief Deep Water" at school was with the girls, especially older girls, whom he loved deeply, to whom he confessed the inner workings of his heart, to whom he promised, each in her turn, lasting devotion and fidelity.

OLIVER SAT down on the couch.

"So you did take those things from Hechinger's," he said.

"I did," Sam said.

"You stole them?"

"It wasn't exactly stealing," Sam said. "I'm going to pay for them."

"You won't be arrested, will you?"

"I won't," Sam said.

Oliver walked over to the window facing the alley and looked out for the police car.

"How come we need a bomb shelter?" he asked quietly.

"Just in case," Sam said.

"In case of what?" Oliver asked.

"Of an emergency," Sam said. "Would you like to see it?"

He moved the table off the rug and pulled the rug back, exposing a square of plywood, which he lifted, then handed Oliver the stolen flashlight.

"Look down there," he said. "Or you can climb down the ladder. The pipes are for support so the dirt doesn't collapse on us."

Oliver leaned over the opening, pointing the flashlight into the hole.

"Creepy," he said, sitting back on his haunches. "What is it?"

"It's a tunnel."

"Where does it go?"

"To a room, but I haven't made it yet."

THE SUN was beginning to fill the room of the garage, a gradual and pale light seeping through the windows, and Sam blew out the candle, leaned back against the wall.

Sam thought of the McWilliams family as a small country, a nation-state of which he was, by virtue of age and vision, the natural leader, and his particular vision was a result of remembering.

Even Charlotte had forgotten all of it: *The Last Supper* in Milan, the train to Rome, the bomb, the Danesi family. Their parents. His siblings didn't understand the need for self-defense, and so Sam saw his responsibility as that of defender, in the oldest definition of the word. His sense of country was actual, not the rented clapboard house on Morrison Street, but tribal, a kind of mental landscape in which the country was themselves.

Sometime in elementary school in Grand Rapids, Sam's science class had studied the defense system of animals, particularly mammals, and each of the students was asked to choose an animal and know its habits and imagine its defense system as personal. Sam chose a porcupine. At night he'd lie in bed and imagine dangerous moments, concentrating on his quills. He could actually feel himself grow larger, feel the prickly things bursting out of his porcupine skin.

"SO WHAT ARE WE GOING TO DO with our bomb shelter?" Oliver asked.

"Live in it in case of trouble," Sam said, replacing the makeshift plywood square, putting the rug back so it covered the floorboards, positioning the desk over the bomb shelter.

"I'm afraid of bombs," Oliver said, crouching beside his brother.

"I'm afraid of them, too," Sam said. "That's why we need the shelter."

The dusty sun fell through the garage window in a triangle of light across Oliver's shoulders, and Sam reached over, boxing him gently in the chin, a gesture familiar to him as if it were one his father had used.

3

THE CAGE WAS ON NEBRASKA AVENUE. It had been built in the late nineteenth century as a private house on a dip of land just where Nebraska slipped off the map into a dark shadow of trees which marked the beginning of Rock Creek Park, a hollow in the damp, dank folds of vegetation where the creek ran. It was actually the Episcopal Home for Juvenile Delinquents, called the Cage by the boys who lived there, although they were free to come and go. It was a place for bad boys too young for prison terms, charged with misdemeanors, stealing mainly, occasionally drugs, breaking and entering, a history of misbehavior, middle-class boys with records.

Sam moved into a room on the third floor, in the back of the Cage, before Christmas, assigned there for six months by Judge Burns of the juvenile court of the District of Columbia, eligible with good behavior for reconsideration in June.

Noli had wanted him to lie.

"Just don't bring up the bomb shelter, darling," she had said, sitting across from him at the kitchen table the day before his court appearance in November. "Or mention the other times you needed to get something at Hechinger's. The judge has no reason to know that."

Sam had confessed to stealing the pipe and flashlight, but he hadn't mentioned to the police any of the other times he had shoplifted during the last eight months. The shovel, coils of rope, a trowel, several lengths of pipe, a metal bucket, nails, a good hammer. The wood he had taken from discards piled at the back of a construction site at Morrison and 32nd.

After the police came and he was charged with shoplifting the pipes and flashlight, Sam had loaded the back of his grandfather's old car with all the stolen items. The manager of the store, an older man who must have been surprised by Sam's simple decency, added up the cost of the stolen items—$326.75—which Sam paid him in cash.

"They're yours," the manager said when Sam turned to go, leaving the merchandise on the counter.

"I don't need them anymore," Sam said.

"You might," the manager replied.

Sam shrugged. "Maybe," he agreed, and reloaded the back of his grandfather's car with his tools.

NOTHING MIGHT HAVE COME OF THE INCIDENT if Noli, with her urgent need for story-making, especially with strangers, had not told the officer that they were from Grand Rapids. And somehow the officer, already suspicious of Sam, irritated at what his teachers thought of as arrogance, an intractable stubbornness, the sense Sam gave of living outside the law, had found out about the incident with Matthew Gray, and the situation escalated.

The way things actually turned out had a lot to do with Sam. Not what he had actually done, but what happened in his presence, the way his entering a room—like the juvenile courtroom or the lobby of the Second Precinct—unsettled the balance, laid bare the arrangement of posturing and conversations, caused a person generally concealed to reveal his ugliness.

He was an observer, not a participant—but the expectation people had of him was that he would *do* something, that he was dangerous to the status quo.

"THINK OF IT THIS WAY, darling," Noli said. "It's not the business of the court that you were planning to make a bomb shelter."

"I wasn't planning, Noli," Sam said patiently. "I made a bomb shelter from things I stole. That's the truth."

"I'd keep that information to yourself," Noli said. "The manager at Hechinger's liked you very much, and he's certainly not going to tell the police."

In a chair beside the kitchen window, William Lucas was drawing the tiny insides of a bisected segment of an egret. He looked up.

"We don't know what the manager's going to say, Noli," he said quietly. "And Sam has a reputation."

"But he didn't do anything to Matthew Gray, if that's what you mean," Noli said.

"That's true," William said. "But people believe that he did."

WHEN SAM APPEARED before Judge Burns the following morning, he told the truth.

Certainly, he thought, the judge would understand why a boy in his situation would feel the need for a bomb shelter. A judge like Mr. Burns, full of decency and seriousness, personable as he seemed to be and warm, would know that essentially Sam was innocent, not of stealing, but of bad intentions.

But he was wrong.

In his final statement, Judge Burns concluded that Samuel McWilliams was a troubled boy, that he should be removed from the agreeable complacency of a home where nobody seemed to have control of him, that he was possibly a danger to society.

The judge recommended the Episcopal Home for Juvenile Delinquents for six months as soon as space was available and told Sam that he might be released earlier than the six-month period if he adjusted.

The word "adjusted" confused Sam. He was adjusted. For the

past seven years, he had had the responsibility for his family. He was smart—that wasn't hard to know in Alice Deal's ninth grade—and he would have been doing well in school if he'd been able to sustain an interest in the subject matter and was willing to do the work. Of course he was adjusted. As Noli said, he could be dropped in the middle of the ocean and make it to shore; he could survive on his own anyplace. He needed no one, was entirely free of the usual adolescent dependencies, except—and this he knew was the clincher—the black beast of his psyche, on which a whole series of reversals could depend, Sam McWilliams's Achilles' heel. He required the presence of his brother and sisters as a constant—his lifeblood, his reason for being.

HE HAD SKIPPED CHILDHOOD altogether, knowing the world in the particular way of children to whom the Angel of Fate has delivered his first terrible lesson before the fragile cells of faith have had a chance to multiply. He was certainly adjusted, because his X-ray eyes, born of disaster, could see straight to the center of things.

"What did the judge mean by adjusted?" he asked his grandfather the night after his court appearance.

"Well-adjusted is what I'm sure he means," William said.

"Do you think I'm well-adjusted?" Sam asked.

"Of course I do, but in this case, I'm not the judge."

William Lucas knew that Sam was more right than wrong, if such a thing as right and wrong existed. Sam's problem, if it could be called one, was that he told the truth.

SAM ARRIVED at the Cage on a Tuesday in early December. The occasion was not what he'd thought it would be; he'd imagined a policeman escorting him, perhaps in handcuffs, maybe even Judge Burns would be there. He'd expected a severe reception, an announcement of the seriousness of the place, a priest or guards or a tank of a woman with tools for child destruction in hand. But in its attitude, the Cage was more like summer camp, half a mile from his house.

Mr. Barringer met them at the door. He was short and broad-faced, with a monotony in his voice and bearing.

He turned to Sam. "Are you called Samuel?"

"Sam's fine." He folded his arms across his chest.

"So, Sam," Mr. Barringer said. "We have rules, as you might imagine. No visitors. No visits home. Two telephone calls a week." He motioned to William Lucas. "Time for you to be on your way. Say goodbye to your grandson."

There was a nastiness to the way he spoke which William Lucas ignored, nodding to Sam, following Mr. Barringer down the steps, across the vestibule, and out into the filtered sunlight of an early-December afternoon. He got into his old yellow Mercury station wagon without looking back, turned on the engine, and drove to the end of the driveway, stopping the car just before Nebraska Avenue. The day was changing to darkness just beyond where he had stopped; the trees, even leafless, seemed a heavy weight above him, the sky closing in. He turned the radio to the classical station, leaned his head against the steering wheel, and wept.

SAM HAD LEFT a complicated list of instructions for his brother and sisters. He had arranged to have math tutoring on Tuesdays when Oliver had basketball practice in the gym at Alice Deal Junior High so they could meet afterwards. On Mondays and Thursdays, he planned to meet Julia and Charlotte on Fessenden Street at 38th near Mirch Elementary on his way back to his new home. And on Friday, when Oliver was out of school early, the plan was to meet at Gifford's Ice Cream on Connecticut Avenue. His siblings believed the arrangement had to do with Sam's anticipated homesickness. But Sam didn't expect to be homesick. He was actually looking forward to the strangeness of a new life, of living alone in a house with people he would have no other occasion to know, of a chance to test himself in the world. He would miss his sisters and brother, but his real reason for daily communication was control.

His list of instructions included a section called WARNINGS:

1. *Set your alarm for 3 a.m. and check the stove in case Noli has been cooking in the middle of the night and forgotten to turn off the oven.*

2. *Do not drive with Grandfather. Make up an excuse so you don't make him angry. But, I repeat,* DO NOT, *under any circumstances, drive with W. W. Lucas, even to a doctor's appointment.*

3. DO NOT *tell anyone at school that I'm at the Cage. They'll think you're creeps or criminals or that our family is screwy. Say nothing about me.*

4. *If Noli decides to stay in her room, do not open the front door to strangers.*

5. *Cross at the lights. This is for you, Oliver.*

6. *If a package comes to the front door, remember the mailbomber I told you about and leave it on the porch.*

7. *Smell the milk before you pour it on your cereal. Noli has a habit of leaving it out all day.*

8. *Do not go on the metro. Somebody got pushed on the tracks last Thursday and is in D.C. General and will probably die.*

9. *Keep the door to the garage office locked, especially if you're working in there. Around Thanksgiving I saw a suspicious man in the alley looking in the trash cans.*

10. *Do not climb out of the bedroom windows onto the roof over the kitchen in order to look into Sally Piscar's bedroom. This is for you, Oliver. You could fall on the patio.*

NOTES: *Please read the daily newspapers, just the front section with the national and international news, to check for my terrorist collection. If you happen to see an article, buy the paper and clip the story for my file. Otherwise don't buy the paper. You can't take it home anyway because of Grandfather.*

In the box marked LETTERS J AND L *in the hall closet are the letters between James and Lucy which Noli has saved. I'd like to read a few of them at a time, so bring a packet once a week and I'll return the ones from the week before so Noli won't know we're reading them. I don't know if she has ever read them—certainly Grandfather hasn't—but she's made a point of telling me that we shouldn't, so I don't want her to find out that we are.*

More later——SLMcW

ON THE AFTERNOON SAM MOVED to the Cage, Julia was kept after school. Charlotte was waiting on the front steps of Mirch Elementary, reading *Madame Bovary*, when Julia came out of the building, her bookbag full to bursting.

"You're late," Charlotte said.

"I'm in trouble." She handed her bookbag to Charlotte. "I'm always in trouble for something. Could you carry this?"

Charlotte hoisted it up on her shoulders.

"What are you carrying? This weighs a ton."

"Everything," Julia said, falling in step with her sister. "I'm not planning to go to school tomorrow. Or for the rest of my life."

Julia McWilliams was small for her age, wiry, with the agility of a spider monkey, strong legs, a mass of black curly hair and blue eyes so striking in their color and size that people stared. She was going to be beautiful.

At Mirch Elementary, she had the reputation for being impossible. She did her work when she wanted to do it and spoke her mind, full of outrage at injustices. Especially toward children. She was upset about something all the time, speaking out without regard to authority or appropriate behavior. But she had an unbearable sweetness. Lost souls sniffed their way to her, settling under her wing, a role she wanted, sought out, taking on the sorrows of others as her own.

AT THE DRUGSTORE, Charlotte picked up a copy of *The Washington Post*.

"Sam said not to pay unless there was something important," Julia said as they walked along Connecticut Avenue past the movie theater to Morrison Street.

"I can't just read the paper and put it back," Charlotte said.

"Sam can." Julia followed Charlotte up the alley between Broad Branch and Nevada, taking out her key to open the door to the garage/office.

"Sam can do anything," Charlotte said, dropping her books on the desk, Julia's bookbag on the floor, opening *The Washington Post*. "He's fearless."

"Scary," Julia said, collapsing on the couch, watching Charlotte bend over the desk to read the front section of the paper. "Are there any explosions?"

On the front page there was the usual political news about President Reagan and the Congress and the economy, a new appointment to the Supreme Court, a terrible accident on Route 495 in which a tractor-trailer jackknifed, a leak in the roof of the Kennedy Center, and a small article in the right-hand column, below the fold, of an IRA bombing of a market in Belfast in which an elderly woman carrying her groceries was injured and a policeman was in critical condition. Charlotte cut out the article without reading further, folded the newspaper, and put it in the trash bin behind the garage.

Julia read out loud: "A young policeman critically injured with head and chest wounds at Queens Court Hospital. Elderly pensioner taken to hospital with superficial wounds and discharged."

"Don't read out loud," Charlotte said.

"Are we supposed to save the stories if the person wasn't killed?" Julia asked.

"I think so," Charlotte said, opening the small file drawer in which Sam kept his collection of newspaper articles, slipping the new one in the folder marked DO NOT READ.

"It's creepy what Sam does," Julia said. "I get nightmares."

"You shouldn't read the stories," Charlotte said. "I don't."

"Well, if you did, you'd know that most of the people in these stories get killed," Julia said.

UNDER SAM'S DESK was an old black metal toolbox which had been in the garage in Grand Rapids. In a tray at the top of the box were hammers and screwdrivers and nails and picture hangers, tape, screws, washers, all old, all a little rusty. Underneath the tray was a large space where Sam kept important documents. That's where the list of instructions was kept, with pictures of their parents, cards from all the presents they had given each other and received from Noli and their grandfather, a sketchbook which had belonged to James, mainly pencil sketches of the places they had lived— "Ashkelon, '73, Chicken House," "Athens, January '70, view from the window of our flat overlooking the old city," "The entrance to Rhodes, holiday, '69." In the corner of each sketch was a tiny profile of a woman, just her head, her small straight nose, her wide-set eyes high on her face, a sort of mythological goddess with long, ropy hair that fell beyond the pages of the sketchbook.

"That's our mother," Charlotte said to Julia, who was standing in the corner of the office looking at the sketchbook.

"Honest?"

"Of course it is."

In fact, Charlotte didn't know. What she knew of their parents she had made up from small bits and letters and pictures, but she liked to think that the curly-haired goddess was their father's image of Lucy, pleased with the marriage she had invented for them, certain of it.

"He must have liked her if he gave her that amazing hair," Julia said.

"He was wild about her," Charlotte said.

AFTER HIS GRANDFATHER LEFT, Sam unpacked his few belongings—a packet of his parents' letters, a small painting his father had done of a river in northern Scotland, his file on terrorism, an empty file marked *Rebecca and Miriam Frankel* which he planned to fill with letters to Rebecca, a haunting, whitewashed picture he particularly liked of all of them on the steps of the Lucas house in Grand Rapids, taken into the sun.

Then he wandered through the sparsely furnished rooms of the Cage, across the wood floors with inexpensive Oriental-look-alike rugs from Sears, plastic couches and oak tables and bookcases with hand-me-down Hardy Boys and Horatio Hornblowers and *Tom Sawyer* and *Robinson Crusoe*, books from the childhood of another generation. There were paintings of darkly colored landscapes, flat lands with cattle grazing or sheep, too small for the walls where they were hanging. No life to the place at all, no specificity, no sense that boys lived here. It was too clean. The dining room was dark-paneled, mahogany-colored, and formal, with long tables and benches, an unpleasant antiseptic smell.

When Mr. Barringer walked in, Sam was standing with his back to the door.

"Isn't it time for you to leave for school?" Mr. Barringer asked.

"I was looking around," Sam said, putting his hands in the pockets of his jeans.

"You better hurry or you'll miss lunch," Mr. Barringer said.

"That's fine," Sam said. "I'm not hungry."

"Pick up the bus on Nebraska just outside the gates," Mr. Barringer said. "I called Alice Deal. They're expecting you."

He was unpleasant, as if his distaste for Sam was specific.

"One more thing." Mr. Barringer followed Sam to the front door. "Your file says you were responsible for seriously injuring a young boy when you lived in Grand Rapids."

"I wasn't responsible for that," Sam said.

"Nevertheless, there'll be no bullying here," Mr. Barringer said. "I just want you to be clear about that."

Sam swung his bookbag over his shoulder, opened the front door, leaving it for Mr. Barringer to shut behind him.

"I'm clear about it," he said.

———

WHEN SAM WAS TEN YEARS OLD and living in Grand Rapids, a story developed that he had been seen beating up Matthew Gray behind the athletic shed in the back of the playing fields of the elementary school. Matthew, small for his age and fragile, born with a crooked spine and an atrophied left leg, tormented by some of the older boys, never by Sam, had made the accusation from his hospital bed at Grand Rapids Memorial, where he spent two weeks recovering from a ruptured spleen.

Matthew hadn't actually seen his assailant. In fact, initially he thought that several boys had come after him, but because he lost consciousness and his memory was unreliable, when Ranier Moore had said it was not several boys but one and that one was Sam McWilliams, Matthew told his mother, who told the school, which called the police.

"I wasn't even there," Sam said, baffled by the turn of events.

Sam wasn't a part of the in crowd in the fifth grade and had no wish to belong to any group, but he wasn't invisible either. Too large a presence to be ignored, too much of a force, a boulder of temperament. No one could get at him.

"I don't remember even being on the playground that day," Sam had said to his grandfather.

But Ranier reported that Sam was on the playground, and so did several others who gave their names to the police and to the principal—Tommy Northrop and Peter Damstra and Felix Ponds and Russ Zeidema and Ray Oates and Johnny Fontana—all claiming to have seen Samuel McWilliams beating up Matthew Gray behind the athletic shed. They signed a statement.

At first no one believed Ranier, but accusation has a way of accumulating its own force. Eventually the children and their parents and the faculty at school and the Lucases' neighbors began to believe that in fact Sam must have been responsible. Even those who had a positive opinion of his integrity assumed they had misjudged him and began to worry about him as a member of their community.

"I didn't do it," Sam said to his family in the weeks that followed. He was perplexed that he could be so broadly misunderstood, having no inclination for fighting, no flicker of the bully in him. But he wasn't outraged. He seemed impervious to the actual injustice, as if he expected it, perhaps, or more likely, as if nothing in his life could injure him after the first injustice delivered by the Fates.

"I know you didn't do it," his grandfather said, "but you've been accused."

"WHY DO YOU THINK they blamed Sam?" Charlotte had asked her grandmother in June before the movers came.

"It's because Sam has a mirror in his brain," Noli said in that serious way she had of making sense out of nonsense. "And when a person looks at him, a boy like Ranier Moore for example, what he sees in that invisible mirror is himself." She took the pins out of her hair so it fell in a gray shawl around her shoulders, took hold of Charlotte's wrist. "So, if the boy's not a nice person, as certainly Ranier is not, he won't like what he sees in Sam's mirror."

SAM DIDN'T BLAME MATTHEW. After all, what did Matthew, who already had enough troubles, know at six years old, if older boys were telling him they knew everything?

What Sam wondered was why. Certainly it must have been Ranier who did the beating—maybe others—and if they wanted to lay the blame elsewhere, as they could, because apparently no one had seen what happened, why choose Sam McWilliams?

"You keep yourself a secret," his grandfather had said when Sam asked him why he was a target for blame. "It must make your peers try to break down your defenses."

"And accuse me of something I didn't do?" Sam asked.

"It's one way to get your attention," his grandfather said.

Sam knew he was a lightning rod for trouble. Perhaps, or so he imagined, this aspect of his chemistry had come of his proximity to the lunch car on the train to Rome. He'd been the last one to touch his father's hand, the last child his mother had kissed, and sometimes he wondered if this accident of fate had created a kind of internal radar which other people sensed about him and wanted to destroy.

THE LONG DRIVEWAY from the Cage was thick with scrubs, weighted with trees, especially evergreens, dark for noon, with a damp, mossy smell of southern winters, a silent path. Sam was not easily frightened, but he had an odd sense that he wasn't alone, that the woods on either side were populated, that eyes took him into account.

Halfway down the driveway, the sign for the Episcopal Home for Juvenile Delinquents just in view, Sam found his mind wandering to the mirror Noli had imagined in his brain. Was it a small reflector as Noli saw it? Did a person have to look directly at his forehead to see himself, or bend down or stand on tiptoe? Did a person instinctively know it was there, or was word passed around?

And as he was thinking about the mirror, even feeling it on his forehead, a rectangular mirror that ran the length of his head, someone came out of nowhere and grabbed him around the neck. An arm, not a terribly strong arm, across his throat, pulling him into the bush along the side of the driveway. The boy, about sixteen or seventeen, with rancid breath and acne, was not alone. There were four boys in a small clearing surrounded by forest. Two of them Sam had seen at Alice Deal.

"So, asshole," said one. "What's up with you today?"

Sam shook free of his assailant and stepped back, oddly calm.

"What do you guys want?" he asked.

One of the boys he didn't recognize was tall and very thin, with a fuzzy blond film of hair on his chin and a cleft. The other was young, small, with spiky red hair. He'd seen the boys from Alice Deal many times and usually together. The talkative one with a low, crackly voice and bad skin was Peebles. His sidekick, who had a look of permanent fright and the eyes of a trapped rabbit, was referred to by Peebles as Banana.

"Dunno," the tall, thin boy called Reggie, the one who had grabbed him initially, said.

"That's what we want to know," the redhead called Bird said. "How come you're at the Cage?"

"I stole some things to build a bomb shelter," Sam said. He put his hands in his pockets.

"Were you figuring to blow things up?" Peebles asked.

"I was building a shelter for protection, not a bomb."

"Protection against what?" the tall boy asked, kneeling down, trying to light a cigarette.

"People blow things up all over the world." Sam shrugged. "Read the papers."

"Like, where all over the world have you been?" Bird asked.

"Everywhere." Sam refused the offer of a cigarette. "My mother's a doctor for places where there are no doctors."

"Yeah?" the boy with the cigarette said.

"That's not true," Peebles said. "I know you. You're Sam McWilliams and you go to Alice Deal and your parents are dead."

Sam folded his arms across his chest.

"You have incorrect information," he said. "My parents are fine."

"Weird," Peebles said. "Everybody at Alice Deal thinks they're dead."

Sam looked directly at Peebles without smiling. "Well, they've got it wrong."

"So tell us what it's like in the jungle," Banana asked, sensing Sam's temper, wishing to change the subject quickly.

Sam leaned against a tree. "What do you want to know?"

"Everything you can remember," Banana said.

"Yeah," Bird said. "Everything."

And they sat around the clearing in the woods, while Sam talked about Botswana, as he knew it from James and Lucy's letters home, about the hippos running over his tent, about a terribly sick child with blue scurvy who'd been saved by his mother, about protecting the revolutionaries in Zimbabwe and dancing naked at Victoria Falls.

"Wild," the redhead boy said. "I wish I could go to Africa. I hate my home."

"You could meet me in Botswana," Sam said.

"Yeah, maybe I could do that," Bird said. "That'd surprise my father. He'd have to find a new punching bag. Bye, Pops, I'll say to him. Off to Africa. See you in September."

"So we can walk around with nothing on and ride camels?" Banana asked.

"Jeeps," Sam said.

"I can drive a jeep," Banana said.

"The women don't wear anything up top, do they?" the tall, thin boy said.

"Nothing but jewelry," Sam said.

"Big breasts?" Banana asked.

"Some big, some little," Sam said. "Same as the women we know."

"The only woman I've ever seen is my Aunt Marty, and her breasts got cut off and now she's dead," Bird said.

"He's got a lot of cancer in his family," the tall boy said.

"Everybody so far but my brother, who's a dickhead, and me."

"So let's say we all go to Africa this summer," Banana said. "What do we do there?"

"Ride around in our jeep, look at women, kill some lions, drink," Peebles said. "Right, Sam?"

"Not exactly," Sam said. "There's a lot of work to do. My mother works all the time."

"We'll be regular missionaries working with your mother. What d'ya think, Sam?" Peebles asked.

"Think?" He shrugged, but he wasn't thinking about them at all. He was thinking about his mother, a kind of joy taking over, almost elation. His mother was a doctor in Africa caring for terribly sick children. His father was with her. Sam could say that. He could make it happen in stories. And who could argue? Who would know?

"I don't know you guys well enough to think anything about you," Sam said.

"So ask," Reggie said.

"I'll tell you why I'm at the Cage," Peebles said. "A lot of reasons. I stole a car and broke into three houses and showed evidence of violence toward family members."

"Me, too," Banana said.

"No, Banana, you didn't," Peebles said. "Tell Sam the truth. You had a gun and you shot it and missed."

"I was shooting at the fence. I hit the fence, Counselor."

"You had a gun. That's the point. That's why you're here."

"Assault," Bird said.

"You probably don't believe it's possible, small as he is," the tall boy said, "but Bird's telling the truth."

"He was a hunk," Banana said.

"He was a kid," Bird said. "And it wasn't really assault."

"I'm here because I'm emotionally disturbed," the tall boy said, lighting another cigarette. "Sexually confused, with the addition of learning disabilities."

"So what are you doing here besides the bomb deal?" Bird asked.

Sam was silent. He could feel the muscles in his face freezing, his eyes going cold.

"Like, stealing?" Bird went on.

"Lay off, Bird. He doesn't want to talk," Peebles said.

"Yeah," Reggie said.

Bird backed away from Sam into the shadows.

"So maybe you could tell us more about Africa," Peebles said. "Especially Botswana."

For the rest of the day, while school, where they ought to have been, was in session, they were in Botswana as Sam described it for them from his parents' letters home, riding in jeeps over the hills and through the shallow rivers, sleeping in tents, run over by elephants, hip-hopping the night away, saving the children from blue scurvy.

THE AFTERNOON FELL into dusk, and the four truant inmates from the Episcopal Home for Juvenile Delinquents sat on damp logs in the clearing, breathing the heavy, rancid air rising from the molding vegetation of late autumn, listening to Sam.

4

CHARLOTTE HAD A BOYFRIEND.
"He has pimples like Rice Krispies across his chin," Oliver said. "It's disgusting."

"A boyfriend?" Sam asked, a sudden terrible feeling in his stomach. "She's only twelve."

"All the girls in the sixth grade have boyfriends," Oliver said. "He gave her a ring."

It was Friday, late January, slate gray and cold, too cold for the ice cream they were eating on stools, looking out the window of Gifford's at the rush-hour traffic on Connecticut Avenue.

"What kind of ring?" Sam asked.

"A cheap ring. It's green because green's the color of her birthstone," Oliver said. "Charlotte told me."

Sam was not amused. "She has to give it back," he said. "Tell her she has to give it back."

"Okay, okay," Oliver said.

Sam pushed away his chocolate ice cream sundae.

"I mean, they're not going to get married," Oliver said. "She's only twelve."

"That's my point." Sam sunk his chin into his jacket. "Tell her to call me tonight at the Cage."

"I thought we weren't allowed to call," Oliver said.

"In an emergency," Sam said. "This is an emergency."

"I'll tell her," Oliver said, staring beyond his brother at the street. "But I hope you won't get mad at her."

"I'm not mad," Sam said. He slipped off the stool and zipped up his jacket. "I'm a little annoyed."

"SAM'S VERY ANGRY," Oliver told Charlotte later.

She was lying on the couch in the office behind their house with her eyes closed, imagining Joshua Rubin kissing her on the lips.

"Are you listening to me, Charlotte?" Oliver asked. "This is important."

"I'm listening," Charlotte said.

"She's not listening." Julia was sitting at the desk in the navy-blue suit her grandmother had worn after her wedding, a very handsome wool suit with a straight skirt and tight jacket—Noli had been thin then—polka-dotted with moth holes. Her small feet were lost in the navy high heels she had borrowed from her grandmother's closet. "Charlotte doesn't listen to anybody, especially me."

"I do," Charlotte said. "Just not constantly." She put the couch cushion over her face, shutting out their voices, lost in the dreamy darkness.

"I want to tell you something," Oliver said, lifting the pillow off Charlotte's face.

"Don't," she said.

"I have to. Sam says it's an emergency," Oliver said. "He's furious about your boyfriend."

THE CROSSTOWN BUS was late, so Sam walked from the ice cream store to the Cage, grateful for the damp cold, the need in such cold to move with some alacrity because his body had the weight of iron, too heavy to carry. Something terrible was the matter with him since the news of Charlotte's boyfriend.

When he got back to the Cage, he called home, explaining to Mr. Barringer that there was a family emergency, and because Mr. Barringer was busy with the social worker, he didn't ask questions.

"You can't have a boyfriend," Sam said when Charlotte answered the phone.

"Not ever?"

"Not at twelve," he said.

"I don't understand," she said quietly.

"It's a betrayal," Sam said. "You understand betrayal."

He asked her to bring another packet of James and Lucy's letters when she met him at the corner of Fessenden on Monday and to check his file for the letter from Rebecca Frankel.

"Have you seen any news reports lately?" he asked.

"Nothing at all," Charlotte said.

She wanted to tell him she hadn't been reading the paper since she'd fallen in love with Joshua Rubin, that she hated to look in the paper for stories of terrorists, and hated to read them.

"Another thing," Sam said, hurrying to get off the phone because the bell for dinner had rung. "Give him back the green ring, since he's not your boyfriend any longer."

PEEBLES HAD SAVED SAM a place at dinner.

"Trouble?" he asked when Sam came back from speaking to Charlotte.

"No trouble," Sam said.

"I hate Tuesdays. Kraut and watery mashed potatoes," Peebles said.

Sam didn't reply. He wasn't hungry, taking only bread, passing on the sausage and potatoes.

"What's up, man?" Peebles asked. "You seem low."

"I'm thinking," Sam said.

"About family night?" Banana asked. "We have a rehearsal after dinner, right?"

"I don't know," Sam said. "I have a lot of homework."

"Homework?"

"I'm flunking math."

"You said we'd be doing my family tonight," Banana said. "The Joseph, alias Banana, Stern family."

"I plan to do your family next," Sam said. "I just don't know about tonight."

"I'm playing the bulimic sister, what's her name," Reggie said. "It's a non-speaking role."

Banana laughed.

"Peebles can play my father." Banana twisted his face into an expression of exaggerated rage. "Peebles knows him. It'll go like this: 'Where the fuck are my blue silk socks, Margery? Where the fuck is the pinstriped shirt my mother gave me for Valentine's Day. For chrissake, Margery, get out of bed and deal.'"

"Sweet," Pebbles said. "I look forward to this opportunity."

"So, Sam, what d'ya think?" Bird asked.

Evenings, when Mr. Barringer was in his room drinking vodka and watching the news, the boys at the Episcopal Home for Juvenile Delinquents who were supposed to be doing their homework rehearsed Family. Family was Sam's idea. He wrote the stories, cast and directed them, but the idea had its beginnings on the first day he'd spent at the Cage, when he'd met Peebles and Banana and Reggie and Bird and they'd spent the afternoon imagining Africa.

Family was a different kind of game. They would choose a family of one of the residents of the Cage, the Banana Stern family, for example—and then Sam would write a play around the stories that Banana told him. The dictatorial father, Bernard, with his habit of kicking the dog when the dog was eating; the bulimic sister, Lola, who shoplifted food from the Safeway and then stuffed herself in the privacy of her closet and threw up in the bathroom next to Banana's room; the tranquillized mother, Margery, sleepwalking through the day in her nightgown; and baby Brian, sitting on the floor of his bedroom tearing off the arms and legs and heads of his action figures, screaming, DEAD, YOU'RE DEAD. DEAD. DEAD. DEAD.

"I want to do my family next," Peter Tripper said. "My aunt committed suicide in our house. I saw her dead on the floor of the bathroom before the medics arrived."

"She was depressed," Bird said. "That's what Peter says."

"My father's in jail," Reggie said.

"Then how come your mother can afford a BMW?" Bird asked.

"I didn't say we were poor," Reggie said. "We're middle-class criminals in my family, bitch. He's in jail for embezzling."

"I thought you told me he was out of jail now," Peter said.

"He's out," Reggie said. "But he was in for nine months. We're doing plays, right, Sam? They don't have to be absolutely factual."

"Right," Sam said. "Emotional truth is what we're after in these plays."

"Whatever," Bird said.

"Sam's right," Peebles said. "Some things you have to invent."

Sam got up from the table.

"You know," Pebbles said, following Sam from the table. "This place was dead until you came here."

"Thanks, Peebles," Sam said, motioning to Banana. "We'll rehearse tomorrow, Banana, but you've got to find some guy to play your mother. Maybe Reggie. I'm headed upstairs."

"See you, Sam," Peebles called after him.

"See you later, Sam."

"Bye, Sam."

"Hasta la vista, Sam."

And the sound of his own name followed him up the stairs and down the corridor to his room.

AS USUAL, HE COULDN'T SLEEP. He sat up in bed, in the dark, with his flashlight, reading the dictionary to take his mind off breathing. He had been reading the dictionary since he moved into his room at the Cage. He liked the simplicity of it, especially at night, when he was afraid of sleeping with his door unlocked, worried that Mr. Barringer would come in and look at him.

He was fearful that if he lay down on his back or turned over on his stomach, the breath would go out of him and his lungs would fill with fluid. He thought about Charlotte, wondering had she called her boyfriend, wondering why the presence of a boyfriend in her life mattered enough to him to cost him his breath.

"JEALOUS" WAS A WORD he had looked up once in the dictionary after he had seen one of the letters his father had written to his mother confessing that he was a jealous man.

Jealous: intolerant of rivalry or unfaithfulness, vigilant in guarding a possession. Sam particularly liked the rare Old Testament definition of a jealous God: . . . *requiring complete devotion.* He understood that definition exactly.

He was fond of the derivation of words, the way one led to another. He'd follow the synonyms. The word "jealous" derived from zealous or zeal. He looked up "zeal," whose synonym was passion: *strong or violent emotion.* Or: *an outburst of intense emotion at fever pitch.* An internal combustion. A bomb.

And as he read the definitions of "jealous" and the synonyms and the derivations with their satisfactory exactness, as he went over and over them, each time sounding like the first, his own feelings began to dissipate. He found himself breathing more easily.

He got out of bed, opened his bookbag, and took out the latest packet of letters between his parents, which he had already read, but it didn't matter. He would read them again and again.

JULIA LAY on the trundle bed and watched Charlotte throw page after page of her letter to Joshua in the trash.

"Are you mad at Sam?" she asked.

Charlotte didn't answer.

"Are you so scared of him you'll dump your boyfriend because he says you have to?"

Charlotte sat on her knees, leaning over her desk, writing in her best handwriting.

"Well, sometimes I am," Julia said, examining her face close up in a hand mirror. "Are you listening, Charlotte?"

"No, I'm not listening," she said. "I'm writing."

Dear Joshua Rubin,

I am returning the beautiful emerald ring you gave me because I can't be your girlfriend any longer for personal reasons. But I am enclosing my favorite poem as a going-away present. "The Song of Wandering Aengus" by William Butler Yeats. I especially like the last lines, which I dedicate to you: "And pluck till time and times are done, The silver apples of the moon, The golden apples of the sun."

> *Love forever,*
> *Charlotte McWilliams*

IT WAS NEARLY MIDNIGHT, the halls of the Cage empty except for Mr. Barringer doing his last walk of the evening, sniffing for smoke, putting his ear against the doors, listening for conversation. Sam turned off the flashlight until Mr. Barringer had walked by his room and he heard the muffled footsteps on the carpeted stairs. Then he turned the flashlight on and opened the packet of letters between Lucy and James.

Edinburgh, July 18, 1961. Wet.
Dear Plum,
It's bear cold here with rain day after day, the color of slate. That's Scotland. I'm ready to leave behind this dreary place with its black castle hanging over the end of town where I live.

I have plans. Bombay now, and later everywhere. I want to know the world first and then DO something in it. What to do is not clear, but I have a sense of destiny and I know you do, too, or

there wouldn't have been that noisy CLICK when we met. All parts
in place.

Love,
Jaggers

P.S. You asked about Jaggers. My mother called me that after a
first-form teacher reported: "James has jagged edges and can't settle
down and sit in his chair." Thus—

Dear dear Jaggers,
I'm fighting with my father, who wants me to go to medical school.
Silent fight. He doesn't do the noisy kind.

And Mother, who doesn't want me to follow you to Bombay
because of the bacteria and worms. She's particularly concerned
about the worms and has described them and what they will be
busy doing in my intestines in some detail.

I count the days until you're back—46 and a half. By hours, by
minutes. When you return, we will never separate again.

And so,
Forever, Plum

P.S. Please help me explain to my parents what you're like.
They're wrecks about us. Especially my father. He calls you Loose
Cannon as if it's your Christian name.

Dear Plum,
I've sent you a painting I made this summer on the river where my
uncle has a cottage. I'm hopeless with words, but perhaps this
painting will help you describe me to your father.

Love, Jaggers

Dear Jaggers,
My father, whom I love—don't get me wrong—is an artist of sorts
as well, doncha know.

And so he asks, "Why does Loose Cannon have all of these
paintings of shorelines?"

"Why do you think?" I ask him.

"It feels like bad news to me," he says.

I wish they had less time to worry. Shorelines make perfect sense.

Love, Plum

Dear Plum,
Goodbye.
Hello.

I'll be the one with the shoe-polish hair and wire-rimmed glasses. You can't miss me.

August 31. 3 p.m. Flight 31 BOAC from London. Idlewild Airport, NYC. Don't dress for the occasion.

Love, Jaggers

5

ON A THURSDAY AFTERNOON in late January, six months after he'd been released from the Cage and the day after his physics exam, which he had flunked, Sam arrived home early just after lunch with a letter to his grandparents in his pocket announcing his suspension from high school.

He unlocked the door to the garage office and opened the windows; although it was midwinter, the air had a spring sweetness and the afternoon was golden yellow.

Last night's Monopoly game was still set up at the table and he pushed it aside, opened his math notebook to a page entitled *Aunt Marty's Missing Breasts*, and took out his pen. From the open window he could see Noli across the garden in the kitchen at the sink and, just beyond her, the shadow of Julia. Looking directly at the kitchen window, he saw in his peripheral vision the first of his father's shoreline paintings described on the back of the canvas as *Loch Lomond Shoreline, 1959. JMcW*. Something about the way Sam's eyes took in the whole, capturing a fraction of his life in a frame which did not include him, translated like language inexactly to a picture in which he saw himself from a place outside. He was sitting at the table alone, a Monopoly game in the center, and underneath the table a rug, and underneath the rug the loosened floorboards, which concealed a small pipe bomb.

Julia interrupted the moment, flying in the side door.

"The principal's on the phone."

"I spoke to him earlier," Sam said.

"But he wants to speak to you now," she said.

He looked up from the table where he was reading his script about Aunt Marty.

"I can't speak to him now," he said.

"I'll tell him that," she called over her shoulder, running back to the house. "I'll tell him you're too busy."

When Julia returned to the office, Sam was reading the letter the principal had given to him for his grandparents.

"The principal called to tell Noli you've been suspended for writing plays during class," she said.

"He told me the same thing," Sam said.

"Bummer," Julia said. "Maybe you should write about us instead of the creeps at the Cage."

"I might," Sam said. "I've thought about it."

It was true. He had been thinking about a family without parents—although in the play he would write, the parents are missing, not dead, the children at risk, although they don't know it.

"The McWilliamses in living color," Julia said. "It could be a very funny play."

AFTER THE CAGE, Sam had gone to a small Quaker school willing to take on difficult problems.

Sam was their first failure.

"He's unreachable," the principal had told William Lucas, his frustration bordering on anger. "Polite, always polite, as if those of us in authority are objects of mockery, but he does exactly what he wants to do, which is to sit in the back of the classroom and write plays."

"I know he writes plays," William had said. Sam had given his grandfather one of the plays, a weird sort of story about a boy called Banana, but William was pleased that he had substituted writing plays for building the bomb shelter. Somehow just the act of writing plays was optimistic. "Aboveground," as Noli said.

"We've read the plays. He keeps them in a notebook and they're quite crazy," the principal told William. "I really hate to tell you this, but they are."

"They're intended to be funny," William said, unable to keep silent.

"Funny? I'm not sure about funny," the principal said. "The one I read is about the sixties and it's very disturbing. I found it very disturbing indeed."

SAM WAS A SELECTIVE READER, seldom of the books he was assigned to read. He had, for example, read everything he could about the sixties. These were the years in which his parents had finished college and married and gone out into the world. The years Sam had been born. Although in memory Lucy and James McWilliams were as clear as if he had seen them yesterday, living somewhere beyond time, always young, he felt a need, an instinct not an intellectual decision, to place them on a time line, to fix them in history.

THERE WERE SPECIFIC THINGS he knew. He knew that his father, after his first year at the Rhode Island School of Design, had become an American citizen because he felt more American than British and wanted to vote for John Kennedy for President. He knew that his mother wore a locket with a picture of her cousin Noah, who had died in Vietnam when he was nineteen years old. Sam remembered the locket attached to a dark, silvery bracelet which she always wore, the fuzzy picture of Noah with a cap of curly hair and a big smile spreading to the corners of the photograph. He knew James and Lucy had been against America's involvement in Vietnam, so they must have spoken about it in front of him.

He thought of his parents as James and Lucy, names he had used for them since they had died, altering his relationship to them, giving him some sense of control, of separation from their permanent absence. But when he thought about them as his mother and father, when the pure rush of feeling took over their imagined lives, insinuating their immortal presence into his heart, they were Plum and Jaggers, always Plum and Jaggers in his mind.

Plum & Jaggers began the winter after Sam left the Cage, the evening he was suspended from high school, when he realized that he wouldn't be going to college. Number 98 in a class of 100, driven only to imagining plays which he wrote in his math notebook, on paper napkins, on the inside cover of *The History of Modern Europe*, even on the envelopes of his parents' letters home. He had no interest in academics, no patience for studying at someone else's recommendation, just a general restlessness, a sense that in some part of his machinery, stone was being ground to sand.

After dinner, they were sitting in the office playing Monopoly, four chairs around the table, Oliver's turn to roll the dice, when Sam stood and pulled up two more chairs.

The gesture seemed to come from nowhere, no conscious thought Sam had, no spatial rearrangement in his mind, just a couple of empty chairs in the office which he pulled up to the table.

"Are those for Plum and Jaggers?" Oliver had asked.

Charlotte looked up from the Monopoly board.

"Plum and Jaggers?"

"They are," Sam said, suddenly drunk with excitement. "These are the chairs for Plum and Jaggers."

"They're just empty chairs," Julia said. "What does that mean?"

"It means the people who sit in them are not at home," Sam said.

Plum & Jaggers came to Sam at that moment out of whole cloth. It was a story of a family of children whose parents are never at home, who have by accident and necessity become their own parents, isolated by the missing generation from tradition and history and long-term memory, from a context in which to live their lives.

It is always evening in the Plum & Jaggers story, dinner hour for the McWilliams family gathered around the dining-room table, underneath which is a rug and, underneath the rug, the floor and, underneath the floor, a bomb.

"Why?" Julia asked when Sam explained the setting for the story. "Will it ever explode?"

Sam shrugged. "It could."

"But will it?" Julia asked.

"I don't know," Sam said. "That's the point of the story."

6

JUST AFTER 7 p.m. on July 18, 1985, a month following Sam's graduation from Shady Hill Friends School, a bomb exploded on the Red Line train at the Cleveland Park metro station. Five people were injured. One was a three-year-old boy.

Sam heard about it on the radio. He and Charlotte were in the office behind their house when the all-music station interrupted with news of the bomb and a warning not to take the Red Line.

"We're going," Sam said.

Charlotte looked up from a play she was reading.

"Something could happen to us," she said.

"I don't think so," Sam said.

They were going to go, of course. Charlotte knew that. They always did what Sam had in mind they should do. But this hot summer evening, coming on dusk, heavy with the smell of roses and honeysuckle slipping through the open garage window, she didn't want to see the scene of a bombing.

"On your feet," Sam said, turning off the fan.

Charlotte put a marker in *The Glass Menagerie* and closed *The Collected Plays of Tennessee Williams*.

In the last year, she had become an actress—"gifted," according to her drama teacher at Woodrow Wilson High School; "inspired" described her roles as Emily in *Our Town* and Juliet in *Romeo and Juliet*.

Sam had taught her. Evenings after dinner when Noli thought they were in the office doing their homework, they played Plum & Jaggers. Charlotte had the lead.

Acting had come upon her unexpectedly, like a sign on the Road to Damascus, a religious transformation. She discovered that she could leave the quiet, responsible young woman called Charlotte McWilliams in her bedroom reading *Anna Karenina* and become somebody else whose life she never had to lead. Somebody new. She was giddy with the pleasure of it. Her grades fell. Her dreamy afternoons, lying on her stomach with a book, were over. Her longing for a love affair slipped away.

"We'll have a company, Charlotte," Sam had said to her one early-spring afternoon in his senior year. "The four of us on the road. Plum & Jaggers Family Comedy Troupe."

SAM TOLD HIS GRANDPARENTS they were going to the eight o'clock show at the Uptown Theatre.

"I hate to lie to them," Charlotte said, settling into the front seat of their grandfather's old yellow Mercury, which Sam drove now, Julia and Oliver in the backseat.

"They don't want to know the truth," Sam said.

"Anyway, we might go to the movies," Oliver said.

"I don't want to go to the movies," Julia said sullenly. "I want to see the explosion."

"That's what we're doing," Sam said.

AT TWELVE, Julia was rail-thin, with tiny breasts, a small bottom the size of a muskmelon, and long, wavy black hair with a purple stripe. She had put a full-length mirror on the door in the office of the house on Morrison Street so she could gauge her sullen expressions.

After Sam went to live at the Episcopal Home for Juvenile Delinquents, she did not return to school. She had read a piece in *The Washington Post* about a girl in second grade who was home-schooled and had persuaded Noli to take on the job of teaching her. She was happy working with Noli, spending her afternoons with Oliver and Charlotte and Sam, keeping up with the culture of her peers by poring over teenage magazines at People's Drugstore, memorizing the vocabulary, the look, the shifting hip, the expression of endless boredom. The magazines gave her a sense of how to speak and act without actually experiencing the growing cynicism of adolescence; she was wise-seeming but innocent, with a fetching honesty that burst forth with whatever was in her mind.

But recently during the slow afternoons, she had become restless, longing for friends, for younger conversation, and she began to think of going to Alice Deal Junior High for seventh grade, just to try it out.

IN PREPARATION, she had dyed her hair and bought dangly silver earrings at the 5 & 10 and changed her wardrobe from jeans to skimpy silky dresses through which her tiny, perfectly formed nipples were clearly visible.

During the summer, Julia didn't wear shoes. On the day of the explosion in the Cleveland Park metro, she had painted her toenails black with small white flowers and drawn a vermilion snake with purple dots slithering up her leg.

She sat in the backseat examining the snake, which was peeling. "I suppose no one died in the explosion, right, Sam?" she asked.

"Right, Julia," Sam said. "No one died."

"Bummer."

IT WAS ALMOST DARK by the time they arrived at the fire station beside the entrance to the Cleveland Park metro. Traffic was rerouted and the crowd filled the street between Newark and Porter Streets. There was nothing to see. The injured had been taken to

Washington Hospital Center by ambulance. The report that Sam overheard from a group of people in their early twenties who had been on the subway when the bomb exploded was that no one was badly hurt. But another group, farther on, described the child who had been taken to Children's Hospital, and the lacerations they had seen didn't sound minor.

"It was an anti-gay statement," a young man next to Sam said. "That's what I think it was."

"You think?" a woman asked. "Or do you have some valid reason for saying so?"

The young man shrugged. "I have a reason," he said. "There was a gay march to the Capitol today."

"I know," the woman said. "I read the paper, too."

"So that's what I think," the young man said. "You don't just throw a bomb for the heck of it. Right? You've got to have a reason."

"I don't know," the woman said. "I don't throw bombs."

SAM MOVED through the crowd, crossing over to the other side of the avenue with Charlotte and Oliver, holding Julia's wrist. Julia, head flung back, was pretending that Sam, with his splendid bones and black hair, was her boyfriend, not her brother, that she was adult and people saw them as a couple.

Everywhere they went, the crowd was arguing, their voices loud and strident, talking about the bomb, the injuries, the reasons for the explosion.

"Let's go home," Charlotte said.

"I thought we were going to the movies," Oliver said. "That's what I want to do."

"I think it's too late for the next show," Sam said, flinging his arm over Oliver's shoulder.

"So let's go home," Charlotte said, an edge of hysteria in her voice. She didn't like large crowds. She was afraid there would be another explosion.

They wandered past the stores on the west side of the avenue, mostly open stores, people milling inside, beyond the doors which were open in the heat of summer.

Just as Sam was beginning to think that Charlotte was right, they should get out of the middle of this crowd, they walked past Gallagher's Pub and Oliver said he wanted a Coke and the man at the door said it was okay for them to come in even though they were underage. It was open-mike night and everyone was welcome.

At the front of the place on a little stage elevated just above the tables was a young girl about Charlotte's age in a tiny flowered dress and a yellow straw hat singing "Carolina Moon" in a thin soprano voice.

"Look at her," Sam said, slipping into a chair at one of the round tables in the back of Gallagher's. He took Charlotte's hand. "I want to do one of our routines," he said. "We're at least that good."

"We're not doing one of our routines," Oliver said. "We don't even know these people."

"These people are drunk. They won't be able to tell the difference," Sam said.

"Count me out," Oliver said. At fourteen he resisted every suggestion, even from Sam.

Charlotte was watching the young comedian who had just come onstage, a small, floppy-eared man with a series of jokes which he found so amusing himself it was difficult to hear the punch line.

"I'll do it," Julia said. "I'd like to do the one about Marigold."

"Because you have the main part," Oliver said.

"Because it's my favorite that Sam's written," Julia said.

"I won't do it," Oliver said. "I hope you guys understand that I won't."

But Sam was getting up, raising his hand at the waiter.

The waiter pointed his finger at Sam. "The young man in the blue T-shirt," he shouted. "You're on."

"Me?" Sam called.

"You've got it," the waiter said.

Sam moved through the crowded tables to the front of the room, stepping up on the empty stage.

"Ready?" the waiter asked.

Sam nodded, taking the microphone.

"My name is Sam McWilliams," he began. "And I'm with the world-famous family comedy troupe known as Plum & Jaggers."

There was a round of applause.

"If someone could help me, I need some props—a table and six chairs."

A group of people near the stage lifted a table and some chairs onto the stage.

"Now I'd like to introduce my sister Charlotte, who plays the role of my sister Charlotte in this skit."

Charlotte walked to the stage and took a seat in one of the chairs.

"My brother Oliver will be playing the role of a particularly intelligent German shepherd–Doberman mix, the family dog we call Anarchy," Sam went on, pulling out a chair for Oliver. "And in this scene my sister Julia plays our cousin Marigold, a young girl who has a reputation as an exhibitionist, recently excused by the juvenile court for the bludgeoning death of her mother, our Aunt Sky Blue or Blue Sky, I forget—her name is mud in our household. The jury concluded Aunt Sky Blue was responsible for her own death because she prevented Marigold from self-actualizing. Thus child abuse, thus Marigold as victim, the failure of the democratic process in late-twentieth-century U.S.A. We all feel terrible for Marigold. Let's give her a nice round of applause."

Julia walked to the stage and stood next to one of the tables, smoothing her small silk dress.

"It's dinnertime. Our parents are not at home. We are sitting—Charlotte and I—at the dinner table eating Cheerios and chocolate marshmallow fudge ice cream with a glass of red wine. We haven't spoken for a year, and I, for one, have forgotten the reason for our disagreement, only that it was significant.

"I should add one detail. Beneath the floorboards on which the table sits is a small pipe bomb, which should not concern you. So far, in all our performances, it has never exploded."

Sam and Charlotte began to eat. Anarchy took a chair between them, sitting on all fours, with his chin on the table.

"The empty chairs are where our parents would be were they ever at home for dinner," Sam says, pretending to take a sip of red wine.

SAM: Anarchy?

(ANARCHY *cocks his head.*)

SAM: Ask Charlotte where Mom and Dad are tonight.

(ANARCHY *barks at* CHARLOTTE.)

CHARLOTTE: Tell Sam that Dad's at one of his twelve-step programs. Overeaters Anonymous or Overspenders, I forget.

SAM: Great.

CHARLOTTE: And Mom's having dinner with the children at the homeless shelter, and then she's spending the night with Al, who's here from L.A.

SAM: Tell Charlotte I said "Great" again.

(ANARCHY *barks at* CHARLOTTE.)

CHARLOTTE: What does Sam think I am? Deaf?

(*Enter* MARIGOLD.)

MARIGOLD: I guess you guys heard what happened. (*She moves next to* CHARLOTTE, *speaking directly in her face.*)

MARIGOLD: So, did you hear or not?

CHARLOTTE: We heard.

MARIGOLD: Did you hear about the abuse charge?

CHARLOTTE: I'm up to my ears in abuse, Marigold. Everybody in my class is abused. It's hard to keep up.

MARIGOLD (*Striking a pose, one hip up, face pouty*): So I'll tell you what really happened.

(CHARLOTTE *and* SAM, *patting* ANARCHY *on the head, continue to eat.*)

MARIGOLD: This is what I told the judge. I come into the house on Friday afternoon, May 11, and Sky Blue is watching her guru on a video. I ask her can I go to the Moon Spew concert with Marco and she says no and I ask why and she says we don't have the money and I say, Bullshit, of course we have the money, and she says no, I can't, on principle, and I say I will, and she calls me a name which I can't even repeat in front of the judge because he could be religious, and so I hit her quite a few times with the VCR and she dies. That's the story. I suppose you two knew the whole thing.

CHARLOTTE: I did.

SAM: So did I.

MARIGOLD: So?

THE MOOD in the hot, crowded room at Gallagher's was uncomfortably silent. The audience was no longer laughing, and Sam looked over at Charlotte.

"Keep going," he whispered.

"They hate it," Charlotte said.

Sam folded his arms across his chest.

SAM (*To* MARIGOLD, *forgetting what line was supposed to come next in the script*): So?

Marigold (*Out of character*): I don't know. I forget.

Oliver got off his chair and crawled under the table, his back to the audience, which was beginning to laugh.

"Let's get out of here," Charlotte said.

And then, in a gesture too swift to anticipate, Julia took hold of the back of her short silk dress, pulled it over her head, dropped it on the floor, and she was standing onstage in nothing but a pair of tiny bikini panties covered with red balloons.

"WHAT WERE YOU THINKING about, Julia?" Sam asked, driving up Morrison Street.

"She thought she was doing the right thing," Oliver said. "She thought she was helping us out of a tough spot."

"No one was laughing," Julia said in a voice thin with tears. "And I made them laugh."

"Plum & Jaggers is not a strip show, Julia," Sam said. "It's high comedy."

"The show isn't funny." Oliver looked over at Charlotte, raising his hands in a gesture of resignation.

In the backseat, Julia was crying.

"What is high comedy?" Charlotte asked.

"High comedy is a mirror of the way we live—our lives inverted," Sam said coldly. "And it's supposed to make us laugh at ourselves."

"Well, this didn't make people laugh in the right places," Oliver said.

"Then I'll work on it until it's funny enough," Sam said.

He parked the car, opened the door to the backseat, where Julia was sitting, and reached in to take her hand, which she refused.

"I'm sorry, Julia," he said.

Julia covered her eyes and climbed out of the car, peering through her fingers.

"Have a little faith," Sam said, following Julia down the sidewalk to the front door, where Noli was waiting for them. "I'll make it funny. Funny enough for television."

THAT NIGHT Sam lay in his bed wide awake in the heat and darkness, looking out the window at the blank space of black where the stars ought to have been, and promised himself, crossed his heart and hoped to die, as he used to do when he was small, when he did hope to die, that he would not let his family down.

7

CHICAGO WAS HOT FOR JUNE and windy along the lake, the city skyline, glistening like silver rain, blinding Sam and Charlotte as they walked along the jogging path off Lake Shore Drive. Sam slipped his arm through Charlotte's.

"Plum is going to China, I suppose you heard," Sam said.

"I heard."

"She has plans to unite the women of China against someone, the Chinese men, I imagine," he said. "She'll miss the Fourth of July with us."

"She always misses the Fourth of July with us," Charlotte said.

"I know," Sam said. "Thank God for Jaggers."

"Thank God for Jaggers?" Charlotte looked at Sam in his new wire-rimmed specs. He wore his regular uniform: faded jeans and Nikes, a cotton Oxford with the sleeves rolled up, one of his father's ties, this one red-and-black-striped, wide, distinctively seventies. Seeing him, who would imagine he was anyone other than a student, probably Midwestern, the eldest son in a conservative family, Republican, Lutheran?

"Why are we thankful for Jaggers?" Charlotte asked.

"Because he's not going to China," Sam said.

"Then I suppose we can expect to have his company for the rest of our lives," Charlotte said.

THE SUN WAS BEARING DOWN on them with almost physical force, and Charlotte pulled the wide-brimmed straw hat she wore over her forehead so it shaded her eyes and she couldn't see in front of her, only under the sides of the hat, an edge of moving lake, a battalion of black tree trunks.

"It's hot," she said.

"And you're wearing too many clothes."

Lately, Charlotte was always in costume, even at Columbia University, from which she had graduated in May with a degree in comparative literature.

Other than the broad-brimmed straw hat which might have been worn by a mother of the bride at a garden wedding in the late fifties, Charlotte wore a long A-line mustard-yellow skirt, a Mexican blouse embroidered at the neck, and boots. She liked white cotton gloves in spite of the heat. Fond of the styles of the fifties, when her parents had grown up, she always wore gloves and frequented thrift stores.

In college, she began to dress in a series of changing looks, discovering that dress was like a house with the blinds shut, the front door locked against uninvited guests. Inside, Charlotte was the perfectly sane, quiet, assessing McWilliams, the compass for the direction of their lives. Her feet were steady on the earth, and under her skin, that whirl of blood and hormones and bile, her heart beating, beating, the climate was generally temperate.

THAT MORNING they had visited Second City, the comedy club where they would be playing. They had spoken with the producer and checked the stage and seen the brochures announcing the summer season.

"Do you like the way we're billed?" Sam asked.

The Second City billing had them playing off and on throughout the summer, beginning in July, twice during the week, and Friday nights as a warm-up act—twenty minutes, time for a single segment. Tuesdays and Wednesdays they were the main attraction.

> PLUM & JAGGERS: sibling comedy troupe—3 kids and a dog—Dysfunction meets hilarity. Join the '90s. Remember your own childhood bliss.

"I think it's amazing, Sam," Charlotte said. "Amazing what you've done."

"Thank you, Charlotte," Sam said, a rare happiness building like fever, a lightness in the fetid summer air that was almost joy. "Joy." What a lovely word, he thought, like bells. A pure sound undiminished by the thickness of the air. His team. His troupe. Plum & Jaggers on the lips of people as they left the theater.

"It's too hot to be out in the sun," Charlotte said.

"We'll head home, then," Sam said. "I want to check on Oliver."

"Why?" Charlotte asked. "I'm sure he's at work."

"I've just had a feeling about him this summer. He's been distracted, and he doesn't look well," Sam said. "When I went into the bathroom this morning, he was looking at himself in the mirror and asked me if the reflection I saw in the mirror in the morning ever looked like the face of a stranger."

"That happens to me all the time," Charlotte said.

"Of course. To me, too. But it doesn't happen to Oliver."

Sam was twenty-three in the summer of 1990, Charlotte twenty-one, and Oliver at twenty had two more years until he graduated from college. Julia, at seventeen, had finished as much as she wished to of high school. During the summers while Charlotte and Oliver were in school, they played in comedy clubs, mostly in Washington, where they still lived in the rented house on Morrison Street with William and Noli. But in 1989, at the suggestion of a scout who had seen their act at the Laugh-Track in northern Virginia, they went to Chicago, playing at several small clubs, and people in the business had taken note of them. By the end of the summer, Second City had invited them to be a part of their next summer season.

They lived on the second floor of a large duplex in Wicker Park and had day jobs: Oliver painting houses in Hyde Park on a crew with a friend from college, Julia on the breakfast shift at a coffee shop, Charlotte in the main library at the University of Chicago. Sam, who had saved enough money housecleaning during the winter to get by for a year, wrote at a corner table of Sharpey's down the street from their apartment.

Their place was large and dirty, with the faint but constant smell of a decomposing animal and garlic in the air.

A VOCALIST CALLED SWOON lived in the apartment beneath them, with some other musicians whom the McWilliamses had not met, but they knew Swoon, and recently Julia had begun to fall asleep at night imagining his splendid face on the pillow beside her.

This early afternoon Swoon was on the front porch when Julia got back from her morning shift at the coffee shop, and he smiled to see her coming up the walk.

Julia had a startling loveliness, a kind of coltish, awkward gait, a surprise in her bearing as if she was expecting an accident to happen, some emergency for which she was not prepared.

Swoon patted the step of the porch for her to sit down.

"You are a sight for these sore eyes," he said.

Julia smiled.

"That's a cliché," she said.

"Well, it's a heartfelt cliché, my beauty."

She sat down next to him, leaned into his shoulder.

"I'm exhausted. You kept us awake practicing last night."

"You should have come on down and told us to lay off," Swoon said.

"I couldn't. We have to practice ourselves," she said.

"You do your funny stories all night long?"

"Once, I took off my clothes." Julia shrugged. "That was funny."

"Onstage?"

She nodded. "Sam hated it, but people in the audience laughed a lot."

"Sam." Swoon looked over at her, his lids half closed.

"He's my older brother. I thought you'd met him."

"I know he's your brother," Swoon said. "He's someone to reckon with."

Julia wrapped her arms around her knees, resting her chin on them. "He's in charge of us," she said. "He's been in charge of us ever since our parents died."

"Oliver told me about your parents," Swoon said, leaning his head against the porch railings. "Strange the way you guys got into comedy."

"Maybe," Julia said. "Except Sam says that comedy is about bad news."

"Laugh until I cry?" Swoon said.

"Like that."

Julia was staring at a fat man across the street walking his very small dog, conscious that Swoon was looking at her, that the look seemed to have an expectation, a kind of aggressiveness, which pleased and frightened her. She wanted to look at him. She imagined herself looking at him, pushing him gently down on his back, lying on top of him, kissing his lips with her eyes open, so their eyes were almost flat against each other, deep, black, secret ponds. She could feel that something was slipping over her, about to happen, and she wondered if she might leap on top of him. Or run.

The man with the dog had gone up the street, around the corner; the street was empty, the air electric.

"Have you ever been with anybody?" Swoon asked, in an offhand kind of way.

"What do you mean?"

"Like a man or a woman, someone real close."

"You mean sex?" Julia asked, her skin prickly, her stomach a little sick. "How come you ask?"

"Because I've been thinking just this morning, just now sitting with you on the step, I've been thinking you're going to have some difficulty if you don't turn down the heat," Swoon said.

"If you want to know, I dream about you before I go to sleep at night and your head is on my pillow," Julia said, leaning toward him so their arms touched. "That's one thing I know."

Swoon didn't smile. He took out a cigarette, lit it, closed his eyes.

He was wearing jeans rolled up, bare feet, no shirt. He had taut, muscular shoulders, not large but confident, and long legs. He was thirty, perhaps less, with impenetrable black eyes, high cheekbones, a tightness in his full lips, a man without attitude but nevertheless pleased with himself in a quiet sort of way.

"You could be bad news and not know it for a minute, not have any idea what you cause coming in a room all-girl like that."

"Don't worry," Julia said. "I have rules. Sam has us living a sort of convent life," she said.

Swoon had gotten up, ground out his cigarette in the dirt, and was headed into the house.

"I don't know what kind of convent he has in mind," he said, "but you're some kind of nun."

JULIA FOLLOWED SWOON into the hall, through the living room to the kitchen, where he stood looking in the fridge. There was a half-eaten apple, a plastic container with something yellow in it, maybe pasta and cheese, a carton of milk, and two beers.

"Not much there," Swoon said. He closed the fridge. "We'll go to lunch."

"Lunch sounds good," she said. "I have money."

"So do I." He took her hand. "You come along now and mind your p's and q's."

"That's a cliché, too," Julia said.

"I'm all clichés, darling. Stick with me and you won't have an original conversation."

SAM PUSHED open the front door to the duplex and followed Charlotte to the second floor. The air inside the building was suffocating and he felt a general unease, not unfamiliar—he thought of his emotional immune system as compromised, susceptible to the smallest change in temperature. Whenever the feeling came over him, he believed someone had died and he was about to be told the news.

So he wasn't surprised to see the note on the door to their apartment—had expected it—a torn piece of the *Chicago Tribune* written in yellow Magic Marker, barely legible:

Guys, it said, *Oliver's at the University Hospital, like in a coma. Drugs. See ya there, Trish.*

"YOU'VE BEEN WEIRD," Trish had said to Oliver that morning on their way to work with the painting crew, driving her blue pickup like a maniac. "Ever since we got to Chicago, it's as if you're on drugs."

"Maybe I am," Oliver said.

"How come I didn't know that? How come, Oliver? We've been together six months and I never thought you did anything but too much sugar, and maybe you're hypoglycemic or diabetic or one of those sugar things." She turned off the music.

They had met in late January in an Asian History class, and by Valentine's Day, Trish had moved in with him. Things happened quickly like that with Oliver. Trish was pretty enough and she had an ease with men which Oliver liked. But she also had an insatiable appetite for constant engagement which by late spring had exhausted him. It was a problem Oliver had with women. He was always ending up with someone who had taken over his bedroom, sometimes his shirts and boxer shorts, and wouldn't leave.

"So what kind of drugs are you on?" Trish asked.

Oliver closed his eyes. A headache was coming on him like a car crash and he was braced for it. He wished Trish Bryant would evaporate and in her place there'd be an angel. He couldn't remember why he had been so fascinated when they met.

They parked in front of the large gray clapboard in Hyde Park and Trish got out of the truck. Already the rest of the painting crew had arrived and were setting up on the front porch, passing out coffee and doughnuts. Oliver leaned his head back against the front seat. He had a sense that his legs were locked in a slow-moving paralysis headed upward toward his heart.

"Trish?"

She leaned in the window of the truck and handed him a banana. "Potassium," she said.

"Do I look funny to you?" he asked.

"You look normal. Too skinny. Eat your banana."

He peeled the banana, put the peel in the glove compartment, and actually felt better after he had eaten.

"I think you should quit this comedy thing," Trish said, walking across the yard with him. "It's not your shtick. It's your brother's, and he frightens me."

Oliver got out of the truck, put his hands in his pockets, and followed her across the yard.

"I really mean it, Oliver. I'd feel weird all the time if I had to play that stupid talking dog Sam insists you do."

"I play a lot of roles, not just a dog."

"Whatever," she said, opening her thermos, handing it to him. "Camomile tea. No sugar."

"No thanks."

Mark Naples, who ran the paint crew, was on the porch giving out assignments.

"We're starting outside today," Mark said to him. "Have you done exteriors?"

"Not much," Oliver said.

"We go from the top of the house to the bottom," Mark said. "It's a piece of cake unless you're afraid of heights."

Oliver looked up. The house was three stories high, with a pitched roof.

"I'm not bothered by heights," he said.

But he had a sudden vision of the ladder in the sky and him on it and the ladder swaying, and he knew he was going to die before his feet were firmly on the ground again.

"We do the trim first, and these windows won't be so hard because they haven't had many paint jobs on them," Mark was saying. "We're using this godawful red color and white on the trim."

"What about the living room? That's not done yet," Oliver said. "I could do the living room while you guys do the trim."

"It's too hot to paint inside today, even with fans." Mark adjusted the extension ladder against the back of the house. "Are you okay, Oliver? You look a little sick."

"He's been weird all morning," Trish said.

"Maybe you shouldn't be on this ladder," Mark said.

"No problem," Oliver said, taking hold of either side of the ladder, giving it a reassuring shake. "If you're interested, my potassium is A-OK."

He finished his coffee, picked up the material he needed, sandpaper and a scraper, and started up the ladder.

What happened and had been happening since May, since exams at Columbia, was an aura inside his head. He'd feel a separation as if a piece of his brain on which he regularly counted for a sense of well-being had come dislodged and in the vacancy was an aura, a kind of vaporous rainbow which he could actually see, although it lived inside his brain. Then the aura disappeared and there was either terror or a terrible headache. He preferred the headache.

At the top of the ladder, his hands wet with nerves, he concentrated on the details, at this particular moment sanding with large-grained sandpaper the loose paint and cracks on the sill of a third-story window. The window looked in on a child's bedroom with a white canopy bed and a white spread, and on the spread a white cat, which caught Oliver's attention. He wondered was it actually a cat he saw sleeping at the bottom of the bed or did he project a white cat there because he wanted one to complete the perfect picture. That is what he was thinking when the cat moved, stretched its long, slender legs, arched its bony back, and jumped off the bed to the floor. Oliver was pleased it had been a cat and not in his mind. He was not, as he sometimes thought, imagining things. The cat was real and so was he and the hands at the end of the extension of his arms were his hands and also real. And that was when he fell.

A careless moment of inattention, a sudden dizziness, a loss of confidence, terror. Both feet went backward on the rung, simply lost their grip. The heels went down and the toes slipped.

WHEN SAM ARRIVED at the University Hospital, Oliver was in a small dark single room, the television on mute.

"I fell off a ladder," he said.

"So the doctor said." Sam brushed the damp, floppy hair off Oliver's forehead.

"Did he say I'm in bad shape?"

"He said you have low blood pressure."

"That's all?"

"Very low." Sam pulled a chair up beside the bed. "Trish left a note to say you're on drugs. That was helpful."

"She's an idiot," Oliver said.

"She was in the waiting room. I sent her home," Sam said. "I know you're not on drugs."

"Are you here alone?" Oliver asked.

"Charlotte and Julia are coming with food," Sam said. "Milk shakes, hamburgers, and french fries. We're staying."

"All night?"

"A sleepover," Sam said. "The quarters are great."

Charlotte and Julia pushed open the door with bags from the deli, handing Oliver the tall milk shake in a plastic cup.

"Chocolate?" Oliver asked.

"Of course," Charlotte said, looking around, rearranging the chairs, putting the lacy shawl she was wearing over the plastic table as a cloth. "I've never spent the night in a hospital." She put her portable radio on the table beside his bed. "Would you like music?"

"Music would be nice," Oliver said.

She turned the radio on low.

The evening was thick with humidity and was particularly dark for late June. Charlotte opened a window in spite of the nurse's request to keep it closed, pulled a chair up next to Oliver's bed, and sat down next to Sam.

OUTSIDE THE ROOM, the lights in the hall painted a bright yellow stripe under the door, and the flat, muffled footsteps of the nurses along the corridor of General Surgery gave an eerie sense of prison rather than a hospital.

The doctor had found nothing besides low blood pressure, except that Oliver's pupils were dilated and his pulse was a little fast.

"Nerves," the doctor said. "That's my diagnosis."

But they admitted him for observation.

"Three stories is a very long fall," the doctor said.

AFTER THE LIGHTS WERE OUT in the room, Oliver sat in the rolled-up bed, wide awake and thinking, his mind clear.

"Sam?"

"I'm here."

He tried to make out his brother's face, a gray shape across from him, the night starless, promising rain, the room too dark to distinguish faces from the space around them.

"What do you remember about the train ride?" Oliver asked.

"What part?"

"You've always said I was the one who wanted lunch."

"Lunch?"

"On the train to Rome."

"No, Oliver," Sam said, suddenly aware of what Oliver was suggesting. "James and Lucy were going to get lunch anyway. They had planned to. We *all* wanted to eat."

"You told me you weren't hungry and that I wanted a chocolate milk shake."

"We were all hungry except Julia, who had a bottle," Sam said. "They would have gone even if we hadn't been hungry."

"I thought I was the one responsible," Oliver said. "That's what you told me."

Sam got up from the chair where he'd been resting and walked over to the window, looking out at the veiled city, the foggy lights shimmering in halos in the sky, the moon a curved line low on the horizon.

"I must have told it wrong," Sam said.

Sam had never considered Oliver susceptible. Of all of them, even Julia, he had thought that Oliver was the least interested in the past, unimplicated in what had happened on the train to Rome, not thoughtlessly, but because he had no memory of it.

Sam felt a sudden, unfamiliar weight. "Do you remember Gió?" he asked, hoping to provide some measure of kindness to Oliver, to invent a story which might compensate for Sam's carelessness.

"You told us about him," Oliver said.

"I just wondered how much you remember from seeing and how much from what I've told you," Sam said. "Do you remember that Gió liked you?"

"He didn't speak English," Oliver said.

"He spoke a little," Sam said.

"He told you he liked me?" Oliver asked.

"I could tell that he did." Sam leaned over the bed. He wanted to touch him, but he didn't.

"I'm very sorry, Oliver," he said. "I didn't know you ever worried about what happened, or I'd have been more careful in the way I told you."

"It's okay."

Oliver tried to close his eyes, but they felt glued open. He won-dered whether there were people who couldn't close their eyes at all, who saw day and night without relief, and whether he was about to become one of them.

"Aren't you at all tired, Oliver?" Charlotte asked when Sam had gone downstairs with Julia to get a Coke. She sat down on his bed.

"I'm never tired," Oliver said. "I'm wide awake except for fainting." His voice was stuck in his throat. "It's a nightmare."

"This isn't like you at all," she said. "What do you think is the matter?"

"I'm going crazy," Oliver said.

"You can't," Charlotte said. "You're the normal one, the ordinary American boy. You simply can't go crazy."

"Don't tell Sam." Oliver turned over on his side toward Charlotte.

"Never," Charlotte said.

AS THE NIGHT WORE ON in a hollow and inhospitable room, in the company of his family, Oliver began to sink into a kind of ease he hadn't felt for weeks, pleased by the sound of their voices washing over him.

"Why do you think they lived all over the world?" Julia was asking. "Do you think they were running away?"

"What would they have been running from?" Charlotte asked.

"They seemed happy," Sam said. "Incredibly happy. That's what I remember."

"At seven you remember that?" Oliver asked. "How can you know the difference at seven when you haven't known unhappiness?"

"I remember exactly. I remember them," Sam said and, then, considering, added, "I think I remember," although he knew how slippery memory is, knew that the scenes he believed he remembered of his parents were fixed in place by necessity, that reality and dream are partners in survival.

He was suddenly uncertain that he wanted the responsibility for his parents' history, or that he had earned it.

They lay in the dark, listening to one another's breathing, to the clatter and muffled thumps outside the door, hoping a nurse would not come in to check Oliver's blood pressure, interrupting what felt like common breath.

"I love it that we're all here lying in the dark telling secrets," Julia said.

"Did Sam mention Second City?" Charlotte asked Oliver.

"It's going to be perfect for us," Sam said.

"Once we decide who you're going to be, Oliver, and then Sam can write some new scripts deleting the dog," Charlotte said.

"I love Anarchy," Oliver said.

"I'm voting for a normal American boy," Sam said.

"At least that's a role I'm familiar with," Oliver said. "A normal American boy, McWilliams style."

OLIVER FELT LAUGHTER, out of nowhere, for no reason, like unexpected nausea. His mind, arched like a cat for combat, fast-forwarded to a vision of himself there in the hospital room with his brother and sisters, and he was laughing, laughing, out of control, the laughter changed to tears and he was sobbing, the doctor coming down the corridor, throwing open the door to his room, sending him to the sixth floor, Psychiatric.

"So good night, guys," Julia said, turning to face the wall. "And Plum and Jaggers, Good night, good night. Are they here, Sam?"

"They're at home for a change," Sam said.

And he saw them, black-and-white shadows silk-screened on the surface of his memory. They were sitting at either end of the dining-room table, talking across the empty chairs.

8

T HE ATLANTIC THEATRE COMPANY was on West Twentieth Street, close to the Hudson River, a small Off Broadway space with 165 seats on a residential block. Plum & Jaggers opened there on a Thursday night in September, a steady blast of rain driving at an angle from the river, so the weather tore under umbrellas, turning them inside out.

"No one's going to come in this rain," Julia said, sitting on a splintery stool, her face pressed up against the mirror, putting on pancake and purple-passion lipstick to give her a witchy look under the hot stage lights.

The date was September 19, 1993, and the McWilliamses had been in New York City for a year, living on West Eleventh Street in a two-bedroom sublet, cheaply had in return for taking care of Meow, the owner's incontinent cat. All year, they had played Off Off Broadway, in the basements of churches and clubs, at New York University and Hunter College, as entertainment at parties. They'd been written up in small reviews in *The Village Voice* and *New York* magazine, and one notice in an article written for *The New York Times* about downtown underground theater. There was a buzz about them, a kind of kettle boil about the "McWilliams Funnies," as they were called among the regulars of comedy clubs and Off Off

Broadway theaters. They were unusual, doing plays, not stand-up routines, actual stories depending on character rather than one-liners. The fact that they were brothers and sisters gave a particular spirit of intimacy to the dark comedy of their plays, as if the audience had been invited to their home.

"What do you think about the rain?" Julia asked.

"They'll come in spite of it," Sam said.

"I wish we'd asked Noli and Grandfather to come later, after the reviews," Oliver said. He was in sweats, the bottoms low on his hips, the shirt too short, so his belly showed. He had a black baseball cap with a bowling pin medallion on backward and high tops untied.

In the corner, in a folding chair, Charlotte was reading.

"I hate it when you read," Julia said.

Charlotte looked up from her book. "Who'll be here tonight, Sam?"

"Reviewers. Maybe a scout from television. Noli and Grandfather."

Sam was also expecting Rebecca Frankel.

On the front of the program was written: PLUM & JAGGERS PRESENTS PHOTO ALBUM WITH THE MCWILLIAMS FAMILY. On the inside right page at the top of the credits, he had written a dedication: "For Rebecca Frankel and her daughter, Miriam."

"Why?" Julia had asked. "We don't even know them, isn't that right?"

"She's the one who wrote to Sam about laughter when he was young," Charlotte said.

"I know about her," Julia said. "I just don't know her."

"We've never met," Sam said.

He assumed he was in love with her.

He had written her letters, which he never sent, during the winter he spent in the Cage. He had large manila envelopes full of all his plays and letters and pictures of the family, thinking that if he ever found her address, he'd send them to her. She was always in his mind, but he hadn't looked for her until the summer at Second City in Chicago. After the incident with Oliver in the hospital, he finally tracked her down. She was living with her daughter, Miriam, who must have been about thirteen, on West Seventy-first Street in New York City and was working as an editor at the Larkin Press.

> *Dear Rebecca Frankel* [he had written when he located her address],
>
> *Perhaps you don't remember, but many years ago, when your son and husband were killed in West Jerusalem, I wrote to you to express my deep sympathy and to tell you about my parents. You wrote back a letter I have read again and again, which has been helpful to me. It is about laughter and despair.*
>
> *I am the writer in a comedy troupe with my brother and sisters called Plum & Jaggers. Should we ever come to New York City to perform, I will let you know.*
>
> *Your friend, Sam McWilliams*

Rebecca Frankel wrote a postcard with a picture by Picasso of a plump young woman with half a face in which she said how glad she was to hear from him, and of course she'd come to his performance in New York City.

FROM THEN ON they communicated with some regularity by post-card, the small white space sufficient to carry the weight of their emotion without embarrassment.

If Rebecca had been, say, twenty-eight when Sam wrote her in the first place, when he was ten, he thought—twenty-eight at least, with a seven-year-old son, no doubt a college education, then she must be forty now. Not too old, he thought, and leaning against the wall in the dressing room of the Atlantic Theatre, waiting for the call to go on, Sam had the terrible excitement of a performer who knows his audience will include the woman he loves.

IN THE SECOND ROW center, Noli was having trouble breathing.

It was her first trip to New York; they had come by Metroliner from Union Station in Washington. In the last two years, since the children were away, she had been going out, but never unaccompanied or very far beyond Washington. The agoraphobia was always present. Whenever she had a sense of sinking into a kind of panic hole, she would imagine herself scrambling out of it, making her way upward to the open air.

Now she concentrated on the theater program, reading the notes on her grandchildren, though she knew them by heart.

"You know, William," she said, leaning against him, "every time I read the program notes about the setting for the show with the stupid bomb under the dining-room table, I feel ill."

"I think that's the point," William said.

The houselights were dimming when a dark-haired woman in a hooded black raincoat rushed into a seat in the front row at the end of the aisle, just to the left of Noli and William, and sat down with a girl about fifteen, her daughter perhaps, a seemingly reluctant traveler.

She turned around, a pretty woman, Noli noted, with sparkling eyes and dimples.

"Do we know her?" William asked.

"I don't think so," Noli said. "I would remember."

She looked back at them again.

"Do you happen to have an extra program?" she asked. "I stupidly forgot to pick one up."

The girl was at an age when public conversation with her mother embarrassed her. She sank lower in her seat.

"I do," Noli said, reaching in her large bag, where she had stashed some programs, twenty at least, to send to friends, handing one to the woman.

"Thank you," the woman said, struggling out of her raincoat. "I'm so glad to have this. I know the writer of the show, so I couldn't miss it," she said, as if she were responding to a question she had been asked.

———

BY MIDNIGHT, the rain had stopped in New York City, the cast party with champagne and flowers and congratulations was over, and the McWilliams family walked, arm in arm, down Sixth Avenue.

"It was perfect," Noli said.

"Not exactly perfect," Sam said. "But better than I'd hoped."

"Wonderful, wonderful, wonderful us," Julia sang, her arm flung over Charlotte's shoulders.

"People laughed," Oliver said. "They really laughed."

"I believe that the woman in the seat in front of us was weeping," Noli said. She laced her arm through Sam's. "She knew you."

"She knew me?" Sam asked.

"A very pretty lady with curly hair and dimples crying her eyes out," Noli said. "I tried to catch her to invite her to the cast party, but she'd disappeared."

There were no stars, but the lights of the city shimmering in the low fog were like a blanket of stars spread over them, as Sam walked with his family, his company, through the muddy puddles of rainwater to their borrowed home on West Eleventh Street.

II

IN THE EARLY WINTER of 1998, *Currents*, a weekly news and feature magazine, devoted a series of issues to what the editors called "The State of Internal Affairs in North America." The first of the series was titled "The Book of Revelations—2000" and included pieces on the apocalyptic nature of the turn of the second millennium, how a kind of craziness was taking over, a proliferation of cults and extreme behavior, of fear and paranoia, even terror—the biblical promise of Revelations.

Another issue was on terrorism. "Terrorism: Warfare as Cult of Self." There had been the trials of Timothy McVeigh and Terry Nichols, the bombing of the World Trade Center, suspicion of foul play in TWA Flight 800, the trial and the plea bargain of Ted Kaczinski, the Unabomber, singly responsible for three deaths and twenty-three injuries. There were random incidents of terrorist-planted bombs in the United States, one in January at an abortion clinic in Atlanta, a detonated bomb found in a trash can outside Macy's Department Store in New York City, an explosion at a mini-mart in New Orleans injuring an employee as he unpacked canned peaches. It was a time, not unlike 1968 following the assassination of Martin Luther King, when an ordinary citizen had a sense that anything could happen.

THE LAST ISSUE of the series in *Currents* was on comedy. Plum & Jaggers was the subject of the cover story.

Sam McWilliams was now thirty-one. In the cover photograph he was standing—a tall, thin, serious-looking young man with wire-rimmed glasses, khakis, a button-down blue shirt with the neck open and the sleeves rolled up, looking by his dress and demeanor like a recent Ph.D. in English literature, except for a dark, untamed intensity evident even in a glossy photograph. Charlotte stood next to him, wearing a long black skirt and a striped man's shirt, over-sized, with the tails out. At twenty-nine she looked twelve, a little plump, with round tortoise-shell glasses and long dark hair pulled behind her ears, an expression of childlike surprise. Julia, her thick curly hair almost wild around a perfectly shaped face, had glasses, too, small rectangular ones at the end of her nose, her blue eyes staring unsmiling at the viewer. She wore a short black skirt, a small tight black turtleneck sweater, and she was thin enough to appear anorexic. She was sitting on the floor. Oliver, crouching beside her in tight jeans and a heavy cable-knit turtleneck, his black-rimmed Buddy Holly glasses folded on his knee, had changed the most since the early nineties, angular, with thinning sandy hair, wispy, long over his forehead, a kind of haunted look on a face which had once been sunny and round. He was almost twenty-eight, Julia twenty-five, though she looked older.

THE ISSUE ON COMEDY was just on the newsstands, and on Sunday morning the McWilliamses lay around the great room reading aloud.

In the kitchen, Noli was making blueberry pancakes on the griddle of the industrial stove her grandchildren had recently given her, as if her days of serious cooking were just beginning. She was eighty-three and losing her sight, but her capacity to flee into a world of the imagination had given her a kind of immortality. She patted the Virginia sausage into small flat circles, stuck her finger in the Vermont syrup, and, licking it, strained to overhear the conversation of her grandchildren.

"Read the beginning again," Oliver was saying to Charlotte.

"The McWilliamses live in New York City," Charlotte began, *"but they spend their holidays in Bluemont, Virgina, on a farm they share with their grandparents."*

Oliver looked over her shoulder, reading along with her.

"They are living the way they have always lived since their parents were killed when a bomb exploded in the lunch car of the Espresso from Milan to Rome in June 1974. The children were seven, five, four, and one."

"Psychic trauma obliterates children of vagabonds," Julia said, assuming a thick accent.

"Your parents were not vagabonds," Noli called from the kitchen.

"Your father was a painter and your mother was . . ." An old memory flickered across William's face. "She was going to be a doctor. She would have been a doctor."

Sam leaned against the table, his arms folded tight across his chest, uneasy listening to his sister read.

"Plum and Jaggers, the invisible parents of this comedy team, may as well be dead," Charlotte was saying. *"Like others of their generation who grew up hooked on the issues of the sixties, they have opted out of family life. The kids are in charge and the spirit of the day is chaos on the edge of disaster."*

"Does it say anything negative about the set?" Oliver asked.

"Nothing negative. Just a description." Charlotte sat up with the magazine in her lap, leaning against the couch, reading. *"The story takes place in the dining room of a row house located in an imaginary neighborhood in a city which could be New York or Los Angeles or Chicago but is referred to as the City of Brotherly Love in honor of the Founding Fathers in Philadelphia."*

"What does it say about us?" Julia asked. "Especially Sam."

"Sam McWilliams, not only the writer of Plum & Jaggers *but its centrifugal force, is mute."*

Noli carried a tray of butter and syrup in from the kitchen, setting it on the table, stopping to listen.

"With the exception of an occasional facial tic stretching his mouth into an exaggerated O, Sam's demeanor is that of an intelligent guard dog."

"Does it happen to say we're any good?" Oliver asked.

"I haven't gotten there yet," Charlotte said, looking over at Sam. "But we are very good, aren't we?"

"We're good enough," Sam said softly.

"Very good. Excellent," Oliver insisted. "Say it, Sam."

"Very good, then," Sam said, in spite of himself.

And they burst into applause, filling the room with laughter.

"But also lucky," Sam added when they had finished clapping. He was anxious about good fortune, with its ultimate promise of extinction. "We've been very lucky."

AFTER THE SUCCESS of *Photo Album* at the Atlantic Theatre Company in the fall of 1993, Plum & Jaggers appeared a few times on David Letterman and twice on *Saturday Night Live*. They did a show in Chelsea which ran most of the winter of 1996, and that was followed by a short-run holiday show called *The Last Thanksgiving*, which played at La Mama to wonderful reviews. Except for a trip to play at the Edinburgh summer festival, they continued to live in New York City, mostly in SoHo, subletting place after place, six months at a time, always temporarily.

In early 1997, NBC Television asked Sam to write a half-hour pilot for *Plum & Jaggers*. Pleased with the results, the network requested thirteen more episodes to air live for half an hour after *Saturday Night Live*, beginning in late October. By the time the article was published, *Plum & Jaggers* was a critical success, with a growing audience of mostly young adults. In early winter, Sam was asked to write nine more episodes, which would continue the series into the middle of the spring and likely promise it a place in the fall 1998 season.

"Plum & Jaggers *is rare comedy*," the reporter had written, "*hyperbolic episodes at the far edge of sanity, combining the psychological strangeness of David Lynch with the plasticity of cartoons.*"

"I don't exactly understand what he's saying," Julia said. "I thought there was supposed to be something sweet about the show."

"There is," Oliver said. "Cartoon characters have a kind of innocence."

"Like dogs," Julia said.

"I'll read how the paragraph ends," Charlotte went on. "*At the corner of the street where comedy turns ultimately serious, these dark stories are about a family of children, forever in exile, turned inside out.*"

"Perfect," Julia said, standing in the center of the room. "I welcome you to the Plum & Jaggers Family Freak Show." She bent in an exaggerated bow. "Broadcast live Saturday at midnight from our living room to yours."

THEY WERE AT BLUEMONT FARM, where they spent time whenever they could. The place, with its old clapboard farmhouse and two-story barn in the process of renovation, was on fifty acres of rolling hills an hour outside of Washington, on the edge of the Blue Ridge Mountains, close enough for the smoky hue of the mountains to form a soft line of color above their house.

The Rappahannock River flowed through the northern section of their land. Oliver, always drawing landscapes on the backs of Sam's scripts, was planning to design houses for each of them which would be built on a hill overlooking the Rappahannock, backing onto the dense evergreen woods. There was the barn, reconstructed as a lodge with an open kitchen and great room on the first floor, an office in the loft above. There was a small one-bedroom cottage where Noli and William lived, which Noli insisted reminded her of Grand Rapids, but that was a matter of wishing and insufficient memory, since the house in Grand Rapids had been brick, built in the twenties, a conventional center-hall colonial. And the ramshackle farmhouse, where the McWilliamses slept, though most of the time they were working or eating or simply talking out stories for *Plum & Jaggers* in the barn.

When William wandered into the open kitchen, Noli was stacking the pancakes and sausage on a platter, humming along with the music.

"The radio's too loud," he said.

"I thought you were losing your hearing." She picked off the edge of one of the pancakes and ate it.

"I can hear perfectly well," he said, carrying the coffeepot to the table.

"Grandfather's hearing is selective," Oliver said.

They slid into their chairs at the table and Noli tapped her glass. She loved to tap her glass, and then she'd fold her hands, looking over the table at all of them as if she had a significant announcement.

"What I want to know is why you all have glasses in the picture in the magazine when you don't need glasses to see?" she asked.

"Except Charlotte," Julia said.

"But Charlotte has always worn glasses," Noli said.

"Charlotte got glasses before James and Lucy died," Sam said. "We were in Israel and the glasses had heavy black rims."

"They wear glasses to give the impression of intellectuals," William said.

"And to suggest that with glasses we see into the heart of things," Oliver said. "That's Sam's idea of it."

"The glasses are a metaphor," Sam said.

Noli nodded happily. She didn't know much about metaphors. She wasn't even interested in glasses or why her grandchildren wore them on the television show when they could see perfectly well without them. She had only wanted to hold her place in the community.

"Well, I for one very much like the idea of glasses," William said. "You have an eye for the particular, Sam. It must be genetic."

AFTER BREAKFAST, they walked along the river. The weather had been unseasonably cold and dry, the river, running low over its rocky bed, the bright noon sun streaked gold across the water's surface. A perfect winter day. The sky was high and cloudless, the air clear. The river meandered in a narrow ribbon through the bottom of the property. Walking single file, the McWilliamses followed the path to the end, where the next farm began. Black Angus cattle, clustered against the fence, stared dumbly across the split rails, mildly curious about their arrival.

"Shall we go to the dance hall?" Julia asked.

"Dance hall?" Oliver asked.

"The vegetable garden, idiot brother of mine." Julia grabbed his hand.

"Why not?" Oliver said. "It's a nice day for dancing."

"Although a little cold," Charlotte said.

And laughing at nothing at all, they ran up the hill to the middle of the property, where a horse barn, falling in on itself, divided what had once been hay fields on one side and corn fields on the other, the residue of stalks still evident, and a vegetable garden with a wire fence to protect the vegetables from deer.

"Do you ever think what you might have been if we hadn't done Plum & Jaggers?" Sam was asking Julia.

"A stripper. It's in my genes." Julia laughed. "A rock-star groupie."

"Not a chance," Oliver said.

"I know I wouldn't have been anything which required school," Julia said. "And I wouldn't have been a mother. That's Charlotte's job."

"Charlotte would have been an English professor," Oliver said.

"Or a translator or a linguist," Julia added. "Something serious."

"A fifties housewife putting out frozen dinners in front of the TV," Charlotte said. "The stay-at-home suburban mother drinking white wine, watching the soaps."

"That's the mother I've always had in mind," Oliver said.

"How can you be a mother if you've never had one?" Julia asked Charlotte. As the youngest, Julia was the mascot, the beloved pet, allowed to roam on a long rope, but watched over like a child in a kibbutz whose economic principles of sharing extend to children.

She didn't think about mothers in the way that Charlotte did. She didn't miss her own mother or long to be one herself.

"I dream a perfect mother," Charlotte said, slipping her arm through Julia's. "Lucy sitting on the end of my bed at night watching me while I sleep."

"I suppose when I think about my perfect mother, I think of Sam." Julia laughed.

THE OFFICE, which they called the viewing room, where the McWilliamses watched videos of past *Plum & Jaggers* shows looking for their mistakes, was on the second floor of the barn. The room was large, the walls painted a rich ocher, with soft old couches and chairs, and books stacked randomly on the worn Oriental rug. Sam's desk, where he wrote his scripts, working first in longhand, overlooked the river. There was a long table in the center of the room where they had script meetings and rehearsals for the next show before they returned on Tuesday mornings to New York.

The room was lined with framed newspaper accounts of the terrorist explosions that had taken place since 1974, Sam's collection after years of saving the stories from the papers. On the walls, written in black in Oliver's elegant hand, were the names of the people who had died, including James and Lucy Lucas McWilliams, as if Sam's memorial to the dead were a public record of names, like the memorial to the Vietnam dead in Washington, and Sam the designated historian for terrorism.

These names were the ones Sam used for the characters he developed, the extras who came in and out of the McWilliamses' dining room in *Plum & Jaggers*, acquaintances of theirs—delivery boys arriving on the set with pizza and an order of live parakeets, solicitors in drag distributing religious pamphlets, an elementary-school teacher tied and gagged under the dining-room table, the town policeman stripped to his undershorts and dumped into the stockpot simmering on the stove. Walk-on parts in the show—Amy and Saul and Marigold and Mavis and Marshall and Samantha and Gloria and Serena. Sam's personal memorial.

Photographs of James and Lucy and their children hung on the walls as well, but for the article in *Currents*, the photographer had selected a close-up of a photograph of James and Lucy taken before they were married, standing on the bank of a river in Scotland which Sam recognized from one of his father's shoreline paintings. They were wearing Wellingtons and heavy parkas and bright-colored scarfs around their necks, like bears, their arms around each other. The white-capped river in the distance splashed over rocks in a sea-spray umbrella, ocean swells of river over the black rocks.

This particular photograph hung next to the large window facing the river. In the reproduction in *Currents*, the frame included Lucy and James and, beyond, the view over the Rappahannock, the spread of evergreen, the rocky bluff in the distance, the sometimes gentle river wandering through the northern counties of Virginia.

In the morning the viewing room got full sun from the east. At night, the shaded, winter moon spread silver light and the room took on a mysterious hush, a feeling of isolation—like the bomb shelter Sam had in mind under the garage promising their small family an escape in the event of nuclear disaster.

But this shelter, high over the river, seemed to extend into the heavens, above the ordinary traffic of daily life. In this place surrounded by his treasures, his photographs of James and Lucy, his family, his scripts, the whole of his life collected in a barn near a village which was not even marked on a map of Virginia, Sam felt, maybe for the first time, a kind of tenuous safety.

LATE ON SUNDAY, before their daily script meeting, Sam was rereading *Currents* when Charlotte came into the viewing room and closed the door behind her, sitting down in a chair across from him.

"Noli loved the picture of James and Lucy in the magazine. We've made them immortal, she says."

"How can she see it?" Sam asked. "She's blind as a bat."

"She sees what she wants to see." Charlotte rested her chin in her hands.

"She's getting old and sentimental."

Sam shrugged, putting the article facedown, looking off into the distance. "Did you like the piece?"

"I did, very much. Didn't you?"

"I thought the reporter did a good job." He got up from the couch, pacing, his hands in his pockets, settling finally at his desk. "But when I actually saw the piece in print, I was afraid I'd made the wrong decision by agreeing to the interview."

Sam had been amazed and flattered that Plum & Jaggers was chosen for a piece in *Currents*, pleased with the reporter particularly and the photographer the magazine had sent. But at that time he had failed to imagine what it would be like when the article was actually on the newsstands, on the kitchen tables of strangers who would discover where the McWilliamses lived, who could form opinions. He felt a sudden unease, a draft of cold air as, taking the manila folder of ideas for new shows out of the top drawer of his desk, he looked over his notes for the meeting.

Charlotte was watching him, the way his dark hair fell over his face, the way he turned his head at an angle when he was thinking.

"Don't you ever wonder about getting married?" She had just reread the section of the article referring to the absence of their personal life. "I mean, have you ever considered a normal middle-class existence?"

"I haven't," Sam said.

"Sometimes I do," she said. "I'd like to have a boyfriend or a house. Maybe even a baby."

Sam looked up from his notes. "You'll have that chance," he said, an edge in his tone of voice. "We'll keep doing *Plum & Jaggers* until it fizzles out. Everything on television fizzles and we will, too. Then we'll live our normal middle-class lives."

But he couldn't imagine a time when the four of them would set up separate lives.

———

AFTER CHARLOTTE LEFT, Sam called Rebecca Frankel in New York. It was close to four, the sun falling quickly, darkness spreading through the room, the weight of winter bearing down. At first the line was busy. When he phoned again, hoping to complete the call before his siblings arrived, a woman answered, her voice familiar, almost a lilt, ending on a high note. "Hello?" she said, and he hung up.

Sam had never spoken to Rebecca Frankel, but he had often called, sometimes listening to the machine—"Hello. You have reached 496–6050. Please leave a message"—sometimes hanging up after her breezy "Hello?" Occasionally, in years past, her daughter, Miriam, would answer in a voice that alternated between sullen and bad-tempered. " 'Lo," she'd say, and Sam would put down the receiver. He imagined Rebecca as Noli had described her the evening she saw her at the Atlantic Theatre Company. Dimpled cheeks, thick, curly hair, dark eyes. He liked to think of her as thirty-two, his age, stalled in the year he first learned about her, a pretty woman, Semitic, with fierce brown eyes and fine wide cheekbones. Her voice on the telephone was girlish.

I loved the show, she wrote in the postcard she sent after the performance at the Atlantic Theatre Company. *It's subtle and heart-breaking.*

She got in the habit of writing postcards once or twice a month, and Sam wrote back, taking hours to compose a paragraph, hoping to communicate everything between the lines.

WHEN OLIVER WALKED IN, Sam was standing at the large window of the viewing room, looking out over the river.

"Where is everyone?" he asked. "It's almost four o'clock."

"Not here yet," Sam said, sitting at the long table, spreading out the sheets of plans for the next show.

Oliver took the copy of *Currents* and settled into the couch to read the parts about himself again. He liked the article. He liked in particular what the reporter said about him, and it pleased him to have special recognition, since Plum & Jaggers was mainly Sam.

"*Oliver McWilliams is Mr. Normal in this clan,*" the reporter had written. "*He's Anarchy, the talking dog, loyal, stubborn, brave, a little stupid. Or himself, a boy whose character is marked by the kind of repeated tediousness and energetic spurts familiar in a fourteen-year-old. Like the fool, or child, he can be counted on to tell the essential truths. And as Anarchy, he never shuts up, compensating for Sam's silence. 'Strong and gentle,' his sister Charlotte says of him.*"

In the photograph of Oliver—each of them had an individual black-and-white shot—he is leaning against a pillar of the lodge with a dog, a large, black, Lablike dog, a mutt belonging to the photographer, who insisted that Oliver was the sort of man to have a dog, especially a large one.

"Do you like what they say about you?" Oliver asked.

"They didn't say much," Sam said. "I like that."

"They describe you as handsome."

Sam laughed.

"And difficult."

"I expected that," Sam said.

"I suppose the reporter thinks that your career as a juvenile delinquent makes you more exciting than the rest of us."

"It wasn't exactly a career," Sam said. He checked his watch. "It's after four. They're late."

SOMETIMES NOLI'S MIND TRIPPED, but she'd usually catch herself before she fell. It happened as Charlotte and Julia were walking with her in the late afternoon, early dusk, the wind picking up behind them.

"Some people in Grand Rapids go to Florida in the winter because it's too gloomy and cold to stay in Michigan," Noli was saying, walking between her granddaughters, her arms slipped under theirs for warmth.

"I don't like the gloom, but the cold here isn't too bad, so I'm staying," she said.

"Staying where?" Julia asked.

"In Grand Rapids," Noli said.

"But we're not in Grand Rapids, Noli." Charlotte took the path that led to the cottage where Noli and William stayed.

"Why did we leave?" she asked.

"Because of Sam," Julia said. "Isn't that why we left?"

Noli stopped on the path, letting her thoughts shake into place and then, hoping to conceal her embarrassment, squeezing Charlotte's arm, she said of course she remembered. She and William lived in Washington, D.C., and had for years, and they'd been forced to leave Grand Rapids because of Sam's trouble with Ranier Moore.

"It was entirely unfair," Noli said. "Sam did nothing at all to that poor boy, whatever his name is, I forget, but the one who got beaten up behind the shed. Ranier Moore did that."

"I remember," Charlotte said.

THEIR GRANDFATHER WAS ALREADY BACK at the farmhouse, still in his coat, tossing wood on the fire.

"It's too cold to take my coat off," he said when they came in the door.

"So cold I thought we were in Grand Rapids." Noli laughed, rubbing her mittened hands together.

"Well, we're not in Grand Rapids," William said. "We're here."

"That's right. Here is wherever we are," Noli said, kissing her granddaughters.

CHARLOTTE AND JULIA HEADED BACK to the barn, late for the meeting, darkness settling in, the taste of winter.

"Don't you think it's strange that they left Grand Rapids just because Sam was accused of something he didn't do?" Julia asked.

"I think Sam was marked as bad by whatever happened and they thought they had to leave," Charlotte said.

Julia pulled her wool hat down low on her forehead and drew her bare hands up into the sleeves of her winter coat, looking over at Charlotte. She very seldom complained about Sam, not that her sister wouldn't be sympathetic. But complaining about Sam made her nervous, as if he could always overhear what was being said.

"Does Sam drive you insane lately?" she asked finally.

Charlotte had taken a flashlight out of her pocket and turned it on to light the path.

"Not insane," Charlotte said. "He's a little overinvolved in everything we do."

"I can't even breathe in my own house," Julia said.

"He worries about us," Charlotte said. "He feels a lot of responsibility."

"Worrying would be okay." She pushed open the door to the barn, heading upstairs to the viewing room. "But he controls us." She turned back to look at her sister, who was just behind her on the steps. "Doesn't he?"

Charlotte shook her head, put her finger to her lips. "He can hear us," she said.

SAM AND OLIVER were were sitting at the long table, their feet up, papers strewn across the table, watching the video of Saturday's show.

"You're late," Sam said.

"We were taking Noli home," Charlotte bristled.

"This isn't a military drill," Julia said, flopping down on the couch.

"So," Oliver began quickly, changing the subject to keep peace, "we have the idea for the next episode." They took their places at the table. "Sam got it from the last lines in the article."

"Read it," Julia said, collapsing on a chair next to Oliver, putting her small, stockinged feet on the table next to his.

"*Exile seems to be the fundamental nature of Sam McWilliams's character and the condition at the heart of* Plum & Jaggers *comedy.*"

"And that's funny?" Julia asked.

"It can be." Sam organized his notes in a measured way, lining the stacks of paper in front of him, then handed out pencils and yellow pads.

LATER, AFTER DINNER, after the rest of the family had gone to bed, Sam went upstairs to the viewing room to work.

It was his favorite time, sitting at his desk at the highest point of land on Bluemont Farm, the barn silent, a wind stirring in the woods beyond, the night cave-black, lights out in the house, his kingdom safely sleeping.

At midnight he checked his watch, turned off his computer, his lamp, and was just picking up a flashlight to go to bed when he heard a rustle outside the window, a kind of sizzle loud enough to penetrate the glass, and suddenly the room was lit as if a multitude of floodlights were pointed at the sky.

THE BARN faced the Rappahannock, on a high bluff over the river. Beyond the river was a vast field kept in high grass where the previous owner had horses. Beyond the field was a dense, dry wood, parched after a long season of drought.

What lit the sky was fire. Gradually Sam could see that the fire had a shape, an extraordinary light beginning just on the other side of the river, where bone-dry grasses, flattened by weather, were bending into winter.

The fire was moving as if it were in the process of igniting before Sam's eyes. A wide curve, a kind of inverted arch, and then a long strip of blaze across what must have been the center of the field, and perpendicular to that line, a shorter one, so what he saw was an inferno, almost glorious in its brilliance, taking the shape of the letter *J*.

10

BY THE TIME the volunteer fire department arrived, the *J* had spread from a curled half-moon at the bottom of the field, closest to the river, to a circle, the clear lines obliterated, so what the firemen discovered when they drove up to the farm not long after Sam's call was a shapeless conflagration ignited by gasoline.

"Do you have any enemies?" the sheriff had asked.

"In Rappahannock?" Oliver shook his head. "We're new to the neighborhood."

"But people know you," the sheriff said.

"I know you," the fire chief said. "Your show isn't exactly my cup of tea, but I watch it because we're neighbors."

"I watch it, too. It's pretty funny." The sheriff put a hand on Sam's shoulder, assuming a kind of intimacy. "We'll be back in the morning when it's light enough to look around. In the meantime, consider your enemies."

THEY SAT ON THE LONG WORKTABLE by the window, pressed together like stockade fence posts, watching the darkness over the back field beyond the river where the fire had been.

"Why would someone write a *J*?" Charlotte asked softly.

"Noli says the *J* is for Jew. Did you hear her?" Oliver asked. "She thinks it was Nazis."

"The article says we lived on a kibbutz in Israel," Charlotte said. "Noli's getting loopy."

"The article is just out," Oliver said. "No one could have read it yet."

"But someone must have known about us and decided to set our field on fire," Julia said, expecting the worst, suggestible by nature, trusting her intuition.

"We'll have to think about our enemies." Oliver turned on the overhead lights.

"Your old girlfriends?" Charlotte asked.

"Real enemies willing to find out where we live and come after us," Oliver said. "Not bad."

"Maybe one enemy," Charlotte said. "Not enemies."

"The show could have made someone angry," Oliver said.

Julia drew her knees up under her chin, her earlier anger at Sam giving way to fear.

"I don't like the idea of floating enemies," she said.

A FAMILIAR SENSE OF DREAD crept through Sam like infection, and he stopped listening, staring into the darkness. As his eyes adjusted, a form was beginning to take shape, like a woman, sliding across the charred field.

He closed his eyes, rubbing them hard, as if the application of pressure could eliminate the projection of bad dreams, but when he opened them again, she was still moving in his direction, holding a long cloth which flew behind her like a sail.

"What's going on?" Oliver asked, aware of Sam's peculiar agitation, the little choking sounds in his throat, as if he had something caught there.

"Do you see anything in the field?" Sam asked.

"Where the fire was?"

Sam nodded.

"Zero," Oliver said. "It's pitch black out there."

"Maybe I see something," Charlotte said, but when she narrowed her eyes to focus, the field was a black sheet hung outside their window, the sky insufficiently bright to illuminate the trees.

"*Someone,*" Julia said quietly. "Not something."

"You guys must be going crazy." Oliver pressed his face to the window, squinting to narrow his focus. "There's nothing to see out there."

Sam put his head in his hand and shut his eyes. With his eyes closed, the shape like a woman wasn't there. But when he opened them, she was close enough for him to see that her head was covered with a hood, like a Muslim woman in her discreet purity.

"Maybe the enemy is someone from the Cage," Charlotte was saying.

"That was years ago. If there's an enemy at all, it's more likely a stranger," Oliver said.

"Someone who doesn't like Plum & Jaggers," Charlotte said.

"Or doesn't like Anarchy."

"Or me," Julia said. "I play such creepy roles."

She pulled a blanket across her shoulders and hugged herself.

Just after midnight, Charlotte fell asleep, as she could always do, even sitting up, and Oliver dozed in and out of consciousness, occasionally leaning against Charlotte. Finally, he lay down on the couch, sleeping until dawn.

Sam couldn't sleep at all, aware that Julia's eyes were fixed on the middle distance, where he had seen the woman.

"What was it you thought you saw in the field?" she asked, leaning into the window.

"A woman," Sam said. "It may be that I've been staring at the darkness for too long, but she's there now and she seems to be wearing a long dress."

Julia cupped her hands around her eyes.

"I think I see her, too," she said.

———

AT DAWN, the sun climbing the horizon striping the black sky silver, a half-moon over the Blue Ridge Mountains, the air damp, promising snow, Sam left the lodge where the others were finally sleeping, walking along the shoreline of the Rappahannock, examining the water as if this walk were a ritual with him. He was interested in the way the light fell in patches on the slate gray turning the water olive, the way the sound of the water changed stone to stone as it rushed over the rocks.

The woman he had seen the night before was gone. He couldn't even reimagine her in his mind, and wondered now whether she had to do with the night's darkness, his sense of dread.

He believed in signs. Not from the outside world, or God, or some rearrangement of the spirits or quirk of nature—but signs from within capable of projecting the image of a Mennonite woman on the black horizon. Had he been older on the trip to Rome, more certain of his instincts, his notion of dread, he would have said to his parents, "We don't need lunch. We can wait until we get to Rome."

THE RIVER was at its widest where he was walking, feeling vaguely uneasy, imagining an arsonist in the woods above the riverbank, although he knew the perpetrator had most likely fled. He wasn't exactly afraid, but occasionally startled by a sudden sound, he moved along more quickly, thinking that he heard someone. Then a bird would fly out of a bush, the light wind rustle the bare limbs of a beech tree, a stone dislodge in the river.

At first Sam thought that the splash of bright red bobbing in the middle of the river was a winter cardinal dipping into the cold water, but it didn't take flight, and as he walked closer, the red grew, its shape changing, until he was walking opposite a large red can with a nozzle—odd to find such a thing in the river as far back as they lived and off the beaten path. He took a long stick and went into the freezing water, knee-high, icy on his ankles, sloshing over his hiking boots. When he got closer, he saw it was a gasoline can, the ordinary kind dispensed at gas stations or purchased at a hardware store, a five-gallon jug, with the smell of gasoline sharp in the winter air. He grabbed the handle, walked out of the water, his jeans freezing in the cold, numbing his legs as he went up the hill to the promontory behind the lodge, where the firemen had gathered with his family.

"This was in the river," he said, handing the can to the sheriff.

"Exactly what I expected," the sheriff said.

AS THE SUN FILLED THE HORIZON, flooding the large east window of the viewing room in the lodge, there were ten people, the sheriff, three firemen, the McWilliamses, Noli, and William, all drinking coffee at the long worktable where *Plum & Jaggers* scripts were read and eating leftover apple pie.

"You *know* the original blaze was in the shape of a J?" the sheriff asked.

"I saw it," Sam said. "It was a J."

"And what do you make of that?" he asked. "Does a J mean anything to you?"

"Nothing," Sam said. In the light of day, he was already beginning to doubt himself, thinking he could have imagined a J—its shape had been so swiftly obscured.

"To any of the rest of you?" he asked.

They shook their heads.

BUT LATER, AFTER THE SHERIFF had taken down the information and the fire department had crossed to the other side of the river to examine the damage and determine that yes, the fire had been started by gasoline, and they were all standing in the vestibule saying goodbye, Julia followed Sam back upstairs ahead of the others.

"I know what J stands for," she said.

"What do you think it stands for?" he asked.

"For me," she said.

"It was probably an accident. Just the way the wind blew the fire last night," Sam said.

"I don't think so," Julia said, and, passing him, ran up the steps ahead of the others.

11

O N THE TUESDAY MORNING after the fire, Sam drove
to New York City, dropping Noli and William off in
Washington at the house on Morrison Street.

"We'll be busy for the next few weeks so I don't know whether we'll
get back to the farm until late February," he told his grandparents.

"That busy?" Oliver asked as they drove north on Connecticut
Avenue to the Beltway.

"We have too much work," Sam said.

But it wasn't the work that alarmed him.

Just after the Delaware Memorial Bridge, it began to snow, large-
flaked wet snow falling in silence on the windshield, and Sam slowed
down. In the backseat of the blue van Charlotte and Julia were chattering. Beside him, Oliver slept, his head resting on his chest.

"Put your seat back so your head doesn't fall off." Sam reached
over and straightened his brother's head.

He was careful of the road, attentive to the dangers around him,
the trucks bearing down the center lane in spite of the increasing
slickness of the highway, the darkening sky obscuring the winter
sun, an occasional screech of brakes, a hatchback fishtailing into
the slow lane, his family sleeping, the wondrous sounds of their syncopated breathing.

Usually he loved the long trips back and forth from the farm to New York. He was always the one to drive, and by Philadelphia the rest of them were sleeping. He did his best work in the quiet interior of the van, whole episodes of *Plum & Jaggers* surfacing, as if a birthmark on his brain had split open, spilling stories.

On this Tuesday, however, midday, driving under 50 on the snow-slick New Jersey Turnpike, Sam wasn't inventing stories. He was thinking about the fire and what Julia had said to him. Of course, it could have been nothing personal. Unspecific arson, a fire set by a couple of kids in a dry field for the fun of it.

But it struck Sam that a person watching *Plum & Jaggers* on Saturday night, watching alone, someone on the fringe of madness, could have attached himself to a character like Julia, playing roles at the far edge of society—Miriam or Marigold or Flo or Beak—particularly Julia, who had defined the parameters of her own role in Plum & Jaggers years before, when she stripped to her underpants at Gallagher's Pub. And this television viewer, obsessed with the story or with one of them, could have discovered where the McWilliamses lived and followed them to Bluemont.

"I think we should move to another part of the city," Sam was saying after they had parked the van in the usual lot on Sixth Avenue and were walking to their apartment on West Eleventh. "A short-term move."

"We're always moving," Oliver said.

"We'll keep the place on Eleventh Street, but if someone read the piece in *Currents*, it would be easy to find out where we live now," Sam said.

"You're sounding paranoid," Oliver said.

"I am paranoid."

IN THE MIDDLE OF FEBRUARY, two weeks after the fire, the McWilliamses moved to a sublet on Varick Street in TriBeCa, keeping the place on West Eleventh, and got an unlisted phone number.

The new place, smelling of turpentine and pine-seed oil and

paint, belonged to an artist with no interest in cleanliness who was out of the country for six months. There were two loft bedrooms, approachable by homemade ladders, a bathroom whose toilet overflowed on their arrival, and a general odor of gas from the old stove. The place was an unlikely one for the Plum & Jaggers Comedy Troupe, out of the way, a haven for visual artists, but Sam felt lucky to have found it.

"If someone wants to find us, they will even if we move to Juneau." Oliver unpacked his small suitcase, hanging his clothes on the plastic hooks lining the wall of the studio, a substitute for closets. "Sam? Are you listening? Do you ever listen?" He gave Charlotte a look of annoyance intended for Sam.

"I'm working," Sam said.

He had set up his books and computer on the long wooden drafting table in the middle of the main room. Beside the computer, the Oxford English Dictionary was open to "paranoia," and on a sheet of lined paper, among his doodles, line drawings of skinny men with big heads, a single strand of hair sticking straight up from the crown, was the notation: *Develop paranoia as megalomania in the character of Sam.*

"What exactly is paranoia?" Julia was asking, leaning over the table reading Sam's notes.

"Madness," Oliver said.

"Delusions of persecution," Sam said.

"If we all believed some stranger was after us, we'd have to rent an attic and lock ourselves in."

Charlotte had become an advocate for optimism, dropping her ordinary reserve in favor of positive thinking, trusting in the goodness of the human race. Sam had taken to calling her Pollyanna.

"Someone needs a level of sanity here," Charlotte said.

"That's Oliver's job," Sam had said.

Julia flopped on the couch, watching Oliver unpack.

"I don't understand megalomania in the character of Sam," she said.

"I don't even know exactly what megalomania means!" Charlotte said.

"Delusions of grandeur." Sam closed the dictionary, gathered his new script, folding it lengthwise. "Personal omnipotence."

"How can you create personal omnipotence in a character who doesn't even speak?"

"Silence is power." Sam put on his jacket, threw a scarf around his neck. "I'm late," he said, going out the door. "I'll see you guys at the studio at three."

"PRETTY SOON WE'LL BE MOVING every day, packing up, slipping away in the dark of night to the next residence, in disguise, probably masks." Oliver was looking in the empty fridge, checking the freezer for ice cream.

"It'll be fun," Julia said.

"It doesn't sound like fun to me."

"I simply don't think anyone is following us." Charlotte was sitting on the kitchen counter reading *The Portable Chekhov*.

"I didn't say someone is following us," Oliver said.

"I did," Julia said.

She was certain. She imagined that one of the peculiar characters, maybe Miriam, maybe Marigold, even Beak, had slipped a hook into the scrambled brain of some calamity out in the wilderness of the world, whose eyes were fixed on Plum & Jaggers, hoping for a personal connection. And that person, whoever he was—in her mind, Julia saw a large, youngish man, possibly deranged—had followed them to Virginia and set a fire in the form of J for Julia. Now he was in New York, close by, thinking about her, probably across the street watching them from the sidewalk.

"Did you happen to read Sam's new script?" Oliver was asking.

"The one with me as Miriam?" Julia asked. "That's what we're doing at rehearsal today."

"The one in which Miriam is a kleptomaniac with a fetish for yellow kittens."

"I read the script last night," Charlotte said.

"Did you like it?" Oliver asked.

"I guess I did." Charlotte was thoughtful. "But I'd never say anything outright to Sam if I didn't."

"But what *did* you think of the script?" Oliver asked, finishing unpacking.

"I thought it wasn't as funny as he usually is."

"Me too. Not sweet," Julia said. "He's usually funny and sweet."

Oliver closed his suitcase and put it on a shelf in the studio.

"That's a worry," he said, searching through his sports bag for running clothes.

The move from the Village had been easy, done in a day, including the cleaning of the new apartment, which was a mess. They moved so often from place to place, traveling light, only a few clothes, a picture of them with James and Lucy, a shoreline painting of James's, some books, the necessities. Vagabonds. The children of vagabonds. They joked about it.

"Reading Chekhov makes me want to get married," Charlotte said, coming to the end of "The Lady with the Dog." "I feel trapped."

Oliver was putting on running shoes and pants.

"It's been harder since we started on television." He tossed his rolled-up socks at his sister. "Julia has been feeling trapped for months. Right?"

"That's the way I was feeling, but ever since the fire I'm just terrified most of the time," Julia said.

"You'll get over it when nothing happens," Charlotte said. "This is temporary."

"I'm going running before the meeting," Oliver said, stretching his long legs, putting on a sweatshirt. "If I'm not back in forty-five minutes, call the police." He opened the door to the apartment. "Watch out for O's. If you see one burning in the middle of Broadway, you'll know I'm done for."

"Shut up, Oliver." Julia sank into the worn canvas seat of a butterfly chair. "You have the sensitivity of a plastic ball."

The apartment in TriBeCa was a fifth-floor walk-up, and Oliver ran down the steps, two at a time. At the entrance to the building, he bent over and checked his shoelaces, pulled up the hood of his sweatshirt against the wind, and stretched, his palms flat on the wall of the building. He was stretching his calf muscles, looking down at the pavement, when a young man, his age, maybe older, tapped him on the shoulder.

"Are you Wade Bull?" the man asked, a gravelly voice, an edginess about him, graying curly hair, medium build. All of this Oliver noticed because the man had moved in so close that even in the cold air Oliver could smell his cigarette breath.

"No, I'm not," Oliver said.

"You look familiar," the man said. "I thought we might have gone to Columbia together."

For a moment Oliver started. Perhaps they *had* gone to Columbia together, but he didn't recognize the man, and he had taken an instant dislike to him. No need, he decided, to begin a conversation on a New York street when he had plans for running.

"No, we didn't," he said, and took off, weaving through the crowds to the far edge of the sidewalk, heading uptown.

IN THE ELEVATOR to the twenty-fourth floor, where the NBC studios were located, a woman, mid-thirties in a heavy cloth coat, a black hat pulled down on her forehead, was talking about *Plum & Jaggers* to an older silver-haired man. The couple had gotten on the elevator in the lobby with the McWilliamses but had apparently not recognized them as familiar.

"The show is worrisome," the woman was saying.

"Worrisome?" The man was in a suit, no overcoat, a stack of papers in his arms, as if he worked in the building and had come from another floor.

"Some of my friends find it too close to the edge," the woman said.

"That's the point of it," the man said.

"But disturbing," she said. "It's too disturbing."

"Then your friends should turn off the television," the man said, following her out the open doors of the elevator.

Julia looked at Oliver.

"What can I say?" he asked quietly.

Another woman standing in a corner of the elevator was giggling.

"I guess that woman didn't recognize you guys," she said.

"I guess she didn't," Oliver replied.

"So she must not watch the show very often if she didn't recognize you. I mean, you look the same in person."

"Thank you," Julia said, following her brother and sister out of the elevator.

"Why did you thank her?" Oliver asked.

"I don't know," Julia said. "I thought she was giving us a compliment."

Jacob Levy was standing in front of the glass doors, his arms folded across his chest.

"You're late."

"Three-ten?" Oliver asked.

"You were supposed to be here at three."

He opened the glass door for them.

Jacob Levy was the executive producer for *Plum & Jaggers*, assigned to the project when the show started on NBC. He was energetic and aggressive, almost frantic in the way that sometimes accompanies a kind of insistent whininess. But he was a good producer, staying current, watching the ratings carefully, attentive to changes in viewer response. He thought of *Plum & Jaggers* as his wings to a future in television.

"So," he was saying as they followed him down the corridor to the conference room, where the three writers—Sam preferred to think of them as editors—who had been hired on the writing team were waiting. "Where's Sam?"

"Sam should be here," Oliver said.

"He should be, but he's not." Jacob opened the door to the conference room.

The woman called Brill, a long drink of water with pale blond spiked hair, was smoking a cigarette. Two men, Andy and Eric, younger than Julia, straight out of college on their first writing jobs, sat at one end of the table making notes on Sam's script.

"He left home at least two hours before we did," Oliver was saying.

"Maybe he had errands," Julia said.

"Not Sam," Jacob said. "He's never late."

They took off their coats and sat down around the table.

"So what are we going to do?" Jacob asked, raising his hands in mock despair. "It's Monday. You don't even have the script finished for this Saturday night."

"We have it in front of us, Jacob," Andy said.

"It's not a done script. We've got to edit before you rehearse. Right?"

"Of course," Andy said.

"And we can't exactly do that without Sam as far as I can see."

"Sam will be here," Oliver said.

Jacob looked at his watch. "Three-thirty?"

"Let's talk about the script. You've read it?" Oliver asked Jacob.

"Yeah."

"I read it," Brill said. "It's hilarious."

"I loved it," Eric said. "All those little yellow kittens which anorexic Miriam keeps in the drawer with her bikini undies."

"There're some problems," Jacob said.

"What kinds of problems?" Charlotte asked.

"I don't want to get into it until Sam gets here."

They waited, sitting in the conference room talking aimlessly, watching the clock, watching the sun fall behind the buildings.

"Why don't you at least call him at home," Jacob asked.

"We don't have the number," Oliver said.

"You don't have the number?"

"We moved. Sam didn't tell you?" Oliver asked.

"You guys are always moving."

"We've moved again," Oliver said. He looked over at Charlotte, her elbows on the table, her chin pressed into her fist; her eyes had the startled expression they got when she was afraid. He slid his foot under the table, gently kicking her ankle.

AT FIVE, Jacob dismissed the meeting.

"Tomorrow, early," he said. "And when you see Sam, if you see him, ask him to call me. Same number I've had for eight years, in case he asks."

IN THE ELEVATOR, filled with people leaving work for the day, Julia slipped her hand in Charlotte's.

"Worried?" she asked.

Charlotte looked over at Oliver.

"Very," she said.

12

SAM HAD LEFT the apartment early for his meeting at NBC, the new script folded under his arm. The air was cold and sharp, the sun a chilly yellow but light enough to color the day, and he decided to walk uptown. He tied his wool scarf a little tighter on his neck, turned up the collar of his jacket. At the top step of his apartment building, six steps down to the sidewalk, he stopped and looked around, a habit he had taken up in the last week, a residual fear or second sense that he ought to pay particular attention to his surroundings.

It was surprising how familiar the people passing by seemed to him, like neighbors or acquaintances, owners of the small businesses where he regularly shopped, people on his subway line he'd come to recognize. Or perhaps they were all strangers and over time the stranger simply assumes a common look and becomes a friend.

A man caught his eye, quite an ordinary-looking man, possibly his age but prematurely gray, medium height and build, a heavy blazer, a long black scarf around his neck. Nothing about him to attract Sam's attention except familiarity. When their eyes connected as they did, the man's expression indicated nothing, but Sam watched him pass in front of the apartment building, watched him walk to the end of the block and turn left. Just before he disappeared from view behind the corner building, he stopped, looked back in the direction where Sam was standing, and then he was gone.

Sam had the feeling that he knew him. Perhaps someone who had glanced off his life at school, or in the theater, or in one of the many places he had lived. But he knew him from somewhere.

He headed uptown. The script on which he had been working before the fire featured Julia as Miriam, a girl about fourteen, a kleptomaniac with an eating disorder limited to grapes and a fetish for bringing home stray yellow cats, dressing them in baby clothes. In this particular episode Miriam is staying at the McWilliams house while her mother, recently renamed Red Azalea, is walking from New York City to Albuquerque, New Mexico, with a group of like-minded white women headed southwest to reclaim their Native American heritage.

The script was a disappointment. Sam knew that. Charlotte had said she liked the new episode, and Oliver agreed that it was fine, not his best, but nothing wrong with it. They were humoring him, and Sam had a mind to toss the manuscript in one of the trash bins along Broadway, to skip the meeting and head uptown to a coffee bar until the next movie show started.

He unbuttoned his coat and slipped the script into his inside pocket, headed down the steps at the subway station two at a time, getting off at Times Square, where the offices of the Larkin Press were located. He had thought of this excursion many times, had imagined the whole trip, straight up to the editorial offices on the sixth floor where Rebecca Frankel worked.

IT WAS CLOSE TO THREE, he noted on the clock over the elevators at Larkin. In the *Plum & Jaggers* studio at NBC, Jacob Levy and the writing team would be gathering. They'd have read the new script in his pocket and the outlines of scripts to come, and would be ready to work. Soon Oliver and Charlotte and Julia would arrive.

The doors opened on the sixth floor and Sam stepped up to the receptionist's desk.

"Rebecca Frankel, please," he said.

"Who can I say is here?" the receptionist asked.

"Sam McWilliams."

"Is she expecting you?"

"No, she's not expecting me," Sam said.

Certainly not. She would be thunderstruck to find him in the lobby of her office. She had gone to a great deal of effort to avoid such a moment, leaving every performance of Plum & Jaggers at the curtain call, depending on postcards, for the same reason that he had avoided meeting her, for the rich perfection of a ghost lover, a consummation without a connection.

"Her line is busy," the receptionist said. "Have a seat in the lobby and I'll call you."

SAM SAT DOWN on a couch. There was no reading material except the Larkin spring 1998 catalogue, but he had in mind the conversation he would have with Rebecca and rehearsed it as he waited.

"I have come for help," he'd say, kissing her first on the temple, not the lips.

"Help from me?" she'd ask, running her small fingers through her thick black curly hair, crossing her splendid legs. Sam thought of her as looking like Julia, her eyes deeper, wiser, her hair short. She'd be slender, but with a figure, not rail-thin as Julia was.

"You started me on the path of comedy in that first letter you wrote me when I was ten years old," he'd say, leaning toward her, his elbow on her crowded desk. "And now I've hit a wall."

He'd tell her about the fire, how worried he was for Julia.

"It was stupid for me to allow that article to be done," he'd say. "I've put my family at risk."

And she would understand what he meant, know its connection to Orvieto.

"This is my latest script." Sam would shrug, taking his script out of his inside pocket. "It isn't at all funny."

Rebecca would shake her head, her face awash in sympathy.

"You're sure?" she'd ask.

"I am."

"What is it, then, if not funny?" she would ask.

Sam would toss the script into the wastebasket beside her desk.

"I think it's cruel."

"I'm sure it's not, Sam," she'd say.

And then she'd get up from her chair, close the door, flip the small lock, kissing him full on the lips.

"Comedy is mysterious and I have the feeling I've lost hold of it," he'd say. "I'm turning mean."

But she had put her hand over his lips to silence him, reaching down, unbuckling his belt.

WHEN THE RECEPTIONIST CAME BACK, Sam was already in his coat and scarf.

"Ms. Frankel will be free to see you in about fifteen minutes, if you care to wait," she said.

"Never mind," Sam said. "I'm late for another appointment. Give her my best," and he punched the Down button on the elevator.

THE NEXT SHOWING of *The Sweet Hereafter* was at 5:15 and Sam sat in a café half a block down Broadway from the cinema and reread the script. He liked working in cafés, not bars, coffeehouses where conversations had the quality of intimacy, a din of voices whose definition was just beyond his hearing.

He thought of calling NBC to apologize for missing the meeting, the first time in his career and all that, but he wasn't apologetic and he didn't call. The script was all wrong, so what use was a meeting? He'd tell them that tomorrow.

As he was reading, he began to notice that he couldn't pay attention to his own words, that he kept looking up, taking in the company. Usually he was captivated by his work. He'd laugh out loud.

He'd read a page over and over, pleased with the dialogue. He could weep for his characters.

He ordered a second cup of coffee, a bagel with cream cheese, and as he left for the movie, he tossed the script in the wastebasket at the entrance to the café.

13

JUST AFTER 8:30, Sam walked into the apartment, carrying groceries.

"We called the police," Oliver said without looking up from the newspaper he was reading.

"The police?" Sam asked, unpacking the groceries.

"The missing-persons bureau," Oliver said. "They haven't come yet."

"Well, you'd better call them back," Sam said.

"We were very worried, Sam." Charlotte had been crying. "If we'd disappeared like that, you would have killed us."

BY THE TIME they had gotten back from the meeting Sam had missed at NBC to find that he wasn't at the apartment—no note, no message on the answering machine—Oliver lost his temper.

"We're supposed to let Sam know every time we look out the window at the great outdoors and it's okay for him to disappear without a word." Oliver opened the fridge and took out a carton of milk.

"This isn't like Sam," Charlotte had said. "Something's happened."

"Nothing's happened," Oliver said. "He wanted to bolt, so he did."

Charlotte, sitting at the end of the couch, was weeping. "We'll call the police now," she said.

"Of course we'll call the police," Oliver said, "but he's fine and the police will think we're insane."

"And they'll probably be right," Julia said.

SAM WASN'T INTERESTED in talking. He made stir-fry, burning the rice, and they sat around the table, no one quite knowing what to say.

"I saw *The Sweet Hereafter*," Sam said finally. "I liked it very much in spite of those children dying."

"It's nice you're able to entertain yourself." Oliver, still irritated at Sam's temporary disappearance, finished eating and took his plate to the sink.

"Is that what you were doing during the script meeting?" Charlotte asked.

"No, it isn't." Sam poured himself a glass of wine, got seconds on stir-fry and burned rice. "I was waiting to see Rebecca Frankel."

"So you finally met her," Julia said.

"I didn't meet her," Sam said. "She was busy."

"Well, they were upset at the studio," Charlotte said. "Jacob was frantic. You've never missed a meeting."

"That's true. I haven't." Sam rested his chin in his fist, a kind of weariness taking over.

"So?"

"There was no reason for me to go. The script is a disaster."

"You could have called," Julia said.

"I could have," Sam said. "I'm sorry I didn't."

He looked across the table at them. "You guys are professionals. You knew the new story wasn't good and you didn't tell me."

"It's not your funniest script," Charlotte said, pushing back from the table. "But I'm not a writer, so I don't know why it didn't make me laugh as much."

"Maybe tone down Julia's craziness a little," Oliver said, his temper relaxing. "I don't like the bit with the yellow kittens."

"I've tossed the whole script. I pressed delete."

He got up from the table and headed to the kitchen.

"I expect the truth from you guys," he called over his shoulder. "We are still a team."

UPSTAIRS IN THE LOFT, he unbuckled his belt without undressing, lay down on the bed, and slipped his arm under his head, staring at the ceiling. They were talking about him. Although he couldn't hear what was being said, he assumed from the somber tone of their voices that the conversation was critical. He was trying to listen, his eyes closed, exhaustion taking over his attention, and he must have fallen asleep, because Oliver, shaking his shoulder, startled him.

"You're sleeping in your clothes," Oliver said.

"But I'm sleeping," Sam said evenly.

"Change," Oliver said. "It's the beginning of the end if you start going to bed fully dressed."

"End of what?" Sam asked, sitting up at the edge of the bed.

"The end of order as we know it," he said.

"You're a bozo, Oliver," Sam said, but he did take off his trousers and shirt, tossed them over the rafters, and climbed back in bed.

THE NEXT MORNING, late, Julia lay on her stomach under a comforter on the couch reading Sam's postcards from Rebecca Frankel, which he kept in a manila envelope at the top of his suitcase.

The windows were open—an exterminator shooting poison at the German roaches, putting out traps for the extensive family of mice who lived under the sink.

"Get a move on," Oliver called to Charlotte, who was following the exterminator around the apartment, opening more windows. "We're going to be late. Yesterday's meeting is rescheduled for noon."

Sam had left early, taping a note of reminders on the fridge with a postscript:

> *When you leave the apartment (every time you leave), stand on the top step of the building and look around. You should be checking for someone who could have a watch on us.*

Charlotte turned Sam's note facedown.

"Something's the matter with Sam," she said quietly to Oliver, not wishing Julia to hear her.

"Of course; he's obsessed," Oliver agreed. "But then, when hasn't he been? At least now he has a reason to think someone is following us." He picked up the note and tossed it in the trash.

"Do you ever wonder if we'll be living together like this when we're seventy?"

Oliver laughed. "Demand your own apartment."

Charlotte rolled her eyes. "Would you?"

"Sure. 'Moving out, Sam,' I'll say. 'Got my own place, my own permanent girlfriend, my own dog, and maybe with a little luck, I've got my own brain back.'" Oliver faked a boxer's punch to Charlotte's chin. "I'll send him a bassett hound called Faithful."

"Be serious, Oliver," Charlotte said. "You'd never leave. None of us would."

"Sometime after *Plum & Jaggers* has a chance to make a go of it." He checked his watch. "Maybe in a year or so, but now we've got ten minutes before we have to leave for the studio and I haven't changed clothes."

Charlotte sat down on the couch beside Julia, lifting the comforter.

"What are you doing under there?"

"Reading Sam's postcards from Rebecca Frankel," Julia said from inside the tent of her comforter.

"Those are personal messages," Oliver called from the upstairs loft, where he had gone to change for the meeting.

"They're postcards," Julia said. "If Rebecca intended for them to be personal, she should have sent letters."

"Read one to me," Charlotte said.

Julia sat up on the couch, wrapping the comforter around her.

"Dear Sam," she read aloud. *"I saw* The Last Thanksgiving. *It's wonderful. What I love about your writing is your ability to be darkly funny and also sweet. It's a gift. Or legacy. Love, Rebecca."*

"Read a newer one," Charlotte said.

"Here's one from this Christmas after the show started on NBC," Julia said.

"Good. Read that."

"Read it loud enough for me to hear," Oliver called down.

"Dear S.," Julia read. *"They're getting intimate. Dear S., love, R. Dear S.,"* Julia went on. *"I saw* Plum & Jaggers *last night. One false note in that episode. When Julia serves Plum's pet parakeet for dinner. Too black. Have you ever considered writing personal essays? I'd be interested in such a book for Larkin Press. You're looking thinner, or else that configuration is a trick of the screen. Eat! Love, R."*

"That's a love letter," Charlotte said.

"No, it's not. They've never met," Oliver said.

"Listen to this," Julia said.

"Dear S., I'd like to call you Samuel. It's a name I'm fond of. You remind me of Saul. Something about your gestures on the show, the way you cock your head, one hand in your pocket. But who knows? I may be inventing Saul, he's been gone so long. That's the sin of it. Forgetting. Love, R."

"I love it," Charlotte said. "It's delicious."

"Delicious?" Oliver pulled the comforter off Julia. "Let's get out of here. We're going to be late."

Charlotte put on a black cape, a long red Chinese scarf, and threw Julia a coat.

"Put the postcards away so Sam won't know you've violated federal regulations," Oliver said, watching Julia replace the postcards in the top of Sam's suitcase.

Julia buttoned her winter coat, putting her collar up, a wool hat low on her forehead.

"What do you really think about Rebecca Frankel?" she asked Oliver.

"I don't think about her," Oliver said, pushing Julia gently out the door ahead of him. "She's a figment of Sam's imagination."

"But it does give us a different sense of Sam, doesn't it?" Julia asked. "Kind of a romantic one."

"He's a hopeless romantic," Oliver agreed. "Who else would try to keep his family together by inventing a comedy show?"

JULIA SLIPPED HER ARM THROUGH CHARLOTTE'S.

"You seem bad-tempered," she said.

"I'm annoyed at Sam," Charlotte replied. "I don't understand why it isn't possible for us to live in separate places and have a private life and still do the show."

"It's not possible until this worry about the fire goes away," Julia said.

"There isn't such a worry about the fire, Julia," Charlotte said. "It couldn't have been personal."

"You really think so?" Julia asked.

"I hope," Charlotte said, going down the steps of the building to the street. "Meanwhile, I dream of flying."

OLIVER DOUBLE-LOCKED THE DOOR and was heading down the second set of steps, Charlotte and Julia on the landing in front of him, when he noticed the graffiti.

On the third-floor wall, gray with accumulating soot and the greasy residue of cooking, there was a new drawing among the old graffiti, love messages and personal confessionals, a picture of two heads kissing. The new drawing was dim, maybe done in pencil or charcoal, but it seemed to represent a small stick figure of a woman, a line for her body, her arms, her legs, her head, two dots on either side of her head for eyes, two dots on either side of her torso for breasts, a squiggly line between her legs, and a mass of curly hair. He made a mental note of it. He would ask Charlotte later.

Julia and Charlotte were standing at the top of the outside steps when Oliver got downstairs.

"What are you doing?" he asked, stopping beside them.

"Checking for suspicious people the way Sam said we should," Julia said, looking up and down Varick.

"Christ." Oliver lumbered down the steps. "How would you know suspicious?"

"If someone was interested in us and knew we lived here, they'd be standing, maybe across the street, or walking back and forth by the apartment," Charlotte said patiently. "That's my guess."

"But they wouldn't be in a hurry," Julia said.

"I don't think so."

"Well, everyone seems to be in a hurry today, so I guess we can go," Julia said, taking the steps down two at a time.

THE WEATHER WAS COLD with the kind of dampness that slips through winter coats, the wind bearing down on them, and they walked with their chins against their chests, crowns forward, their arms wrapped around their bodies.

In the subway, Oliver took a seat next to Charlotte. Julia stood by the door, holding the rail.

"Did you see what was on the wall of our apartment building?" he asked.

"I didn't notice," Charlotte said.

"A nude stick figure with lots of curly hair. A woman. It's very dim, maybe even drawn with pencil."

"I didn't notice that," Charlotte said. "You're thinking it's Julia?"

"Well?"

"Don't get like Sam, Oliver," Charlotte said as the train arrived. She led the way through the turnstile. "Graffiti is everywhere."

"I love that about New York," Julia said, following Charlotte up into the shaft of sudden sunlight lighting the subway stairway. "See?" She pointed to an abstract of a dog painted black with his ears straight out. *Sweet on you Beatriz*. Signed. *DDT*. "It's so personal."

And they wound their way, single file, against the crowds and blustery wind, to the studio.

14

WHEN SAM ARRIVED AT NBC, people kept their distance. No one mentioned the fact that he'd missed the meeting on the previous day, and neither did he. The other writers on the script team were already in the conference room with coffee and sandwiches, the new script in front of them. He took off his jacket and scarf, tossed them on a chair in the corner, and took a seat at the round table.

"We'll forget this script," he said, turning a copy of the new episode of *Plum & Jaggers* facedown.

"What do you mean, forget it?" Jacob asked.

"Just that," Sam said.

"But I love it, Sam," Andy said. "It's so odd and funny. That's what NBC likes about us."

NBC had high hopes for the family comedy. "Cozy, edgy," they called it. And the young writers who worked with him loved Sam, although he took no particular interest in them personally. A "genius," they told Jacob Levy.

"You ought to try to be nicer to the writers," Charlotte said.

"I don't like to work with other people," Sam said. "I never did."

"But they adore you," Charlotte said.

"I can't imagine why they would," Sam said.

He had resisted NBC's decision to hire a team of writers to work on his scripts.

"I've always worked alone," he told them. This is television, he was told, not live theater, and without further discussion the writers were hired. But during the script meetings Sam kept a chilly distance, always polite, but he showed no interest in pursuing a social relationship with any of them.

JACOB LEVY PICKED UP A COPY of the script.

"What do you mean, forget it?" he asked. "The script is good."

"I liked Red Azalea," Brill said. "She's dynamite."

"It's wild the way she paints her body with all those red flowers like Georgia O'Keeffe vaginas," Andy added.

"It's second-rate," Sam said without inflection. "I don't know what's gone sour with me the last two weeks, but something has."

A sense of doom. A growing dread, rising like water seeping into the corners of his brain. He was losing his sense of humor. He could actally feel it leaking, as though the stitches on a fresh wound had torn.

Sam looked around the table. "I gave you some suggestions for new episodes, so let's go over them instead."

"The ideas are good, don't you think, Jacob?" Andy asked. "Eric and I agree."

"The ideas are great, but we've only got so many more shows before the network decides on next year and we've a couple of negative letters about the parakeet you strangled. The one you served with garlic mashed potatoes," Jacob said.

"What negative got said?" Sam asked.

"People didn't like it, so I was wondering what you thought about adding a new parakeet to the next episode?" Jacob asked. "Like the kids give Plum a baby parakeet for her birthday."

"I don't like it." Sam got up and opened a window enough to cause a draft. "Death is irrelevant in comedy."

Jacob paced the room, back and forth, tearing at his thick mop of black hair.

"Nothing is irrelevant," he said.

"I like some of the next episodes, Jacob," Brill said quickly. "You're not going to get rid of anorexic Miriam with the cat-fetish problem, are you?"

"I have no problem with her—but since we're doing audience response, I've got a question about the fact that the character of Sam doesn't talk," Jacob said.

"Sam's mute," Sam said. "That's his character."

"It's just that I had some letters about his being weird," Jacob said, settling into his chair. "I guess that's the point."

"Weird isn't the point," Sam said, putting on his coat.

"I thought we could build up the episode when Plum disappears to go with Red Azalea to New Mexico," Eric said cheerfully. "Maybe with telephone calls back home."

"My favorite idea is where Miriam dances to Frank Sinatra with the tomcat."

"But we'll have to cut the cat's erection, gang," Jacob was saying as the rest of the McWilliams family arrived, taking their seats around the table.

"We're talking about viewer response to help you guys think about the direction for the next episodes," Jacob said to the McWilliamses. "One of the other problems that's come up is the static nature of the set. Every Saturday night, the same dining room. Know what I mean?"

"What would you suggest?" Oliver asked Jacob, closing the window, taking a seat next to his brother.

"Maybe street scenes, you know. Maybe they go to Red Azalea's house for dinner. Maybe a bar. What do you say, Sam?"

"I don't think very much of that," Sam said.

The group around the table was quiet.

"As I see it in these final episodes, random incidents of terrorism have increased, violence is on the rise, no one seems to be in charge," Sam said with a kind of exaggerated patience, looking wearily around the table. "Like everybody else in the City of Brotherly Love, the McWilliamses are afraid to go outside."

He got up from the table and, taking his bookbag and gloves, stood beside the closed door as if he were expecting to leave in a hurry.

"The point all along with *Plum & Jaggers* has been one set. A dining-room table, six chairs, two of them empty, and an invisible bomb."

"But the country is doing fine. I mean, there's violence and terrorism here and there, but hey," Jacob said.

"*Plum & Jaggers* isn't a newspaper account," Sam said, trying to maintain an even tone. "It's an imagined story of a family and what could happen to them."

He opened the door to leave.

"I'll get coffee and meet the rest of you on the set."

But he didn't get coffee. He went into the bathroom and locked the door, looking at his unfamiliar face in the mirror, sitting on the toilet with his head in his hands.

Sometime in the middle of the meeting, he wasn't sure when, he could feel a temper coming on like a sickness, as though he were ignited, waiting to detonate.

15

SAM WAITED for his family at a café on West Thirteenth Street where he often wrote. The café was a small, earnest, vegetarian lunch place with a variety of Asian teas and burning incense, and the customers were quiet. Sam usually worked at a table in the window, but this afternoon, recovering from the wave of anger, he wasn't writing. He was thinking about his mother.

He seldom thought about James and Lucy as parents—not since he had stolen their affectionate names for one another, appropriated their unanticipated absence from his world and invented Plum and Jaggers as intentional truants from family life. He knew that his sense of them was a shadow of the truth—their history incomplete, dying as they had before they had a chance to fail. In the stories Sam wrote, Plum and Jaggers were members of a generation of parents who had abdicated the responsibilities of family life by choice. But somewhere between his idealization of James and Lucy and the parents he had invented for Plum & Jaggers lay Sam's true feelings about his own.

He was thinking about the last moments of his mother's life. He had a clear picture of what had happened in Orvieto. Without struggling through the murky air of memory, he could bring everything from that day to the main screen of his mind.

He imagined his mother and his father walking through the railroad cars to the lunch car, where they ordered sandwiches for their children, laughing at the pleasure of their adventure, probably buying small Italian cakes as a surprise dessert, Lucy leaning against James in the narrow passageway.

One moment they were standing with eleven other people in the lunch car. The next moment they were dead. Not even the warning of an automobile accident. There and not there.

But if James and Lucy had known, if there had been an abbreviated moment, an apostrophe in the clock's ticking, time enough for them to have a sense of consequence, they would have been devastated for their children. One alteration in the arrangement—Lucy remaining with the children, for instance, or James stopping at the men's room—and the history of the McWilliamses would have had a different text.

It mattered deeply to Sam to believe they knew. To believe that for a moment of consciousness before the final darkness, they had understood the cost of their innocent adventures, that unlike Plum and Jaggers they were not entirely responsible for leaving.

CHARLOTTE NOTICED A CHANGE in Sam as soon as she sat down in the Café Rosa with her pot of tea and fortune cookies, reading the fortunes aloud to Julia, who took the two she wanted—"Love beckons" and "The heart is a lonely hunter"—sticking them in her pocket.

Sam's eyes were narrowed, his mouth drawn taut, his lips thinned across his face, his body wound tight, hard as a baseball.

"So what did you think of the meeting today?" Oliver asked.

"Not much."

"Jacob misses the point about the setting," Charlotte said.

"The setting is exactly right as it is." Oliver ordered more tea and ginger cookies. "But I do worry about Julia's role."

"My roles are too extreme?" Julia asked.

"I'm afraid they're a magnet for crazy people, and New York has a lot of those," Oliver said. "We need to be disturbing, but just this side of sick."

Sam had opened the notebook in which he listed his ideas and was drawing dogs with long snouts and angular heads.

"I worry about the line of safety we're crossing," Charlotte said.

Sam looked up from his notebooks. "That's the line we cross," he said. "That's who we are."

"We have to be careful, though," Oliver said. "This is television, not a small theater audience who have come to see *us* because we're Plum & Jaggers."

"But we've hit a funny bone." Julia leaned against Oliver. "I don't think we should change the show completely."

"We're not changing it at all," Sam said, getting up and putting on his coat. "I know exactly what I'm doing." He took his papers and stuffed them in his bookbag, walking out of the café ahead of them, turning left downtown.

IN THE CAFÉ, Sam had been thinking about one of his father's paintings, a small and particularly detailed one that he especially loved. He had in mind to stop at the old apartment on West Eleventh to pick up some clothes and the painting as well.

The wind had settled to an occasional bluster of cold air at the cross street, a pale invisible sun gave the afternoon a suggestion of light. From time to time, he stopped at a corner and looked around to check the pedestrian traffic. He was aware of a young man, well scrubbed, in jeans and a leather jacket, walking just behind him from Rockefeller Center to Chelsea, a walk Sam and his siblings often took but didn't expect of others who worked regular hours.

"Do you have the time?" the young man asked at one corner.

Sam checked his watch. "Four-thirty," he said.

"You're taking quite a long walk," he remarked at another intersection.

Sam turned away. He didn't expect incidental conversation in New York City and was bothered to have been noticed by this man.

Perhaps it was nothing, or perhaps he thought he knew Sam because of *Plum & Jaggers* and was interested in friendship.

"See you later," the man said, ducking into Tall Men in Chelsea. Sam didn't acknowledge his goodbye.

THE PAINTING Sam had in mind was a Scottish shoreline of exquisite detail, with small brushstrokes in various shades of green, particularly lush, lit from an angle beyond the painting, the sun setting behind the landscape. A single red Wellington belonging to a child lay on its side in the grass. The sea was dark olive, a spray of orange lit the water in the distance, and under the arch of white-caps, a dangerous blackness.

How strange a painting it was for the father Sam remembered as lightness itself. He slipped the painting in his bookbag and was immediately relieved, feeling almost a rush of happiness as if something significant had been missing in his life before. He planned to prop the painting up on his desk in the new place in TriBeCa, let it shine on his computer.

What he wanted to do with the stories of Plum & Jaggers was to walk his characters into the sea as far as they could go without drowning.

IT WAS A LONG TRIP to TriBeCa and almost dark by the time Sam arrived at their front door. He assumed he would be the last one home, even if they had walked, because of his stop on Eleventh Street, and he was hoping Charlotte had picked up dinner on Broadway. His mind was on the beginning of a new episode.

In the last script, the lips of the character of Sam are fixed in the permanent shape of an O. The scene begins when Sam places Jaggers's empty chair in the middle of the dining-room table, climbs up on it, and sits facing straight forward, hands folded on his knees, in an attitude which acknowledges silence as a separate character.

Sam wasn't even thinking when he opened the mailbox for Apartment 4A.

OLIVER, SPRAWLED ON THE COUCH with a beer, could hear Sam run up the steps to the second floor and slam open the front door. He strode across the room and dropped a postcard on Oliver's stomach.

"We got mail," he said.

"Mail?" Oliver asked. "Who knows our address?"

"The person who sent the postcard," Sam said.

The postcard, from the Museum of Modern Art, was a long-faced Modigliani, just the elongated head with black hair and tiny black eyes and a brilliant green necklace. It was addressed to Sam McWilliams in an elegant, masculine script, nineteenth-century in its perfection. In the space for messages, the writer had drawn a small cursive *J.*

"We're moving tonight," Sam said.

Oliver put his head against the back of the couch, staring at the ceiling. "Where in God's name are we going now?"

"I'll find a place."

Julia sat down on the couch next to Oliver. "I was right." She covered her face with her hands. "Someone is following me."

Oliver put his arm around her, kissing the top of her head.

"I want to quit," Julia said. "I want to move back home with Noli."

"No one's quitting," Sam said. "Not now. Not yet."

IT WAS WINTER DUSK, the darkness beginning to settle just beyond their studio windows, and they packed quickly, to be out before night. Sam ordered a car.

"Where are we going?" Julia asked as they headed down the steps with their luggage.

"Hotel Moronna, until we find another place," Sam said.

16

SAM'S PLAN WAS TO MOVE from place to place under cover of darkness, a small army of foot soldiers, or else rats, traveling the sewers, surfacing for food. They lived at Hotel Moronna for a few days without incident, and then moved on, first to the Village Garden on West Thirteenth and then to a small hotel on the Upper West Side. It became a regular pattern in their lives. On the third or fourth day at a new location, Sam would begin calling around the city under an assumed name for a new hotel, a small place where ideally they wouldn't be recognized, although occasionally they were.

When Sam called the New York Police Department, Detective Howell was assigned to meet with them.

"What can you do?" Sam asked. "We're living like fugitives."

Detective Howell wasn't optimistic. "Not much to do," he said. "There isn't enough to go on. You have a gasoline fire in Virginia, which is out of our jurisdiction. Only the *J* on the postcard is associated with New York."

"We *know* someone is following us," Sam said. "This isn't a guess."

Detective Howell shook his head. "I believe you," he said. "It isn't exactly surprising. You're in a high-risk profession, comedy, and likely to attract problems. But there's nothing we can do until something more happens."

"That's a consolation," Oliver said.

"You could hire a bodyguard," the detective said. "A lot of people in your situation do."

"But the police department can't assign someone to keep a watch on us?" Sam asked.

"Not on the basis of what you've told me," Detective Howell said. "One postcard, evidence of arson in another state, no known enemies or past failed love affairs, no actual signs of someone following. Really, what you're talking about is your own fear, which is not to say I don't believe you have reason to worry." He got up, indicating their meeting was complete. "Keep me up-to-date as you move around," he said.

BY THE FIRST OF MARCH, an unusually soft and warm winter for New York City, except for a pervasive dampness, the McWilliamses' lives had settled into a routine in which the only serious inconvenience was their constant change of location. Sam's plan, which they had followed without consequence for quite a while, was based on surprise. A highly developed series of arrangements which had them moving around New York in twos or threes or fours, a different pattern every day. Even for a professional criminal, they would have been difficult to follow. Until Oliver's March 12 birthday, they had begun to believe they had shaken the enemy.

They were living at the Berrial Hotel off Central Park West. It was a large, impersonal establishment catering mostly to foreign businessmen, and Sam liked the anonymity of it, the unfamiliar foreign conversation in the lobby. He was beginning to talk about returning to the apartment on West Eleventh and had arranged to have a cleaning crew come and painters for the kitchen and bathroom, with plans to move back around the first of April.

———

IT WAS THURSDAY AFTERNOON, early, still light, after rehearsal of a scene with Julia as Miriam and Anarchy on Prozac for his repeated depressions. Sam had stayed at the hotel rushing to finish the next episode.

The strategy for the evening—every day had a plan designed by Sam—was that Julia and Charlotte would walk up Sixth Avenue. First they'd stop at Vacés for gourmet takeout and a birthday cake, and then at the bookstore in Rockefeller Center for a book of Italian landscapes which Oliver had seen, and finally they'd walk along the park to the hotel.

But Charlotte had a terrible headache and went home by taxi with Oliver, leaving Julia with the birthday chores.

"It's light outside," Charlotte said to Julia. "Don't worry. You'll be fine."

"What about Sam's hysteria?"

"Just do the shopping and take a cab home," Charlotte said. "There're a zillion people on the street."

IT WAS RUSH HOUR when Julia left the studio. She walked to Sixth, hoping for a cab, but none was available, so she decided to walk uptown, stopping for the hot chocolate at Leona's teahouse on the corner of Seventh and Fifty-second. Leona's was a small, cozy restaurant with crisp white tablecloths and sprays of flowers in tiny vases, sticky sweets rolled to the table on a trolley, a winter refuge where she and Charlotte sometimes stopped to read *The Village Voice* or fashion magazines, to smoke an occasional cigarette out of Sam's sight and talk about men and babies. Sitting in a cushy chair in a corner of the room beside the window, the *Voice* open on the table, she was suddenly conscious that someone was watching her.

She looked around. Two middle-aged women at the table next to her, lost in a conspiratorial conversation; a young man in a romantic quarrel with a beautiful Asian girl, whose head was turned away to avert his look; a full table, probably of students, books open, chatter-

ing across a pot of tea; no one specific, unless it was a waiter standing by the cappuccino bar looking in her direction, but not at her
exactly, beyond at the street. She was suddenly agitated and got up.

"Do you need something?" the waitress asked.

"Just the bill," Julia said, drinking her hot chocolate quickly, putting on her coat, her bookbag over her shoulder, dropping the sugar
cookies in her pocket to eat on the way.

Outside, she headed toward a bookstore, walking quickly, weaving through the crowd, alert to strangers on the street. The sense of
being watched had followed her.

"Stupid," she told herself.

It was all in her mind—she had caught Sam's paranoia. But she
couldn't help it and sped along the street as if she were being
chased, rushing into the safety of the bookstore.

She was kneeling down in the section for garden books when
something brushed across her hair, and she jumped up face-to-face
with a man, taller than she was, although not tall, with graying
curly hair, an oddness about him, a long black scarf wrapped
around his neck.

"Sorry to startle you." His face had an expression of amusement.

Julia said nothing, grabbing the book for Oliver, taking it to the
counter.

He had touched her hair. Certainly that's what had happened,
she thought, taking deep breaths, watching the man still standing in
the Garden section looking at books. But she could feel his eyes on
her when she turned her back to him and paid the bill. It could not
have been an accident, touching her hair.

Four blocks to Vacés. She thanked the clerk who had wrapped
Oliver's book and hurried out of the bookstore, checking behind her
to see if the man was still in the Garden section. But he had disappeared.

At Vacés, she got two Moroccan chickens and grilled vegetables
and roasted potatoes and a ficelle, a raspberry-and-chocolate birthday cake and candles, two bottles of sauvignon blanc. Loaded down,

she went out to the street to hail a cab, scanning the crowd for the man from the bookstore with a growing sense of peril.

The cabs traveling uptown were full, darkness coming quickly. Her arms, weighted with packages, felt as if they would fall off her body, but she headed with the traffic toward home, walking close to the buildings, checking for reflections in the glass.

"Marigold."

She heard the name distinctly above the noise of the traffic, spoken by someone close. She turned around. Marigold? Who else would have a name like Marigold?

At the corner of Fifty-ninth there was a young man standing with his Labrador retriever, and something about the dog gave Julia a sense of safety.

"Excuse me," she said. "I need your help."

He was younger close up than she'd thought he was, maybe only fourteen, but he stopped and stood with her on the corner while she told him that she was being followed, her arms were too full of packages, and would he help her get a cab.

"Who's following you?" he asked.

"I don't know," she said. "I'm sure it sounds crazy."

"Oh no," the boy said, standing just off the curb, his hand in the air. "I mean anything can happen in New York."

"I guess that's right." She scrambled in her pocket for money, finding only the sugar cookies. "I can't find my money," she said, breathlessly climbing into the taxi he had hailed. "Only sugar cookies."

She stuck out her hand with the cookies.

He laughed and shook his head. "Be careful," he called as she shut the door to the cab.

AT THE HOTEL she paid the driver. Standing for a moment to readjust her packages, in the confusion of luggage belonging to new arrivals, she saw a man with graying curly hair and a black scarf, just the back of him.

She turned into the hotel, rushing through the lobby, into the elevators, pushing 4. At the fourth floor she hurried down the carpeted corridor, falling against the door to their suite.

"Do something!" she planned to say to Sam.

But Sam, ashen-faced and quiet, met her at the door and took her by the shoulders, pulling her into the circle of his arms.

Noli was dead.

17

WILLIAM WANTED A CHURCH FUNERAL.

"She was religious," he said.

"Noli?" Oliver asked, astonished at this news.

"As a girl, she was very religious," William said. "So I have decided on a church funeral at First Methodist in East Grand Rapids, where she went when she was growing up."

"The service should be very small. Does First Methodist have a chapel?" Charlotte asked, thinking that certainly no one would come. They'd been gone so long from Grand Rapids, their tiny family would be lost in the vast Methodist church, with its long rows of white pews.

But William shook his head.

"People will come. We lived there all our lives."

THE OBITUARY in the Monday-morning Grand Rapids *Express* had the lead:

NICOLE LUCAS, GRANDMOTHER TO
PLUM & JAGGERS DIES AT 87

On Tuesday afternoon, the church pews were full, people crowded in the back, standing on the lawn in the damp, gray March weather, the collars of their coats up.

"People know us," Julia whispered to her grandfather. "As if we've existed in Grand Rapids all along."

"Of course people know us," William said. "This is our home."

Few of the people who came had actually known William and Noli. Their friends were very old or dead. Friends of Lucy's came and cousins several times removed, or friends of friends, but the majority of the crowd inside the church were young, the McWilliamses' age, people who had known them in grammar school or known them before they moved to Washington. This crowd had come to Noli's funeral because the McWilliamses were on television.

"*Plum & Jaggers* brought them here, don't you think?" Charlotte asked Sam.

"And my criminal record in Grand Rapids," Sam said.

AFTER THE SERVICE, the McWilliamses stood with their grandfather at the entrance to First Methodist, greeting people who formed a long line to speak to them. In the corner across from the door where they were standing, Sam noticed a young man with a boyish face, pale, thinning yellow hair, a look of illness about him, blowing the smoke from his cigarette out the side door of the church. He didn't come over to the line of people shaking hands with the McWilliamses and their grandfather, but neither did he show any interest in leaving.

"Who's that?" Julia asked. "He keeps watching Sam."

"I don't know," Oliver said. "He's a stranger to me."

Sam watched the man for a moment. There was something out of the ordinary about the way he carried himself, the way he held his head at an exaggerated angle, the way he looked at Sam, unembarrassed to be staring.

"My guess is Matthew Gray," Sam said.

"That's a familiar name," Charlotte said.

"Do you remember him?" Sam asked Oliver, breaking out of the receiving line.

"I don't," Oliver said.

"He's the reason we left Grand Rapids."

Sam crossed the room and put out his hand.

"I'm Sam McWilliams," he said.

"Oh yes, yes, yes," the young man said. "I'm Matthew Gray. Matthew Laster Gray."

"I thought that's who you were," Sam said.

"I shouldn't be here," Matthew stumbled. "I didn't even know your grandmother."

"We're glad you've come," Sam said.

"I see you on television." Matthew had watery blue eyes more in the shape of a rectangle than an oval, absent of expression. He seemed not to know what to do with his hands, and so they hung at his sides, and he shook them as if they'd gone to sleep.

"Do you know who I really am?" Matthew asked.

"I do know who you are," Sam said gently.

"Yes, yes. Well, some people said you left town because of me," Matthew said. "I don't think so, but that's what my mother said."

"Your mother is right," Sam said. "That is why we left Grand Rapids."

"Too bad, too bad," Matthew said.

"It is too bad, because I wasn't the one who hurt you," Sam said, surprised at the control in his voice when he felt on the edge of internal catastrophe. "It was a Tuesday and I was at recess playing with some friends—I don't remember who—but I do know that everyone had recess at the same time and you were in my brother Oliver's class."

"Yes, Oliver. He threw up on the art table. We were doing our pumpkins."

"Oliver never mentioned that, or else I've forgotten," Sam said.

"But on the day that you were hurt, I was on the blacktop, where I usually played. I never went behind the athletic field, where the shed is, because I was afraid to be too far from the building where my brother and sisters were."

"I was afraid, too," Matthew said. "I was afraid of Ranier Moore." He lit another cigarette. "Ranier Moore hurt me behind the shed."

"No one told me who hurt you," Sam said. "I only know that I didn't."

"It was Ranier. Ranier Charles Moore. He hated you. Hated you," Matthew said. "That's what my mother told me after my brain got better and I suddenly remembered it was Ranier, not you. Or I think I remembered," he said, offering Sam a drag of his cigarette, which Sam took, although he didn't like to smoke. "I got hit in the head, you see."

SAM NOTICED that people were stopping in the church hall with their cups of strawberry punch and sugar cookies, pretending to have a conversation but actually watching Sam and Matthew Gray.

"Has Ranier come to the funeral?" Sam asked.

"Ranier isn't here. He's someplace else, but very smart. Brilliant, my mother says. He went to college and had a good job and then went crazy and had to go to a hospital for a long time. My mother says he's a sex maniac." Matthew shook his head. "She says he's the only sex maniac that has ever lived in Grand Rapids."

Sam took Matthew by the arm and stepped just outside the church door, aware that the young man was warming to him, pleased with Sam's attention.

"Do people in Grand Rapids know that it was Ranier, or do they still think it was me?"

"My mother knows. She said not to tell anybody. Ranier would kill me dead as a doornail."

Sam waited while Matthew finished his cigarette.

"After you moved, people in Grand Rapids forgot all about you, and then you got on television sitting at the dining-room table on the TV screen and people remembered how your parents were dead and that's why you beat me up." Matthew laughed, putting up his hand to cover his mouth as if he were coughing instead. "Only you didn't do it, after all." He put out his cigarette, came back into the building, and shut the door. "But people don't know that, so when your grandmother died, everybody wanted to come to the funeral to look at you, in the flesh. That's what my mother said. In the flesh."

"So it seems," Sam said.

"I go to funerals in Grand Rapids all the time," Matthew said. "Everybody's funeral, and this is the biggest one I've seen, the very biggest of all."

THE CROWD WAS THINNING and Sam moved back to where his family was standing, taking a place next to his grandfather.

"At least two hundred people are here," William said to Sam. "Isn't it remarkable how kind people can be."

"It certainly is," Sam said.

"I wonder why we ever left Grand Rapids," Williams said. "We were very happy here."

"We were," Sam said kindly, taking his grandfather's hand, leading him out of the church.

LATER, AFTER DINNER, Sam walked the streets of his old neighborhood alone. The evening was damp and cold and empty, with a wet snow beginning to fall. Occasionally Sam saw a person walking his dog or hurrying home late from work, but mostly he had the sparsely lit streets to himself.

East Grand Rapids was an older section of town, with some enormous houses where the furniture barons had lived, and less pretentious brick or clapboard houses for the workers, with aluminum siding, built close together, with small yards, in walking distance from the business district and schools. The house where Lucy Lucas grew up, to which the McWilliams children moved when their parents were killed, was a brick colonial painted yellow, with a front porch and a swing and a small front yard, where Noli had had a cutting garden.

Sam laced through the streets where he had once walked or ridden his bike. Gradually, as the night darkened, the stars concealed in the heavens, snow accumulating, the neighborhood came back to him as a place he knew in his bones, the smell of winter, the rising streets over the Grand River, the way the houses were built in close proximity. He circled back to the Lucas house again and again in order to get his bearings, a swing set in the yard now, the front door bright blue under the porch light, young children, three or four of them flying past the windows in pajamas. As he walked, he began to remember specifics. Matthew Gray's house, two blocks south from his on Wicket Street, where he had gone with his grandfather to apologize for something he had not done. The house where Tommy Meeuwsen had lived was dark except for a light in the back. Sam had gone there for a birthday party just after his parents had died, and the Meeuwsens had had a pony in the back yard who bit his fingers when he gave it sugar, and he had called for Noli to pick him up before the birthday cake. Next door was the piano teacher's house, where he used to sit in the hall while Charlotte had her lesson, looking through what was then a very small collection of terrorist bombings which he kept in a folder in his bookbag.

Several times he tried to find Ranier Moore's house, starting at the Lucases' old house. He had gone to Ranier's for a sleepover and for dinner once when Mrs. Moore made sweetbreads, soft and white as brains. "It's the Clean Plate Club in the Moores' house," she had said. He and Ranier hadn't been friends. Nevertheless, Ranier had pursued him, asking him to cookouts and sleepovers and birthday parties, which he refused to accept in spite of Noli's insistence that he be polite.

"I don't want to go to Ranier's," Sam would say to Noli.

"But you should," Noli would reply. "Ranier likes you so much."

"I don't think he does like me," Sam said, sensing even before the incident with Matthew Gray that Ranier's interest in him wasn't based on friendship.

He came upon the Moores' house by surprise. He knew it was the Moores' because of the six-foot chain-link fence around the small back yard where they had kept their dog, Bloomfield Hills. It was the only house with a wire fence, and the neighbors complained about the dog and the unattractive fence and the fact that when the Moores cooked out on the grill, they had to do it in the front yard and eat on the front porch because Bloomfield Hills was behind the fence in the back and wasn't fond of people.

This evening the Moores' house was brightly lit, crowded with furniture, and in the dining room Sam could see a young, blond, frizzy-haired girl working at a table. On the wall behind her, quite visible from the street because of the size of it and the light over it, was a cloudy reproduction of *The Last Supper*.

THE DRUGSTORE was closed, but Sam could see Matthew Gray at the back unpacking boxes in the hair-products aisle. He knocked on the glass and Matthew looked up, smiling when he saw who it was.

"Sam McWilliams," he said happily, unlocking the door. "We're closed, you know. Closed to the public."

"I know," Sam said. "I came by hoping to catch you."

Matthew smiled broadly. "So here I am, right here in my place of employment, where I work," he said.

"I don't want to keep you," Sam said.

"No problem." Matthew took a Coke out of the cooler and handed it to Sam. "On me," he said. "The Coke is on me. A gift."

"I've been walking around my old neighborhood."

"I live on Wicket Street," Matthew said.

"I remember. I saw your house."

"In the same room where I have always been, only my mother got me a plaid comforter and matching curtains for my birthday. Red and green."

"Well, I just walked by Ranier's house," Sam began.

"Bloomfield Hills was killed by a Good Humor truck in front of the house. I was on my bike and saw it happen." Matthew shook his head. "I wasn't sorry. A dog is like his master, is what my mother says."

"I remember Bloomfield Hills and I know what you mean," Sam said. "Do the Moores still live there? When I walked by just now, a blond girl was in the dining room."

"That's Veronica, who lives with them. She's their niece."

"And you don't know where Ranier lives now?"

"Someplace," Matthew said, suddenly brightening. "I remember now. Ranier came home for Christmas and he was at church and I asked him had he seen *Plum & Jaggers* and he said yes, and I said wasn't that something, you on television after beating me up."

"So he isn't crazy any longer?" Sam asked.

"Oh yes, yes, very crazy, but he smokes cigarettes even in church," Matthew said, excited by the conversation, slapping his hands together, a giggle bubbling in his throat.

"I wonder if I'd recognize him," Sam said.

"No, no no." Matthew shook his head. "He's very old."

"He's my age." Sam smiled. "He has always been my age."

"He's older than you now," Matthew said solemnly.

SAM LEFT WEDNESDAY AFTERNOON to get back to work and resettle his family in their old apartment on West Eleventh Street. William was confused, forgetting for the moment why Sam would be going to New York, even forgetting his house on Morrison Street in Washington and what had happened to bring his grandchildren to Grand Rapids.

He wasn't returning to Washington. He didn't want to leave Noli in Grand Rapids by herself. That's not the way he said it, but they knew it was what he meant.

"This is home" was what he said.

All he wanted from the house on Morrison Street was the great oak bed in which he used to sit regarding himself in the mirror over the dresser while Noli leaned against the pillow next to him.

So the others stayed behind in Grand Rapids to settle their grandfather in an apartment.

"I'll call you every morning as always," Sam said, kissing William on the top of the head. But hearing his own voice, he thought his remark came across as casual, even patronizing. Later on the plane he wondered about himself. Why this absence of sadness at Noli's death? What he did feel, had felt since Oliver's birthday, when his grandfather called to say that Noli had died during her afternoon nap, was more like the memory of sadness, a short story he had read, an aftertaste, but not sadness itself. The wires of the synapses clipped, a cold emotion, not death, but the absence of life. He felt nothing at all.

On the plane, in the middle seat of three in coach, Sam suddenly saw himself behind the screen of his own life—the creation of Sam McWilliams on *Plum & Jaggers*—an actual representation, a cardboard replica, an empty vessel which the inventor of Sam McWilliams had made substantial for a television audience.

THE MCWILLIAMSES stayed five days, securing a first-floor apartment in a house on Wicket Street near Matthew Gray, two blocks from the house where they had lived. William was pleased. The house on Wicket Street was familiar to him, he said, wondering had he lived there when he was young or after he and Noli were married?

"He loves the apartment," Charlotte said to Sam on the telephone. "It has a garden out back."

"He never liked gardens," Sam said.

"Well, he likes them now. It's what he wanted more than anything. He says he likes cutting gardens," Charlotte said.

"He's changed, then, hasn't he?" Sam asked.

"Especially with us," Charlotte said, motioning to Julia to ask her if she wanted to talk to Sam.

Julia shook her head.

"It's odd not to have Sam here, isn't it," Julia said, looking out the window of her grandfather's new apartment, at the bare trees accumulating light snow in a late-winter storm as they were packing to leave Grand Rapids. "Sort of like death."

18

SOMEONE WAS FOLLOWING JULIA. Not all the time, not even every day, but persistently. She'd walk out of the apartment and feel that someone was watching. The street could be empty. She'd look up and down the block, checking the windows of apartments, and hurry to the subway, to the market, to get a coffee on Sixth Avenue. She never saw anyone specific, not close enough to identify. But a person in a crowd would catch her attention, on a subway or across Fifth Avenue on her way to work or coming out of a crowded elevator. An attitude about him which struck her as personal. Every man with graying curly hair was immediately familiar. It was spring, too late for wool scarfs, but often she thought she saw the man from the bookstore who had touched her hair, and then he'd disappear.

Once, in an elevator with Charlotte on her way to the dentist's, she turned around to see a man about forty, with a beard, leaning against the back of the elevator, staring at her, and he didn't turn away.

"He probably recognized you," Charlotte said once they were in the dentist's office.

"I don't think he was the sort to be watching comedy at 1 a.m. on Saturday nights," she said.

"You're turning into an agoraphobe like Noli."

"Who wouldn't?" Julia said. "I'm asking Sam if we can get a bodyguard."

SAM AGREED. At the Actors' Studio they found a large all-state wrestler from Massachusetts who had flunked out of college and come to New York City in the hope of developing a career as a character actor. His name was Baldridge and he was a member of the thin-blooded residue of failed aristocracy, too little challenged to rise to occasions. They called him Heartbreak, and he loved the name, believing it reflected their affection for him.

His job was Julia, although he often found himself responsible for all four of them, waiting in a coffee shop next door to 142 West Eleventh Street in the village, the brownstone to which they had returned the first week of April.

"You can count on me absolutely," Heartbreak said.

But occasionally something attracted his attention, and like a hound dog he'd simply vanish on a new scent.

One afternoon shortly after he'd been hired, Julia was trying on clothes for Marigold at a thrift shop when a friend of Heartbreak's from college walked by the shop. Heartbreak forgot entirely what he was supposed to be doing outside the thrift shop door and went with the friend for a beer. When Julia came out with her bag of clothes, he was gone, catching up with her just as she was hailing a cab on Sixth Avenue.

"Don't tell Sam," he said. "I'll never do it again. I just forgot."

"You can't forget."

"I know I can't forget, and I never will again."

But he did.

SAM WAS WORKING TOO HARD, sometimes way into the night after the rest of them were sleeping, getting up early, if he slept at all, before they were awake. He had set up his computer at the dining-room table of the apartment. It took too much time, he said, to pack up his work and walk to the coffeehouse for the day. Too much distraction. He had lost interest in the company of strangers.

"I can't stand it that Sam's working at home," Julia told Charlotte in early April on their way to the studio for rehearsal, Heartbreak close on their heels.

Charlotte said nothing. She was exhausted by their lives with Sam, overcome by a constant need to sleep. He filled the living room like a gas leak, poisoning the air.

"Can't you move your office into one of the bedrooms, where you'd have some quiet?" she asked.

"The noise doesn't bother me. I like the sound of talking," Sam said to them.

There was no point in arguing.

He wrote in a kind of manic fever, sometimes working all night, fifty new pages by morning.

"What do you think?" he'd ask Oliver, who was lying on the couch, trying to keep up with Sam's writing.

Oliver shook his head. "I don't know, Sam. There's too much."

"What do you mean, too much?"

"A hundred and fifty pages for a half-hour episode?" Oliver put the pages facedown on his stomach. "You used to do half that and we hardly needed to edit it at all."

"So you guys edit," Sam said. "I don't want those clowns at NBC touching this work. They haven't got a clue what it's about."

"Me either," Julia whispered to Charlotte as they sat in the living room trying to cut the scripts in half, to make some sense of Sam's obtuseness. Not even a standard for absurdity was observed.

"Something new needs to happen to Sam in these stories," Oliver said to his brother. "We now have three episodes in which he's got Jaggers's chair in the middle of the dining-room table and is sitting in it for the whole half-hour show."

"It is supposed to be funny," Sam said coolly. "Amusing. Remember? I'm a comedy writer."

"I wonder if it doesn't go on too long."

"It goes on for just the right amount of time."

Sam knew he was losing his bearings. The line between himself and the invented character of Sam McWilliams was disappearing, and he was beginning to think of himself as a genius. He would sit at his worktable reading what he had just written, even the stage directions, out loud to his siblings. He didn't allow interruptions. Not even music, which disturbed his thinking patterns, he said. Sometimes he was too busy to eat.

THE RATINGS for *Plum & Jaggers* were falling.

"We have bad letters and bad insider reports," Jacob told the others at rehearsal in mid-April, when Sam was at home furiously writing to finish the final two episodes for the season.

"Tell Sam," Oliver said.

"You tell him."

"That's your job, Jacob. We're his siblings."

"I showed him the letters and they didn't make a bit of difference," Jacob replied.

"Sam's going through a crisis. Writers do."

"I know about your grandmother and the possible stalker." Jacob paced the room. "I know it's been a bad time for you guys, but he won't listen to anybody."

"Try talking to him calmly," Charlotte said.

"Calmly? I may as well be dead," Jacob said. "He blows me off and writes exactly what he wants to write. It just doesn't happen to be what people want to watch at the moment."

"We know that." Charlotte put on her cape.

"Well, help me, then."

It was a Monday, the second week in April. Julia was staying at the studio to rehearse a solo scene which had been going badly and Heartbreak was waiting for her. She had plans to go to dinner with Andy and Eric and then to a dance club.

"You're sure I'll be okay?" she asked Charlotte in the ladies' room.

"Don't you want to go?" Charlotte asked. "You never get to do anything."

"I do want to go," Julia said. "I'm just a little scared."

"Then make sure Heartbreak sticks right beside you and call us at midnight."

"WHAT ARE WE GOING TO DO about the show?" Oliver asked as he and Charlotte headed home.

"I'll tell Sam what Jacob said."

They were walking from Fourteenth Street to their apartment, a cold, wet spring day, the wind pushing them forward, the rain soaking their hair.

"I don't think you should tell him."

"He needs to know how much trouble we're in," Charlotte said.

"He knows," Oliver said. "He knows everything that's going on."

"I still plan to say something."

CHARLOTTE HAD BEEN UNFLAPPABLE for weeks, steady and cheerful, with an astonishing calm. But the cost of her supporting role in their fragile family was accumulating. Since Noli had died, she couldn't concentrate for long enough to read a book. Sometimes she couldn't sleep. She went days eating nothing but bread and butter and hot tea. The only real pleasure she had had since Sam had turned crazy was naming babies. She had picked up a small spiral notebook, and while they sat around the apartment editing Sam's excessive scripts, she'd make lists of names, mostly for girls. She hadn't even told Julia she was naming babies, although Julia was a name she had chosen. Julia Lucas. And Lucy, of course. But so far her favorite was Miranda. Miranda McWilliams. She hadn't imagined a father.

AT THE APARTMENT, Oliver struggled to open the rain-swollen front door, leading the way up the steps to the second floor, stopping at the landing.

"What's up?" Charlotte asked.

He turned. "Do you smell something?"

Charlotte caught up with him, sniffing. "I do."

"Something's burning," he said.

"No kidding."

IN THE LIVING ROOM Sam was working at the computer, his back to the kitchen, smoke around his shoulders like a cape.

Charlotte rushed into the kitchen. "What's on fire?"

"Nothing that I know of," Sam said without looking up.

"Can't you smell the smoke?"

In the toaster oven on the Formica counter under the cabinets a piece of toast was on fire, ribbons of black smoke seeping between the seams of the glass door. Charlotte pulled the plug, smothered the toast with a towel, and opened the window facing the alley.

"It's an incinerator in here." Oliver threw down his umbrella on the couch. "What is going on?"

"Toast," Charlotte said.

Sam looked up from the computer. "I smelled nothing. I'm working."

"Working?" Oliver turned the toaster upside down and dumped the charred remains of toast in the sink.

"I did put bread in the toaster oven," Sam said.

"You could have burned up," Charlotte said.

"Don't be extreme," Sam said, printing the pages he'd been working on. "If I wanted to die of smoke inhalation, I'd be more professional than toast."

"I didn't say you *wanted* to die," Charlotte said, opening more windows. "I said you could have."

The rain from the east rushed through the open windows in thin sheets, soaking up the smell of burned toast. Charlotte took out the bucket of soaps from under the sink and cleaned the kitchen, sprayed the living room with lavender toilet water, tossed the toaster oven in the trash, and scrubbed the counters sticky with the residue of smoke.

"Are we going to mention the ratings?" Charlotte asked Oliver quietly, but Sam overheard her.

"I don't care about the ratings," he said, assuming a voice of exhausted rationality. "What I'm writing now is the best work I've ever done."

He had some pages in his lap, editing with a pencil, his feet on the dining-room table next to the computer, his Orioles cap on backward.

"Do you want to read me what you've written so far?" Oliver asked.

"Nope, I don't," Sam said.

JULIA TOOK THE N TO SOHO. Heartbreak was standing at the other end of the car, holding on to the pole in the center aisle, looking over at her, as he had a tendency to do, smiling. She wanted to keep his attention so he wouldn't miss the stop at Prince Street. At the same time, she wished he wouldn't watch her so enthusiastically.

At the newsstand just outside the subway stop she pretended to look at the new issue of *Currents*, motioning for Heartbreak to stand beside her.

"I'm meeting my friends at the Blue Mango for dinner and then we're going down Broadway to a place called Pewter's," she said. "Stay close."

From the Prince Street stop, Julia walked to the Blue Mango on Mercer, checking behind to see if Heartbreak was close by, which he was, although the second time she turned her head, he was looking at some small carved boats in an antiques store, his hands on the glass, his face against it, so that he easily could have lost her if she hadn't waited for him to catch her eye and trot along, keeping half a block behind.

From time to time, she could see him through the window at the

Blue Mango, walking by, peering in, always with the broad smile he insisted on giving her. She'd have to mention it to him.

After dinner they went to Pewter's—Eric and Andy and Brill, some of their friends with whom they had eaten. As they left the Blue Mango, Julia saw Heartbreak across the street and made eye contact.

IMMEDIATELY INSIDE PEWTER'S, Julia was nervous.

The place was dark and crowded. Blue and yellow strobe lights splashed across her face and beyond her, across the room and back, a kind of syncopated light show which split the face of a person in half and she could feel the coming of panic. She grabbed Andy's hand.

"Dance with me," she said.

Andy was a good dancer, weaving in and out of the other dancers, holding her firmly at the small of her back, moving light as air over the whole dance floor, into the middle and out again.

"Just stay with me," she said, out of breath, when the music stopped.

In the corner, she could see Eric and Brill leaning against the bar.

"Let's go over to Eric," Andy said, leading the way.

At first he had hold of her hand, but when someone pressed between, he dropped it. As Julia looked up, orienting herself in the brightly dotted darkness, she couldn't find Andy. She pushed her way to the bar, searching up and down for Eric and Brill, and they seemed to be gone as well. But instead of standing where she was, waiting for them to find her, as certainly they would have, she bolted.

Outside, there was a long line of people waiting to get in, and she walked along the inside until she spotted Heartbreak. He was just crossing the street headed in the other direction, away from Pewter's.

"Heartbreak!"

He turned around and, spotting Julia, waited while she hailed a cab.

She saw him clearly as she got into the cab. The plan had been that he would follow her in another cab and when she looked he was standing on the other side of Broadway just opposite and watching her. She thought she saw him nod his head, give a little wave as if he were hailing a taxi himself to follow hers.

"One-forty-two West Eleventh," she said to the driver, looking out the window, expecting Heartbreak any minute to appear in the backseat of one of the cabs. But when she looked behind her at the first red light, Heartbreak wasn't in any of the taxis, and she could no longer find him on the street across from Pewter's.

She opened her purse and counted out six dollars, slid down in the backseat so the occupants of a passing taxi wouldn't be able to see her, so the man with graying curly hair who had been watching her, even this afternoon on Broadway while she had a cup of tea, wouldn't recognize her should his taxi pull up alongside hers.

142 WEST ELEVENTH was a four-story brownstone in the middle of the block between Sixth and Seventh Avenues—eight steps up from the sidewalk, a glass front door, then a small vestibule where the mailboxes were and a second glass door to the stairs—an apartment on each floor, four apartments in all. No doorman. Sam had been willing to forget about a doorman when he hired Heartbreak.

Julia paid the driver, asking him to wait till she got safely inside. He didn't speak very much English, so she repeated, "Wait." And he nodded as if he had understood.

"Thank you," she said, shutting the car door.

But by the time she had zipped her wallet and stuffed it in her backpack the cab was halfway down the block, and Heartbreak was nowhere to be seen.

There was a light with low wattage above the glass front door, and as she put the key in the lock, she could see her own reflection in the glass.

Behind her she heard or thought she heard a sound of footsteps, maybe in the street, maybe on the steps. She didn't need to turn around and couldn't have turned had she wished to, her hand frozen on the key, her heart pumping.

In the fuzzy gray reflection in the glass door, she saw someone coming up the steps behind her, his head rising to her waist, her shoulders—it happened quickly—and before she had a chance to scream or ring the bell to her apartment, he had put his palms on the glass on either side of her, trapping her in the arc of his arms, his smoky breath floating around her head, his shadow surfacing to familiar features in the glass.

Swiftly, before he had a chance to pin her hand, she reached under his arm and punched 4. Moments passed, maybe only a matter of seconds extending in her imagination, and then Oliver's voice came over the speaker.

"Who is it?" he called.

The apparition in the glass put his hand over Julia's mouth, flattening her lips against her teeth.

"Sam McWilliams," he said in an ordinary voice, barely audible above her muffled cries.

19

UPSTAIRS IN THE APARTMENT, the McWilliamses were alert to trouble. It was almost 2 a.m. No one had gone to bed, Oliver pacing, looking out the window for Julia; Charlotte sitting up, half-sleeping, *Sense and Sensibility* face-down on her lap. Sam was at the dining-room table, too agitated to work. When he heard the buzzer, he jumped up.

"Who is it?" Oliver asked, and Sam was out of the apartment just as the man announced himself.

By the time Sam got downstairs, Julia was gone. The street was dark, the streetlight in front of their apartment burned out. The rain had stopped, but the night was heavy with an early spring fog. Sam caught his breath.

The man with Julia couldn't have had time to hail a cab, not on West Eleventh Street after midnight. Sam turned right toward Sixth, walking slowly to check the dark caves along the street, basement apartments, an alley in the middle of the block, corners where people chained their trash cans to trees, garden squares out of the circle of streetlights.

Someone appeared to be stuffed in a rectangle between two buildings, flattened against the wall, his head tilted up, arms at his sides. Sam would not have seen him in the darkness if some animal sound, a low, almost inaudible groaning, had not escaped his lips as Sam walked past the buildings. When he turned to look into the black space, a form began to take shape, and as his eyes adjusted to the night, he saw a man whom he had seen before. He didn't see Julia until he was between the buildings himself, and then he saw her on the ground, a pile of clothing, laundry, not even her head showing.

At first the man didn't even try to escape when Oliver, running from across the street, grabbed him by the shoulders and held him against the wall.

A small crowd gathered from the apartments nearby. Someone had a flashlight, and Sam sat in the circle of light holding Julia's head. She was making funny kitten sounds in her throat, a breaking noise like dry twigs, and in the distance Sam heard the siren of the ambulance coming in their direction.

Later, not one of them knew what had happened or how—the ambulance came, the emergency medical team moved in, Sam and Charlotte stood back with Oliver, the small crowd withdrew along the sidewalk, and sometime in the moments between the arrival of the ambulance and finally the police, the man struggled out of Oliver's grip and disappeared.

WAITING IN THE EMERGENCY ROOM of St. Luke's Hospital, Sam couldn't stop talking.

"I don't know how he got away, Oliver," he said, pacing in front of the chair where Oliver was sitting. "Now he's loose somewhere in New York City. Loose, for chrissake."

Charlotte was in the room with Julia, only one member of the family permitted. The wait for news from the doctor went on and on. A shooting victim had come in, a drug-overdose who was comatose brought in on a stretcher, an elderly man on oxygen.

"Would you check?" Sam asked Oliver.

"They'll let us know when they have some news." Oliver was thumbing through an old *Life* magazine to calm his nerves.

"God, Oliver. You won't ever act. You simply turn catatonic in an emergency situation." Sam thrust his hands in his pockets. "The whole thing—the whole family responsibility is on my shoulders and has been forever."

"Your choice, Sam," Oliver said, checking the waiting room for reactions to Sam's temper.

"I thought the guy after Julia was Ranier Moore. Didn't you?"

"Nope," Oliver said. "I always thought it was a stranger."

"I had an instinct, especially when we were in Grand Rapids." He sat down next to Oliver. "We've seen that curly-haired guy before, haven't we?"

"We've all seen him. I saw him in TriBeCa. He came up to me and asked had I gone to Columbia. Julia saw him. He's been around," Oliver said. "I gave the police a detailed description."

"He called himself Sam McWilliams," Sam said. "You heard that."

"He's a sick man," Oliver said.

Sam got up and walked over to the patient entrance to the Emergency Room, ringing the bell.

"They'll never find him," he called back to Oliver. "The police are completely incompetent." He pressed the bell again.

"Is anybody planning to let us know about my sister tonight?" he asked when the nurse appeared. "Or do you all assume we're just enjoying the company in the waiting room?"

"As soon as the doctor sees your sister, sir," the nurse said. "We've had a heart attack and a cardiac arrest. It's a busy night."

After the nurse left, Sam was asked by the woman sitting at the Admissions desk to step outside the waiting room because he was disturbing the other families.

BY THE TIME OLIVER HAD SPOKEN to the doctor and followed Sam to the street, Sam was silent.

"She has a concussion," Oliver said, leaning against the building next to his brother. "Apparently the guy hit her head against the wall of the building where they were hiding. The doctor doesn't think it's serious and he's going to release her, but we have to watch her for the next forty-eight hours."

"She'll live?" Sam asked, without looking at Oliver.

"Of course she'll live," Oliver said. "Did you think she wasn't going to?"

"What else would I think?" Sam asked quietly, his arms folded across his chest, his eyes closed. "Welcome to my mind, Oliver."

It was dawn, the golden beginning of a day which would be clear and bright, when Sam went out after the stranger.

Julia lay in her own room next to Charlotte, who was reading *Sense and Sensibility* aloud to keep her awake, as the doctor in the Emergency Room of St. Luke's had recommended.

"Let the police find him, Sam," Charlotte begged.

"Or Detective Howell." Oliver stood at the door to the apartment, hoping to detain him.

"I'll find him myself," Sam said.

PLUM & JAGGERS WAS RUINED, Sam thought, heading uptown. At least his capacity for writing the kinds of stories he had always written had left him since the man who had set fire to the dry field at Bluemont had crept into the privacy of Sam's imagination. Before the fire, even in moments when Sam's spirit had been shattered, there was a kind of sweetness seeping through the dark skin of comedy in his scripts.

Wandering the streets of the city, joining the morning commuters who poured onto the sidewalks with umbrellas tucked under their arms although the day was going to be pure sun, Sam had a vision of the graying curly-haired man who was pursuing Julia. He began to see him as an agent of fate, a materialization of danger, the enemy, related by blood to the other agent—whoever he might have been—who had blown up the lunch car of the Espresso to Rome in 1974.

Someone who had Sam in mind from the start.

BY NOON Sam was beginning to feel estranged from himself, an abstract painting of the head of a man in which the sides of the face do not line up, the brain broken into jigsaw pieces, the expression unspecific. He stopped for coffee, but even a small amount of caffeine made him nervous, so he tossed the full cup in the trash.

In Chelsea, he wandered into Barnes & Noble, standing for a long time in the Fiction section, checking the inside covers of newly released books to see which ones were published by Larkin Press. There were several, and he wondered if Rebecca Frankel was responsible for them.

"How do you find out who the editor of a book is?" he asked the young man at the cash register.

"Call," the young man said.

"I'm looking for a book edited by a woman named Rebecca Frankel."

"What book?" the young man asked.

"My question exactly," Sam said.

"Do you know the name of the author?"

"If I did, I'd tell you now, wouldn't I?"

"I'm sorry, sir. I can't help you." The young man looked up at Sam finally. "Do you want me to get the manager?"

"No, I don't," Sam said.

He wondered what would happen if he were to hit the young man directly in the face.

On his way out of Barnes & Noble, midday, sunny and crisp, he felt better. He considered walking to Larkin Press or calling to ask what books Rebecca had recently edited.

He hadn't heard from her for a couple of weeks. The last postcard, a strange one for a woman who was extremely careful in her choice of pictures, was a charcoal drawing by a German artist Sam had never heard of, a black-and-white of a woman with melon breasts bursting through an iron corset, an expression of hopelessness in her tiny eyes.

Sam, the card had said. P & J *is getting too dark. Go dancing tonight. Love, R.*

He walked uptown, through Central Park and west to the Cathedral of St. John the Divine and on to Columbia University, where he sat for a long time in the main cafeteria listening to the voices of students chattering, imagining Sam McWilliams, the character from *Plum & Jaggers*, seated at the table next to him, his legs crossed, his arms folded on the table, drinking a cup of coffee at sufficient distance for observation. It occurred to him that he was losing his mind.

BY THREE O'CLOCK, the apartment on West Eleventh was spotless. Charlotte had cleaned it, even the woodwork and the floors, the grimy corners of the rooms accumulating dirt and dead spiders. She went out early when the shops opened and bought new white comforters and sheets and towels and dishcloths, Indian throw rugs for the living room, flowers everywhere, on the dining-room table, where Sam worked, and the kitchen window and the bureau in the entrance hall. She had put up their father's shoreline paintings along the west wall of the living room, lined there as if the apartment were a gallery. She had even cleaned out the closets and the cupboards and bought shelf paper, opening every window to let the dead air of other people's lives escape.

Oliver helped. At least he did the floors, but every time Charlotte left a room where he was working, he flopped down on the couch or bed or even the floor and fell immediately asleep.

In the early afternoon, Charlotte showered, dressed, and sat in a rocker in the living room, surveying the apartment with a sense of arriving clarity, like health after a long illness. In the next room, Oliver was sleeping on the floor.

When the telephone rang just after three, it was their grandfather, his daily call, just catching up. He had no interest in bad news, so Charlotte didn't give him any.

"Was that Sam?" Oliver called from the next room.

"Grandfather," Charlotte answered.

"Where *is* Sam?" Oliver called.

"I don't know," Charlotte said. "I guess he's still looking for that man."

A young man called, and when she picked up the receiver, he said in a high falsetto, "Is this the Plum and Jaggers residence?"

She hung up the phone.

"Who was that?" Oliver asked.

"A crank call."

It was nearly 4 p.m. and Sam had been gone all day.

"Don't answer the phone anymore," Oliver said, and when it did ring again, he put his hand on the receiver in case Charlotte was tempted.

"Turn up the answering machine so at least we can hear who it is," Charlotte said.

It was Jacob Levy.

"Give me a call," Jacob said in his soft, anxious voice. "We do have real trouble now."

"Erase that," Oliver said. "Sam doesn't need to hear it when he comes home. *If* he comes home."

"He'll be back."

IT WAS SHORTLY AFTER FOUR O'CLOCK when Sam arrived, rushing up the steps of the brownstone, bursting through the door.

"Any word?" he asked.

"No word," Charlotte said.

"How's Julia?" Sam peered into her bedroom.

She was lying on the bed, on top of the covers, in her nightgown, her arm slung over her eyes.

"Better," Charlotte said. "Her head still hurts but she's better."

Sam collapsed on the couch.

"I see you cleaned up," he said.

"We're starting over," Charlotte said. "A new and perfectly sane life."

"Sane?" Sam shook his head. "That's a leap of faith."

Oliver leaned against the entrance to the kitchen, his thinning hair flying, his shoulders slumped.

"Where were you?" Oliver asked. "We called NBC."

"I wasn't at NBC."

"Oliver thought you had gone to see Rebecca Frankel," Charlotte said.

"I was walking all over town," Sam said. "I'm sure he's nearby making plans for a return visit."

"The police will find him," Oliver said.

"Fat chance!"

WHEN DETECTIVE HOWELL CALLED from the precinct, Charlotte was making carrot soup and Sam was lying on the couch, his eyes fixed on the ceiling. Oliver took the call.

"Now what?" Sam asked when Oliver handed him the phone.

"No luck so far," Detective Howell said. "This could take a long time."

"I'm sure it could," Sam said.

"We're lucky nothing worse happened," Charlotte said when Sam had hung up the phone.

"Lucky?" Sam got up, gathered his scripts from the dining-room table, and went into his room.

"If the phone rings," he said, closing the door, "don't answer."

20

OLIVER WAS AT CAFÉ ROSA waiting for Charlotte at the table where Sam usually sat. He had a large sketch pad and was drawing a river front, a park with wooded walking trails and bike paths and gardens. Domesticated community land attracted him, a sense of safety and friendship with strangers. Just in the last few days since the call from NBC he had been drawing landscapes, one after the other, mainly cityscapes with communal land. It was as if he'd already drawn them in another time, locked them away, and forgotten until this moment, when they spilled out of his mind.

AT THE APARTMENT, Sam was finishing the final episode of *Plum & Jaggers*, living on coffee and granola bagels, working through the night.

No one had spoken to him about "The End," as Julia referred to the final episode. They didn't know what to say or how Sam really was or if he would or could survive without the four of them, like fingers doubled over in a tight fist. For the several days since *Plum & Jaggers* had been canceled, they'd walked around the apartment on cat's feet, watching Sam, stealing sidelong glances at him, peering out of their bedrooms at night to check if he was still there, still working.

CHARLOTTE ARRIVED at the café with the mail, setting it down on the table next to Oliver's sketch pad. She ordered lunch.

"Bills," she said. "And a letter from Rebecca Frankel."

"A letter?" Oliver held it up to the light. "That's something new."

"I hope it's sweet," Charlotte said. "He doesn't need to hear any more about how gloomy his writing has become."

"Has he finished the edit?"

"He has to be finished," Charlotte said. "The end's tonight."

"Have you read the edit?" Oliver asked, folding up his riverfront design, removing the mail so the waitress could set the table for lunch.

"Everything but the very end, which he says is a secret. It's sweet. Like the old Sam," Charlotte said.

IN THE APARTMENT, Julia lay on her bed with the door ajar so she could see Sam working.

He sat with his back to her in the same khakis he'd been wearing since Tuesday night, when he'd pressed Play on the answering machine and gotten the message from Jacob Levy that *Plum & Jaggers* was finished for television, canceled after the next episode. He was barefoot, the legs of his trousers rolled up, a black T-shirt hanging off his bony shoulders. His face had the hungry, haunted look of a child of war. In days, this diminishing.

He hadn't been able to sleep. If he closed his eyes, even for a moment, even sitting with his hands on the computer, his head full of story, he'd see the lunch car explode. In his mind there was a glossy color postcard of a burning train split down the middle, spewing bodies like lava out of the center of a volcano; it was as if his

sense of sight and hearing were one, the image of the train replicat-
ing the sound of the exploding bomb. The end of *Plum & Jaggers*
started with this waking nightmare. They had been rehearsing the
final episode all week. But Sam had in mind a conclusion to the
story beyond the one they had rehearsed. He had decided he
wouldn't tell his siblings. That way the story would unfold to its
inevitable conclusion with the element of surprise.

"Stop watching me, Julia," he called over his shoulder. "I can feel
your eyes."

"They're closed," Julia said.

She still had a headache from the concussion she'd gotten—a
constant, dull pain, a general exhaustion, an absence of hope.

Sam got up from the table, took off his glasses, and stood in the
doorway to Julia's room.

"We've got rehearsal late today for the last show."

"I know," Julia said.

"Where are Charlotte and Oliver?" he asked. "Planning their marvelous lives after we're kaput?"

"At the café having a late lunch," Julia said evenly. "We're meeting at the studio."

She was steady with Sam. They all were, refusing to rise to combat, addressing his constant challenge as if it were ordinary conversation. It took effort, particularly for Julia.

"And you've been left on suicide watch," Sam said, a quiet hysteria skimming the surface of his conversation.

Julia didn't reply.

He went into the kitchen to get another cup of black coffee—bit-
ter, too long in the pot. But he drank it slowly, turning on the printer
to print out the final finished episode of *Plum & Jaggers*, twenty
pages at a time, finding some small pleasure in the emerging words
as they appeared on the page.

Julia could hear the low grinding of the printer taking its slow
breaths, but sometime before the manuscript was printed out, she
must have fallen asleep. When she woke up, the apartment was

silent except for the construction crew working in the building across the street. Sam had left.

HE LEFT in a wave of high spirits, the script in his bookbag flung over his shoulder, a kind of jumpiness in his brain that felt at once like happiness and fear, as if the two were one, the division of a common cell. It was almost four o'clock, hours before they were supposed to meet at NBC for rehearsal, plenty of time to go to Fortieth and Broadway and pick up props.

What he had in mind was noise with reverberations and smoke. An illusion of disaster.

IN THE FINAL STORY, Plum and Jaggers are expected for dinner.

"Together for the first time in years," Charlotte was to say.

Oliver was to be Oliver, with the exception of Anarchy's curled black tail attached to his blue jeans and wagging so he wouldn't be able to sit down at the dinner table. Sam was cooking dinner, nouvelle cuisine. Salmon with dill and cucumber sauce, garlic mashed potatoes, slender asparagus in vinaigrette, a carrot cake.

Welcome Home Plum and Jaggers, Julia would write on the white icing. When the show opened, she would be decorating the dining room as well, streamers above the table, balloons tied to every chair.

That would be the scene for "The End." No extras, everyone playing the role of himself in giddy preparation for Plum and Jaggers's return home.

"It isn't as bleak as other episodes have been lately," Sam had told Jacob over the phone when he called to say the script was done. "Nothing to complain about in this script."

Sam had the balloons and streamers and cake-decorating kit and a cake from the bakery and other props from Maxi's, Items of Illusion, arriving at NBC just before four o'clock.

Down Fifth Avenue just below Rockefeller Plaza, he saw his

brother and sisters, three abreast, the crowds of afternoon shoppers weaving around them. Sam didn't wait.

"WE'RE IN GOOD SHAPE for tonight," Sam said to Jacob, who was sitting on one of the dining-room chairs on the set when Sam arrived. "I've done the final edits and we're reheasing one more time."

He handed Jacob a final script.

"The others are on their way. I saw them when I came in."

Jacob skimmed to the back of the script.

"I don't get it," he said, when he had finished reading the end.

"What don't you get?"

"It's just stage direction. Plum and Jaggers come back. Right? We assume they sit down on those empty chairs."

"That's right," Sam said.

"No fanfare." Jacob shook his head, watching Sam put the cake on the dining-room table, dump the bag of balloons and streamers and candles.

"So you guys are just there when Plum and Jaggers come in, and that's it. No comment?"

"The story is simply over," Sam said coolly. "That's how it ends."

THERE WAS A NERVOUS EXCITEMENT in the studio Saturday night, a sense of uncertainty, a community sadness.

At 12:50 a.m. the McWilliamses took their places at the dining-room table.

Sam pulled the chairs for Plum and Jaggers away from the table and brushed off the seats.

"Tell us the end once more," Oliver said to Sam as the crew was adjusting their cameras, checking the microphones.

"Plum and Jaggers have presumably arrived. You have that chatter back and forth as we've rehearsed. And then we all take our seats."

"The lights dim and kaput." Julia was fixing her hair with her fingers.

"Ready?" the cameraman asked.

"Ready," Sam said.

PEOPLE GATHERED in the studio, the writers and cameramen, a reporter from *Currents*, several others laughing.

"Sweet," Jacob said to Brill as the episode unfolded.

"I love it," Eric said. "Like it was in the fall. So sad and funny."

"You guys were pretty quick to cancel," the reporter said.

"Bad ratings," Jacob said. "Television is merciless."

THE EPISODE was rushing to its conclusion—the set cheerfully decorated with colored streamers, the cake shimmering with candles, dinner on the sideboard in the dining room, a sense of expectancy, a knock from somewhere.

"They're here," Oliver said, wagging his black, curly tail.

"They must have forgotten their key." Charlotte rushed off to answer the door.

"They're here, they're here, they're here at last," Julia sang, twirling around the table, falling into her chair. "Hello, Plum and Jaggers. Hello, Plum. Hello, Jaggers. Hello, hello."

SAM WAS STANDING by the sideboard, his arms folded across his chest, his head facing the door through which Plum and Jaggers were expected to come.

He took a lighter from his pocket, reached over to light the candles on the dining-room table, and then, pulling out the chairs for Plum and Jaggers with a kind of exaggerated flourish, he got down on his hands and knees and crawled under the table and lifted the top of a barely visible box.

There was a sudden small flash, the smell of burning in the studio, a sizzling sound like a high-pitched musical note, and then an explosion—a huge, flat noise, metal on metal.

Thick gray smoke swooped up from beneath the table, filling the set.

BARELY VISIBLE in the cloud of charcoal smoke, assuming a familiar posture, his legs slightly apart, his arms folded across his chest, his expression severe, Sam spoke above the commotion.

"Goodbye, everybody," he said in his first-ever speaking role since the beginning of *Plum & Jaggers*.

"Goodbye and thank you for coming to dinner."

III

21

SAM WAS GONE.

Mid-August, a heat wave in New York City, no air conditioning in the McWilliamses' Eleventh Street apartment, which they were in the process of vacating. Boxes stacked in corners, Julia's clothes in one corner, Charlotte's books, her treasures, her costumes packed for Goodwill. Oliver had the largest number of boxes with their parents' letters and photographs, the shoreline paintings, the *Plum & Jaggers* scripts. He was to be the keeper of records, the historian, the only one among them moving to a house with an attic, one in Boston, where he was going to study landscape architecture.

In preparation, Oliver and Julia were scrubbing out the kitchen cupboards, washing the woodwork, the scabby linoleum floor.

"Charlotte said she'd get groceries on the way back," Julia was saying.

"I hope she remembers." Oliver filled the large black trash bag with residue from the cupboards. "I'm starving. I'm always starving lately."

"Me too," Julia said. "Since Noli died, we never eat."

Charlotte had traveled the daily route she usually took with Oliver uptown to the studio on West Seventy-second where Sam had moved days after the show was canceled in April. He lived alone, without furniture except for a futon and an ancient television. Nothing on the walls or in the fridge or in the closets, only what Charlotte and Oliver brought him, dinner or a large lunch, bagels, books or magazines, always the newspaper, hoping that something, perhaps the report of an act of terrorism someplace, would bring him back to himself.

They had tried everything. Psychiatrists and physicians, a psychic healer, even a clown, whom they had actually made the mistake to bring to the apartment. But Sam refused help. He seldom spoke.

Once, sometimes twice a day, Charlotte or Oliver went to West Seventy-second, fourth floor back, and Sam answered the door in his cut-off jeans, no shirt. Sometimes he couldn't or else wouldn't get out of bed. He moved like an old man, the smallest gesture requiring too much effort. His skin was the color of pale ocher, his breathing uneven, as if he were willing it to cease. They believed he must be dying.

JULIA DIDN'T VISIT.

"I hate him," she told Charlotte and Oliver after the fiasco of the last *Plum & Jaggers* episode. "He could have blown us up right in the studio."

"He wasn't going to hurt us, Julia," Charlotte said. "He knew exactly what a smoke bomb would do."

"I almost choked to death," Julia said.

WHEN THE AIR HAD CLEARED after the smoke bomb, Sam was already on his way out of the studio. The small audience who had gathered to watch the final episode were too stunned to notice that he had left.

"That's one way to exit with a bang," Jacob said to the press at the post-show party held at the studio without Sam. "Everybody knew there was a bomb under the dining-room table and that it wasn't interior decoration."

The McWilliamses didn't speak to the reporters. Sam stayed in his bedroom with the door closed, and the others, wandering through the apartment in a state of nervous agitation, had nothing to say to the press. They didn't want to let on that the smoke bomb had been a shock to them as well, and they didn't wish to claim responsibility for it by lying.

ON MONDAY, after the final show, the story was in the entertainment sections of papers all over the country. The viewing audience registered by the Nielsen ratings had been the largest ever for *Plum & Jaggers*.

SAM MCWILLIAMS TAKES CONTROL was the lead in the piece by the *Washington Post* television writer, who went on to give a detailed psychological analysis of Sam as a victim turned perpetrator, referring at length to the death of his parents and his tenure at the Cage.

The *New York Times* story was an intellectual assessment of the history of the show, the importance of comedy, the particular power of live television. The writer described the final episode as "heartbreaking," especially the last lines, when the character of Sam finally speaks. He made little of the smoke bomb, dismissing it as a gesture of adolescent fury.

Oliver had read the *Times* piece and handed it to Charlotte.

"Tell me what you think," he had said.

"About the smoke bomb?" Charlotte had asked, taking the paper.

"It was under the dining-room table as a warning," Julia said, lying on the couch on her stomach, looking at pictures in trashy magazines, contributing little to the discussion. She didn't want to read the stories about *Plum & Jaggers*. She couldn't bear the criticism, especially of Sam, in spite of her anger at him. "I never never expected that stupid bomb to explode."

"I like this piece about the show because it takes us seriously," Charlotte had said, finishing the story. "Maybe what he says about adolescence is true and Sam knew it, too."

The door to Sam's room had opened and he stood in the shadows in boxer shorts, his arms folded across his chest.

"This apartment is a Nuclear Free Zone," he had said without a trace of humor in his voice. "Any discussion of Plum & Jaggers is finished."

IN SEPTEMBER, when Oliver moved to Boston to begin school, Julia and Charlotte were planning to rent an apartment near Columbia University so Charlotte could go to graduate school in literature. Her plans were clear. She wanted to read books and have a baby.

"A baby?" Oliver asked. "You're free finally to do whatever you want and that's what you want to do with your time?"

"What else?" Charlotte asked.

She had a recurring puppy dream. She was lying on a soft dog bed—not a dog herself, but a woman—human arms and legs surrounding a tribe of golden retriever puppies with velvet ears and cold wet noses pressed against her bare skin. The joy of it.

"We need a baby. We're too small a family without one," Charlotte said.

Oliver shrugged. "I don't know that a child is the answer to our situation."

Julia had been given the role of a mildly disturbed teenager in a new ABC comedy series about a family on the brink of disaster.

"I'm surprised you want to keep on acting," Oliver said.

"I don't," Julia said. "I just don't know how to do anything else."

THEY WERE SITTING on the counter drinking lemonade when Charlotte came back from Sam's apartment.

She dropped the mail on the dining-room table, the bag of groceries she had taken to her brother, the newspaper.

"Sam's gone," she said. "The apartment is empty and he's taken his clothes."

DETECTIVE HOWELL was sympathetic.

"You kids," he kept saying, shaking his head. But after what had happened with the graying curly-haired man, still roaming at large, probably in New York City, the detective took them seriously. He asked for a list of every place Sam could be—the farm in Bluemont, or Washington, or Grand Rapids, even Chicago, although he had not been back there for some time. Anywhere in New York.

"When a person disappears, it's often to a place they've been before," Detective Howell said.

He wanted a complete report from childhood.

"Everything you can remember which might be of help to us," he said.

The McWilliamses told him about the home for juvenile delinquents, about Sam's collection of newspaper articles on terrorism, about his imagined love affair with Rebecca Frankel, and what had happened in Grand Rapids with Ranier Moore and Matthew Gray.

After Detective Howell left, Oliver walked the city, taking it in sections, winding through the blocks from the Hudson to the East River, one square area at a time. More than once he thought he saw Sam walking in front of him, his head cocked, his tense athletic gait, but when Oliver hurried to catch up with the stranger, it wasn't Sam, nothing like him, and besides, he realized, Sam no longer looked the way he had just a month ago. He stopped by NBC to see Jacob Levy and left a note at Larkin Press for Rebecca Frankel, who was off taking her daughter to medical school and would be away for ten days.

WHILE OLIVER WAS GONE, Julia made signs on postcard-size heavy art paper—burnt orange, so the message would show up. At the top of the postcard she drew a chair, and in black block letters she wrote: SAM CALL JULIA AT HOME.

She planned to post the signs everywhere—in coffeeshops and on bulletin boards, on electrical posts, in telephone kiosks and the NYU bookstore, all around the Village and SoHo and Chelsea, downtown and midtown.

That Sam had disappeared was her fault for hating him.

Charlotte spent the day on the telephone calling people who might have news of Sam. When Oliver came in, she was talking to Jacob.

"He hasn't heard anything from Sam for weeks," she said, replacing the receiver.

"Sam's not likely to call Jacob," Oliver said. "They didn't exactly part friends."

"But I'm trying to get in touch with everybody who might have news. I talked to Brill. She had a crush on him."

"What about the superintendent in his building?"

"He didn't even know that Sam had left, but he did check the apartment again."

"No trace of him, right?"

"Something which I didn't notice when I was there this morning," she said. "The super said there was a used razor with some hair still on it on the back of the sink."

"So Sam shaved before he left," Oliver said. "That strikes me as a good sign."

"Maybe it is." Charlotte brushed her hair, twisted it up on the top of her head with a comb. "Who knows?"

"He hasn't shaved in weeks." Oliver collapsed on the futon.

"Then I suppose it's a good sign." Charlotte took some of Julia's postcards and slipped them in her backpack.

"If what you're planning to do is put up signs, I don't think Sam's in New York," Oliver said.

"What does that mean?" Charlotte asked.

"It just doesn't feel like he's still here," he said, as if Sam's presence in the city, even diminished to the silent skeleton he had become, would be known.

THE STREETS WERE EMPTY for a Tuesday, too hot even for August, the steam from the subways hovering just above the sidewalks, the air pudding, thick enough to eat.

"I know you don't think these will make any difference," Julia said, pinning an orange card on the crowded bulletin board of the Chelsea Barnes & Noble bookstore.

"Anything helps. If he's here, he'll see your posters," Charlotte said, walking uptown along Sixth Avenue.

"You're humoring me," Julia said. "That's the point we've come to, isn't it, and we used to tell each other the truth." She taped a card to the telephone box at Twenty-third Street.

"Sam was the one who insisted on the truth. Certainly not me," Charlotte said, feeling suddenly old as she watched Julia taping her message on the telephone kiosk among the cards for yoga instruction and transcendental meditation and lost cats, and roommates, the hundreds of *seeking* messages, some with photocopied pictures, dim black-and-white shiny faces, pasted smiles—*SWF, leggy, beautiful, intelligent, sensual, seeks everything in one. Call 684-3212,* and *Homosexual visual artist seeks monogamy plus sun and fun in shared house on Fire Island for the summer.* There was a full-length picture of a buzz-cut male about thirty in a wrestling position—*SWM seeks temporary trouble and joy.*

"Did you read that one?" Charlotte asked.

"Which?"

"Trouble and joy."

Charlotte thought she would weep. Something she couldn't name had happened to them, as if the landscape had emptied and they could no longer find one another in such infinite space.

She didn't *know* Julia. Not in the way she had just days ago, a matter of months, when her sister had been an extension of Charlotte in another body. Or Sam's invention of Marigold or of Julia or Miriam—retrievable.

She saw them as they had been before *Plum & Jaggers* was canceled, before Sam moved to Seventy-second Street. A mass of radiating arms, rubbery-skinned, a bright sharp-eyed octopus scuttling along the ocean floor. The image pleased her.

Julia slowed her pace until they were walking shoulder to shoulder. She leaned closer so Charlotte could hear her speaking above the dull roar of passing traffic.

"I think the smoke bomb on the set worked," she said.

"What do you mean, worked?"

"It broke us apart."

She slipped her arm through Charlotte's, a gesture familiar to them, a way they often walked, especially in New York, but this afternoon it felt contrived, as if loss has a way of spreading out of control.

AT THE NEWSSTAND across from Macy's, Julia got a pack of peanut M&M's and cigarettes and scanned the front pages of the newspapers lined up in stacks on the open shelf, half expecting to see Sam's picture there, as if by now the news that he was missing would be national. She paid for the candy and cigarettes, stuck them in the zipper pocket of her bookbag, but turning to leave, she had a sudden urgency to look at the newspapers again. Something familiar had caught her attention.

The image her eyes had slipped across was on the front page of *The New York Times*, in color, an Israeli child, eight or nine, with a cap of black curly hair, high cheekbones, deep-set black eyes, a look of expectancy.

FOUR CHILDREN KILLED IN BUS EXPLOSION IN TEL AVIV, the headline read.

Julia walked on in silence, heading up Broadway.

"She looks like you did when you were little," Charlotte said finally.

"You saw her, too?" Julia asked.

"She flew off the page," Charlotte said, reaching down, taking hold of Julia's hand.

DURING THE DAY, Sam kept the television on mute. He lay on the futon, usually on his side, and waited for night, for the sun filtering in stripes through the dusty window facing east to move across the city and rush to the other side of the world. Not that he slept. It seemed to him as if he didn't sleep at all, his eyelids pasted open—the sparsely furnished room a still life except for the moving images on the television screen. When Oliver or Charlotte brought him food, he ate out of kindness or exhaustion, and he drank water because he couldn't tolerate the feeling of panic that came with dehydration. From time to time, he got up from his futon and filled his glass, pleased with the growing weakness in his legs, the sense that his body was separating from him, that soon he could discard it, a glimmer of promise that one day he would fall asleep forever.

Intellectually, he knew what was going on with him, what had gone on. He saw it as a headline in the Metro section of *The New York Times*.

ASHES OF YOUNG MAN DISCOVERED IN
UPPER WEST SIDE APARTMENT

Samuel McWilliams, 32, formerly of Washington, D.C., exploded yesterday in his New York City apartment. Mr. McWilliams, whose parents were killed in the bombing of the Espresso to Rome, June 11, 1974, has been undergoing the process of evolving into a human explosive for the last 20 years, most recently disguised as the writer of the now defunct Plum & Jaggers *television show, culminating successfully in yesterday's conflagration. His ashes have been distributed among his heirs, Charlotte, Oliver, and Julia McWilliams.*

Sometimes he could still amuse himself. Not often. Mostly his days were a desert, empty of thought, his mind traveling a long, redundant path leading back always to itself.

And then, on Thursday, August 10—later he marked the date—August 10, 1998—three days after the terrorist bombing of the American embassies in Kenya and Tanzania had filled the news on CNN with repeated scenes of death and horror and devastation—

something happened to Sam which changed the course of internal events as if his body were an actual war zone and the balance of power on the field had reversed.

On the tenth, the news of the bombings over, Sam, his eyes half closed, was lying as usual on his side on the futon watching the frames of up-to-the-minute news on CNN meander across the television screen. Suddenly he was astonished to see a still shot of Julia at eight or nine years old.

He sat up and turned on the sound.

The child pictured had a mass of curly hair, deep-set dark eyes, a broad forehead, an expression of trust.

She wasn't Julia.

Leah—he didn't get her last name—a small and perfect black-haired angel—was one of four children who had died in Tel Aviv that morning, when a bus carrying families out of the city for a day's holiday blew up, killing the children seated in the back of the bus.

In his mind's eye, he could see the four of them scrunched in the backseat of the bus, giggling in unison, whispering back and forth, the way children do when they are just far enough away from parents to feel at once a sense of freedom and safety.

"You children sit in the back and have a good time," their parents would have said to them, herding them down the bus aisle. "We'll be sitting just ahead."

And off they went to their holiday, maybe by the sea. The television report did not say where they had been going.

Julia. Leah. They were the same.

His heart leapt—he could feel it in his chest. And something like life, long absent from his company, came in a rush.

He got out of bed, pulled on his khakis, his socks and shoes, searched his closet for a starched shirt like the ones he'd always worn, the sleeves rolled up, the collar open. He got a glass of water. In the fridge, Charlotte had left applesauce and half a piece of herb chicken, which he ate. He needed nourishment. In the bathroom, he shaved for the first time in weeks, washing out the sink when he finished, forgetting the razor on the ledge. He packed his bookbag, filled a garbage bag with trash, threw out the dead flowers—Charlotte was always bringing flowers, sticking them in a vase on top of the television. He swept the floor of the apartment spotless, slung his bookbag over his shoulder, locked the door, and walked down the steps. At the newsstand on West Seventy-second Street and Columbus, he picked up a copy of *The New York Times* and walked in the direction of Central Park, light-headed, the blood warm against his skin.

REBECCA FRANKEL WAS AT HOME.

Sam stood in the hallway of her apartment building on West Seventy-first Street while the doorman called upstairs.

"Nine D," the doorman said. "You can go up." He indicated the elevator.

SAM'S HEAD WAS THROBBING. He was so thin his trousers, even with a belt, were hanging on his hips, his shirt like a hospital sheet around his shoulders, and in the lobby mirror—the first time in weeks he'd actually seen himself in the light of day—he had the impression of a cadaver. Nevertheless, in spite of his heart thumping against his shirt, so little flesh, he felt a promise of health.

He punched 9. When he stepped out of the elevator—running his fingers through his too-long hair, slipping his hands in his pockets, assuming, he hoped, an attitude of tentative confidence—Rebecca was waiting across the hall.

She was older than he'd imagined her. Plumper, wearing black slacks, wide in the hip, belted around her small waist, a black T-shirt with RANDOM in large white letters, her hair, in springy gray curls, piled up on her head, with pins sticking out like so many tiny birthday candles.

On second thought, he decided, she wasn't exactly old. There were the childlike dimples Noli had described, the dark, fiery eyes, high color in her cheeks, a liveliness about her. She had been pretty, surely, just as he'd imagined her. But he had also imagined her young. His age, his love.

"Hello," she said, putting out her hand, and as he reached to take it, she kissed him, wrapping her arms around his neck, kissing him firmly on both cheeks.

"Sam McWilliams." She shook his shoulders gently. "You need to eat."

IT WAS AS IF SHE'D BEEN EXPECTING HIM. There was chicken salad with walnuts and grapes, thin slices of red roast beef, and thick slices of rosemary bread with grainy mustard, small honeycakes dusted with powdered snow.

"I loved the last episode of *Plum & Jaggers* with the smoke bomb," she said, full of bright happiness in his company. "Bravo, I said to myself."

HE STAYED ALL DAY, talking and talking, filling in the missing lines from years of postcards, watching the sun move out of the rectangle of her east-facing window, arriving as sheltered light on the other side of her apartment, the shadows changing as they fell across him as if he were part of an Impressionist painting, a study in changing light.

Rebecca gave him tea and bread pudding, salted a roast, which she then put in the oven for dinner.

"Don't leave," she insisted. "Stay the night."

Staying the night was exactly what he'd had in mind that morning when he'd seen the frame of Julia become Leah, the fibrillators of desire recharging his heart, thinking of Rebecca as young.

And here to his great surprise, not disappointment, which is what he might have expected, but something sweeter, was Rebecca Frankel materialized as his mother, aging with Sam as Lucy Lucas

hadn't had the chance to do. And all along he'd been thinking of
Rebecca, like his mother, locked in a perfect, crystal moment of
youth, trapped in a bell jar beyond his reach.

"I don't think you ever met my daughter, Miriam, who was a baby
when you wrote me," Rebecca was saying.

Sam laughed.

"I never met *you*."

"I sometimes forget," Rebecca said. "We've been so close by postcard."

"I remember about your daughter. My grandmother saw her at
the theater once."

"She's started medical school at Tufts in Boston. I just got back
from taking her."

She produced pictures of Miriam and spread them out on a glass
coffee table. Miriam looked the way Sam had thought Rebecca
would look, but her expression was sharper than her mother's, her
features more angular, her presence bolder, combative. There were
a few pictures of Rebecca's husband and son, who had been killed,
pictures of West Jerusalem, of Miriam as an adult, standing at the
Wailing Wall.

"I went back," Rebecca was saying.

"To Jerusalem?" Sam asked.

She nodded. "I thought I never would, but last May, when Miriam
graduated from college, we did. We went to the school where they
died and just stood there outside the building in the play yard for the
longest time, and then we went to the apartment where we'd lived."
She put the pictures back in the box. "You should do that."

"Maybe," he said.

"When it happened, you were on your way to Rome?"

"We were. Connecting with the past. My father loved that word.
'Connecting.'" Sam said "connecting" with a Scottish accent, surprising himself with the familiar sound in his ear, as if only days ago
he'd listened to his father's voice.

Rebecca smiled. "Is that how he spoke?"

"As I remember, but I was only seven," Sam said.

"But your memory has perfect pitch," Rebecca said.

"I've never been to Rome," he said.

"No, I haven't either. I've actually not been anyplace since Saul was killed except that trip to Jerusalem with Miriam." She smiled. "Miriam has been to Rome," she said. "She's been every place. A regular vagabond."

It was late when he left Rebecca's apartment, wanting to stay, wishing to say something deeply personal to her equal to what they felt—what he knew she felt—for each other. But it was after dinner; he had had too much wine, too much food after long abstinence, and was woozy in the head, without a plan for where he would spend the night. He didn't want to go to the apartment on West Seventy-second Street where he'd been living with the memory of death, and he wouldn't go home to his family.

As far as his family knew, and this was what Sam intended, he had disappeared without a trace. If they wanted to find him, they would have to follow.

HE WENT TO PENN STATION by subway. When he arrived, it was 10:30 by the clock over the information booth and the next train to Boston left at 6:58 in the morning, so he purchased a one-way ticket, found a bench in the passenger waiting section, and slept off and on, more than he had slept in three months, comforted by the company of strangers. Once after midnight, when he had been wakened by a homeless woman requesting money for coffee, he called the apartment on West Eleventh Street, but when Julia answered at the first ring, he hung up—pleased that she must have been sitting right by the telephone, at the kitchen counter perhaps, Charlotte and Oliver in the living room, still awake after midnight, worrying about him.

THE SMELL OF COFFEE BREWING woke him before dawn with a kind of gnawing hunger, and he noticed a boy seated across from him, probably fifteen or sixteen, staring at Sam unembarrassed.

"Hi," the boy said.

"Hi," Sam replied.

"Are you Plum and Jaggers?" the boy asked, leaning across the aisle.

"I wrote *Plum & Jaggers*," Sam said.

The boy smiled broadly.

"So in real life you talk," he said.

"Sometimes I do," Sam said.

"When the show stopped being on TV, I thought you might be dead," the boy said.

"Well, I'm not dead," Sam said.

"I'm very glad of that." The boy got up, stood for a moment looking at Sam as if he wished to commit him to memory, and then wandered off in the direction of the trains.

Sam arrived in Boston at noon on the eleventh of August and went directly to the medical school at Tufts University, where he was given Miriam Frankel's address on Beacon Street.

WHEN REBECCA FRANKEL CALLED on the afternoon of August 13, Charlotte had just returned from Sam's apartment to check if he had possibly been back, although the super had told them he'd be glad to keep an eye out.

"It's good for us to walk around Sam's neighborhood, just in case," Oliver said.

"In case what?" Julia was short-tempered, angry at herself.

"He could be wandering the neighborhood."

"I don't think so," Julia said. "He isn't in New York. You said so yourself." She turned to Charlotte.

"So what did you see?" she asked.

"Nothing," Charlotte said. "Nothing, nothing, nothing."

"Don't say 'nothing,' " Julia said, pacing the apartment, wringing her hands. "I hate that word."

"Cut it out, Julia." Oliver put his arm over his eyes so he didn't have to watch her. "This isn't a hospital waiting room. Take a tranquillizer."

"Leave her alone." Charlotte had picked up *Persuasion* and was sitting on the kitchen counter, but she didn't have the patience to read.

In the four days since Sam had disappeared, they had become irritable with one another. No one slept, even Charlotte, who counted on sleep as her defense against the uninvented world. They didn't shop for groceries, ordering in chips instead and soft drinks, Oreo cookies, gallons of lemonade. They lay around the living room waiting for the phone, afraid to leave in case they'd miss a call, afraid to separate, too restless to stay.

"We have to have a plan," Oliver said.

HE'D TALKED ABOUT MAKING A PLAN often, a sensible list of alternatives—one of them could go to Grand Rapids, another to Washington—but none of them could think of a reasonable plan worth leaving the apartment for.

When the phone rang, they jumped—each time it rang, they jumped. But this time Julia, pacing by the kitchen, was closest and picked it up.

"This is Rebecca Frankel." The voice was soft and crisp. "I'm a friend of Sam's."

"Oh yes, I know. We know. We know all about you," Julia said.

"And I know about you."

Julia covered the receiver. "It's Rebecca Frankel."

"I just returned to work today and found a note at my office from your brother Oliver," Rebecca said.

"Thank God, you called. We've been hoping you would." Julia told her about Sam.

"I don't know very much," Rebecca said. "But I did see him."

She told Julia what she knew. Sam had come by and spent the afternoon and evening—that would have been the day he disappeared.

Monday, August 10, she said. He didn't seem entirely well. He was shaky and certainly too thin, but his mind was sharp. He ate, she added. He ate almost three meals in the short time he was there, as if he hadn't eaten for weeks.

"You'll think this is crazy, but did he seem as if he might be dying?" Julia asked. "That's what we've been worried about."

There was a long pause.

"When a person is ill, his pupils often become opaque." Her voice was thoughtful. "You know that."

"I didn't know that," Julia said. "Were his eyes opaque?"

"No, they weren't opaque, but they were clouded," she said. "I noticed that."

"Clouded?"

"Milky. I wouldn't worry about it," Rebecca said.

"So what did she say?" Oliver asked when Julia had hung up the telephone.

"She says Sam's ill." Julia dropped to the floor and buried her face in her hands. "She says his eyes are opaque, and how can she know what his eyes look like up close? Tell me that."

"Shut up, Julia." Oliver put a couch pillow over his face.

"What did she actually say?" Charlotte asked.

"I told you," Julia said. "She said he ate and talked and seemed okay except for his cloudy eyes."

The telephone rang and Charlotte picked up. It was Rebecca again. She was afraid that she had given the wrong impression.

"I had no idea Sam had disappeared until just now when I spoke with you," she said. "When he came over to see me, I assumed of course that he had come from your apartment. I even mailed a postcard there for him the day before yesterday. I had no idea that things were as bad as you've described them."

"They've been very bad," Charlotte said. "He doesn't speak to us at all."

There was a long, soft silence, as if Rebecca were arranging the tone of her voice for absolute kindness.

"He was better than that when I saw him. He talked a lot."

She asked them to keep in touch.

"We should check the mail to see if her postcard has come," Julia said, and followed Oliver downstairs to the mailboxes.

The mailbox was, as usual, full. They got mail, often harassing letters forwarded from NBC.

"Don't expect fan mail," Jacob said. "The fans don't write unless you're on a winning team."

There were bills and letters for *Plum & Jaggers*, an announcement of summer sales at local shops, a letter written in the slanted, curly printing of an older woman postmarked Grand Rapids, and the postcard from Rebecca.

Dear S,
I cannot tell you how wonderful it was to finally see you in the flesh. Miriam's address—did you ask for it or is that my imagination?—is 420 Beacon Street, apt. 403, Boston, Ma. 02115. The summer has been awful for terrorism. We didn't even talk about the embassies. Come again soon. R.

At the bottom, she had drawn a long, skinny heart.

"Think about it," Julia said, sitting on the edge of the couch. "There he was, lying on that stupid futon, with his opaque eyes looking at the mute TV and then he sees—he must have seen—every terrible picture of the bombings in Africa."

"And then he probably saw the picture of you," Charlotte said, leaning on the counter next to the telephone.

"Her name was Leah," Julia said.

"You know what I mean," Charlotte said. "Rebecca Frankel told you his eyes were cloudy."

THE AIR in the apartment was still, rancid with the heat, the odor of aging produce, the sickly sweet smell of mice, and exhaust from the traffic floating in the open windows.

Oliver stood at the window overlooking Eleventh Street, his forehead against the glass, watching the slow-moving scene on the street below.

"I think I have a plan," he said finally, opening a bag of chips. "So listen."

TWICE SAM HAD SEEN HER FROM A DISTANCE, once coming out of her apartment on Beacon Street the first day he arrived in Boston and the second time that evening at a café downtown, sitting at an outside table. She was alone.

But at the time something had stopped him from going over to speak to her, a kind of physical paralysis, his legs limp, the old familiar breathlessness. Leaning against a building, he waited for the blood to travel to his extremities again, and by then the opportunity had passed.

So she came up to him.

He was sitting in the same café where he'd seen her the day before, reading the personals from the *Globe*, wishing he had a notebook, even though there was nothing he had to say in it. His head was down, so he didn't see her until she had slipped into the wrought-iron chair across from him and said, "Aren't you Sam McWilliams?"

"Yes," he said with some hesitation, uncertain whether he wanted to be or not.

"In hiding, right?" She put her chin on her fists and smiled at him. "I think you know my mother, Rebecca Frankel."

She looked exactly as he'd thought she would, a mass of black curly hair pushed behind her ears, dark lidded eyes, high cheekbones, full lips, a tiny mole or birthmark in the place where her mother's dimple was.

"I'm Miriam." She ordered ice cream from the waitress, doubledip vanilla swirl and butterscotch.

"I know about you," he said, hoping to sound surprised but not too enthusiastic, hoping his voice wouldn't tremble.

"I felt terrible about *Plum & Jaggers*," Miriam said, taking a packet of sugar from the bowl, emptying it in her hand, licking the palm. "Energy," she said. "I want you to know I think you're an amazing writer."

They talked. Mainly Miriam talked at first about going to medical school and how her choice to be a doctor probably had something to do with the deaths of her father and brother, but who could have saved them, certainly not a doctor. She told him about the trip she had taken with her mother to Jerusalem in the summer and how strange it was to be in the place where her family had died.

"Don't ask me how I felt," she said. "That's what everybody has asked me and I don't know yet."

She put her hand on top of his in a gesture not romantic, maternal perhaps, and Sam suddenly felt something like tears simmering. Tears. It almost made him laugh out loud. He couldn't recall that particular feeling of arriving tears once in his whole life, not even as boy.

"I got this for you," she said when the ice cream she'd ordered arrived. She stuck her spoon in the butterscotch ball and reached across the table, putting the spoon to his lips.

"Eat, eat," she said, laughing, and he took the spoon from her.

"Where is the place your parents died?" she asked.

"South of Florence," he said. "It's a small place, not even a town, on the side of a hill near Orvieto."

"And you've been back there?"

"Never," he said.

"You should go."

"That's what your mother told me," he said, finishing his ice cream, and he was just about to ask her to go someplace, to a movie or a park or her apartment, when she picked up her backpack, weighted with books, leaned over, and kissed his cheek.

"I'm so happy we've met."

She wrote her telephone number on a napkin. "Are you here for long?"

"Maybe," Sam said. "I haven't decided."

"If you stay, I hope you'll call."

He watched her walk down the street, past the cafés and shops, her pale yellow dress lifting in the light wind, her black hair striped silver from the sun. And when she'd disappeared around the corner, he paid the bill and hailed a taxi for Logan Airport.

As it turned out, there were two seats in coach on the 7 p.m. Delta flight to Milan. Round trip was less expensive, so he chose at random the morning of September 16 as the return date, paid full fare, and was asleep before takeoff from Boston. His plan was to take the same trip they had taken with James and Lucy, by train from Milan to Orvieto.

"Holiday," he gave as the purpose of his visit to the officer checking passports at Malpensa Airport in Milan. "Holiday," from holy day.

On the train, he'd looked the word up in the tiny dictionary he carried—looked up "holy" from the Old English *hal* or *hole*. Holiday was the right definition for this voyage or excursion, this odyssey, he thought, traveling to Orvieto.

He had read about Orvieto in *The Rough Guide: Italy*, at the edge of Umbria, east of the Tiber, rising high above the valley as if it were a city hanging from the sky. The description was familiar to Sam's childhood memory of his first sight of Orvieto from the train, so when the the city filled the window next to where he was sitting, the breath went out of him.

The conductor stepped outside of the train ahead of Sam.

"Orvieto?" he asked.

Sam nodded.

"American." This seemed to please the conductor, a small, rigid man, maybe in his early fifties, with sun-washed hair the color of sand, deep watery blue eyes, a long sad face, although he was smiling.

"Okay, okay," he said, climbing back aboard, waving to the engineer.

It was three in the afternoon. Hot and dry, an oven wind blowing from the south. Sam walked to the end of the platform in the direction the train had gone, headed to Rome, looking out over the yellow fields scattered with squat, craggy olive trees.

The station was a squarish stone structure, the building empty except for a young man in blue jeans stretched out on his back on the flat bed of a baggage cart, his cap pulled over his eyes, his legs crossed at the ankle. He showed no sign of interest in company until Sam started to walk in his direction. Then he pushed his cap back on his head and sat up on his elbow.

"Taxi?"

"No taxi," Sam said.

"Funicular?"

Sam shook his head.

"American," the man said with some disappointment, pulling the cap back down over his eyes.

Sam planned to walk.

The Danesi house must have been located in the hills overlooking the train tracks, hilly but not hilly enough to take the funicular. The McWilliamses had walked up a hill to the house, but it wasn't terribly high or Sam would have remembered.

He walked over to the baggage cart.

"Danesi?" he asked.

The young man lifted his cap, his eyes squinting into glittering sunlight, which slipped under the roof of the station.

"Danesi," he said, raising his hands in a gesture of what-can-I-say? "Danesi here. Danesi there. Many Danesi in Orvieto."

Sam leaned against the cart. He had the young man's attention now. He had sat up and was swinging his legs over the sides, pointing to himself in an exaggerated gesture.

"Danesi," he said proudly. "I am Antonio Danesi."

"Do you know Gió?" Sam asked.

Antonio Danesi looked at Sam, cocking his head, folding his arms across his chest. He was small and young and handsome, and Sam could tell from the sweet smell of liquor on the hot wind that he was also a little drunk.

"Gió." The young man pursed his lips, nodding his head north, in the direction of Florence. "Gió Danesi."

Antonio walked around the side of the station, motioning for Sam to follow. "You come with me, Mr. American," he said, laughing.

There was a narrow cobblestone path through the low brush at the front of the station which led up a hill directly in front of them. The hills surrounding the station were brown and rounded like anthills, the brush dry, low to the ground, clustered with brilliant scarlet desert flowers. Antonio had taken a cigarette and offered it to Sam, who took a drag, not inhaling, but pleased to have the company of Antonio, a shared cigarette, the heavy, sweet smell of Italian tobacco, the odor of a burning bush in the unforgiving heat.

The path, marked by an occasional crucifix or a painted replica of the benevolent Virgin Mary set behind glass and nailed to a tree, was not an easy walking path, winding, steep, the stones unevenly placed, the ground dusty. At the top of the first anthill, Antonio stopped, spread out his arms, and pointed to a small cluster of buildings scattered on the next hill. Tiny colored houses ran up the side of the hill, a toy village, a sprinkling of trees and yellow flowers. Beyond, the funicular looming above him crawled up the hill to Orvieto.

GIÓ DANESI STOOD BEHIND THE BAR at a small trattoria on the edge of town, his back to them, making coffee. He was surprisingly tall—that was Sam's first impression—and striking in his darkness, wearing a white starched shirt with the sleeves rolled up, black trousers, his hair long, over his collar and straight, a demeanor of gentle repose.

"Gió," the young man said.

Gió turned toward them, smiling at Antonio, passing the cup of coffee to an elderly woman with her marketing in a string bag, a black shawl loose around her shoulders. She looked over at Sam suspiciously.

"American?" she asked.

Sam smiled and nodded.

"Gió," Antonio said, a kind of bark in his voice. He pointed to Sam. "Your friend."

Gió came from behind the counter. "My friend?" he asked.

"Do you speak English?" Sam asked.

Gió gave a shake of his shoulders. "A little bit," he said.

Sam was breathless with excitement. "I'm Sam McWilliams," he said.

"Yes," Gió said patiently.

"When I was a little boy, I came to your house after an accident."

"Accident?" Gió asked. "Accident. Yes?"

"There was a bomb."

"A bomb."

"A bomb," the elderly woman said, pleased to join the conversation, clapping her hands together, making a hard flat sound. "Like that. Bomb."

Gió looked at Sam, his face changing. He was taller than Sam, even leaning with his back against the counter, his brow wrinkled, a hand across his lips.

"Bomb," he said, his eyes narrowing in thought. "In the train. I know." His face took on a sudden dark intensity. "The American boy."

And then he caught his breath, his eyes softening, flooding with tears. He grabbed Sam in his arms and kissed him on the head and turning to the elderly woman, he raised his hands in a gesture of despair, his head shaking back and forth as if the full force of the explosion in Orvieto had finally come to him in the presence of Sam as a young man.

THE HOUSE WAS THE SAME—a sand-colored stucco cottage washed in white light, at the top of a long, dusty road. Sam remembered the road—not the walk up to the house, but the drive down in Mr. Blake's long American car, Gió at the bottom of the hill standing in a field of sunflowers, his palms over his eyes.

SUSANNA, SMALLER THAN HE HAD IMAGINED her, whirled through the house on her short, plump chair legs with dishes and glasses and pots of tomato sauce and thick crusty rosemary bread with olive oil and anchovies, oregano from the garden outside the window, bottles of red wine. She spoke very little English, and moved too quickly, in any case, to speak directly even to Gió, but the music of Italian was swimming through the hot, claustrophobic air. Somehow by noon the long table was set, glasses of wildflowers winding down the center, and a banquet of people, mostly young, Sam's age, several children, streamed through the front door, filling the small cottage to its full measure of space.

Sam stood at the door with Gió.

"This is my brother Filippo," Gió said, and there was Filippo and his shy wife, Marisa, a baby in each arm, kissing Sam on both cheeks.

"My sister Beatrice," Gió said.

Beatrice, younger than Sam, with lovely thick brown lips and sun-colored cheeks, took his hand and kissed the fingers.

"My sister Patrizia speaks good English," Gió said. Patrizia had come from Florence, taking off work for the afternoon to see Sam McWilliams, the bad dream of their childhood, rise from the dead of memory.

"We are so happy you remember us," Patrizia said.

She turned to her mother, saying, "He remember us, Mamma."

And Susanna passed a glass of wine to Sam, raised her hands in the air, throwing kisses to the sky.

"Remember, remember," she repeated in English.

AT DINNER he told them about his life with Charlotte and Oliver and Julia, with his grandfather and Noli. He told them about Plum & Jaggers, how the stories had come from his parents' deaths, about his childhood collecting stories of terrorism, and about Rebecca Frankel. They listened, Patrizia translating, sometimes with laughter and tears, their eyes fixed on Sam as if he were some kind of miracle.

"The other children will come to Orvieto?" Filippo asked. "The girl, the boy, the baby girl." He smiled. "See, I remember."

"Not now," Sam said.

"They must come," Gió said.

"Maybe," Sam said. "Maybe they will."

He had called them from Boston before he left and then from Milan, but the answering machine was on, the message the same, Oliver's crisp voice: "Please leave your name and number and we'll return your call."

Perhaps they had gone to Grand Rapids or Washington or to the farm.

But even if they had answered, he had no plans to speak with them. He'd hang up when he heard one of them say "Hello." They would know it was him.

AFTER LUNCH, Sam slept. The room where Susanna put him was very small, with white walls and a starched white spread, a blue-and-white Della Robbia Virgin in a circle of colored fruit over the cot, the shutters closed against the heat.

Day fell into night without his stirring, and when he did get up, his head swirling with the wine, the taste of garlic thick in his crusty mouth, it was dark outside.

Gió was at the kitchen table drinking an espresso, his chin resting in his hand.

"I was drunk," Sam said.

"Very drunk." Gió laughed. "It's good."

"Not so good for me." Sam sat in a chair across from Gió, running his hands through his hair. On the table, a red ceramic bowl was filled with small yellow cakes and he took one and then another.

"What time is it?" he asked.

Gió held up five fingers.

"Five in the morning? What are you doing up?"

Gió smiled.

"I watch out for you," he said.

For a long time they sat in a comfortable silence, watching the flat lemon sun come over the horizon, obscuring the details of the landscape.

"I go to work soon," Gió said.

"I'll come with you."

"To work?"

"Is there work for me to do?"

"Work?" Gió laughed hard. "Scrubbing, washing dishes, taking garbage. Not good work for you."

"I'll do it," Sam said.

"You stay here, then?" Gió asked, taking Sam's head in an arm grip, tousling his hair, giving his chin a gentle box. "Good. You stay here. This is your new home."

SAM HAD FALLEN into an agreeable pattern so familiar it was difficult for him to remember what his life had been like with Plum & Jaggers, as if he were beginning again as a child to whom nothing has happened but a simple repetitive life of dependency and pleasure. He loved his room in the Danesi house, getting up at dawn, making his bed, pressing the crisp white coverlet with his hands until the wrinkles were gone. And then he'd stand in the doorway to admire the purity of the place where he had slept. Nothing on the walls but the blue-and-white ceramic Virgin, a tangerine rag rug on the tile floor.

At the trattoria, he washed dishes in water so hot his hands turned bright red—mustard-yellow dinner plates, olive-green dishes for antipasto, tiny white espresso cups. It gave him aesthetic satisfaction to watch the stack of dishes, the colors of the earth, fill up at the end of the day, waiting for the next.

AT NIGHT he wrote postcards to Miriam Frankel, love letters he wouldn't send, accumulating at the bottom of his bookbag.

Dear Miriam, he wrote on the first postcard, a picture of the Piazza XXIX Marzo in Orvieto. *Thank you in particular for the ice cream. I had no idea I'd be so fond of butterscotch. Yours, Sam McWilliams*

When he thought of her, which he often did, he saw her lovely face half covered with shiny black curls. She was licking the sugar from her palm.

SHORTLY AFTER HE ARRIVED in Orvieto, he had called his grandfather in Grand Rapids, hoping in fact for news of his siblings.

"It's Sam," he said when his grandfather failed to recognize his voice. "We must have a bad connection."

But it wasn't the connection.

"I don't know Sam," William said in a thin voice with an unfamiliar edge of impatience. "You must have gotten the wrong number."

ONE EVENING after work at the trattoria, still light although quite late, the sun crouching in the corner of the village, Sam asked Gió to show him where the lunch car had exploded.

"You really want to see?" Gió was hesitant.

"Why do you ask?" Sam said. "Is it something I shouldn't see?"

Gió shook his head.

"Nothing is there," he said.

THE TRAIN TRACKS came closest to the village in the hills below Orvieto to the north, and it was there at a bend of track headed toward the station that the event had happened.

Sam and Gió walked off the hilly path which they took every day back and forth from the trattoria to the Danesis' house, across a field with low brush and lavender wildflowers, to the bend in the tracks.

"There," Gió said. "The train stopped there."

"And where were we?" Sam asked. "The children."

"Here," Gió said. "Where you are standing."

They were halfway between the tracks and the cluster of small farms, including the Danesi's above them, although Orvieto itself was no longer visible, and so it seemed as if nothing were there, certainly no sound but the sounds of birds, the crackling of dry grass, nothing but train tracks and open field.

Sam folded his arms across his chest.

"You see," Gió said apologetically. "Nothing is here."

"It happened a long time ago," Sam said quietly.

"Yes, a long time," Gió said, but he seemed unhappy that there was no evidence.

THE NEXT MORNING there was a dust storm. Italy had gone weeks without rain, a heat wave out of northern Africa. The vegetation everywhere was struggling for life.

Sam woke up at dawn, a roaring wind filling his perfect room with dark brown sand. He had slept poorly, with bad dreams he couldn't remember, and wakened with an articulated question for Gió, who was sitting with his parents at the long wooden table, already awake and eating when Sam came into the kitchen.

He poured himself a small cup of ink-black coffee and sat down next to Gió.

What he wanted to know was where the bodies from the explosion had been placed. Surely the people who died must have been somewhere on that hill, moved there by the medics before they were taken to a mortuary. Sam knew that his parents' bodies had traveled on the plane with them from Florence to Brussels to New York—his grandfather had promised Charlotte—that they were buried in East Grand Rapids Memorial Cemetery, where he'd been only once, and that was before they had moved to Washington. Maybe there had been a funeral, but if so, Sam had not attended it. And he had never asked questions, protecting his grandparents from a conversation they didn't wish to have.

GIÓ TURNED TO HIS MOTHER, speaking to her in Italian.

"You really want to see?" he asked Sam after his mother had spoken. "Mama kept the newspapers."

Sam studied the front page of the *Corriere della Sera* for June 12, a large picture of the wrecked train—and on the jump, page 5, two other pictures faded yellow, one of a medic on his haunches next to a line of swaddled bodies, lying side by side along the bend in the track. The other of a boy, not Sam—he checked carefully—sitting on the hill, his head resting on his knees, his arms over his head, as if he were expecting a second disaster.

HE LEFT FOR WORK at the trattoria later than Gió, after the wind had subsided, only tiny tornados of sand stinging his bare ankles as he walked down the winding path away from town, turning right across the circumference of the hill above the bend in the track where his parents had died. In the distance, he heard the sad wail of a train whistle, maybe the same one he had taken from Milan.

When he sat in the place where he might have been sitting when the Danesis found them, the wind had picked up slightly, and in the open field, he could no longer hear the train's whistle, only a tintinnabulation in his ears.

For a long time he sat staring straight ahead. Nothing but the long ribbon of black tracks and yellow-brown fields—above him Orvieto was concealed by the configuration of hills. Alone, at a place he'd never imagined he would actually see, a kind of wild abandon came over him. He stretched out on the dry grass, brittle enough to cut into his skin like tiny needles, and lying on his back, his eyes closed in the sunlight, he began to roll.

THE HILL wasn't at its steepest where he was rolling, but was steep enough for his body to gain momentum—over and over he turned, his arms drawn up against his chest, his legs tightly crossed at the ankles, a rectangle of brilliant blue sky and then a square of hard brown earth, dust in his nose, in his eyes, his face littered with tiny scratches, faster and faster, until his brain was scrambled. And then he rolled to a stop.

What the engineer must have seen was an object coming toward the train just after he had begun to apply the brakes in his approach to Orvieto. Some of the people on the left side of the train saw something rolling toward them as well, and braced themselves for an impact.

The train slowed down to about fifty miles an hour as it passed Sam, lying ten, maybe fifteen yards from the bend in the track, his hands over his ears little protection against the deafening sound. All of this happened in a matter of seconds.

It didn't occur to Sam until later that he might not have stopped before he reached the tracks. There'd been no way to know in advance that the terrain flattened yards from the bend. Nor had he anticipated the possibility of danger. It was as though he were just a boy, wonderfully invincible, rolling down a hill, trusting the force of gravity.

WHEN THE TRAIN HAD GONE, leaving in its wake a virtual hurricane of dust, Sam rolled in the dirt, rubbing his back and shoulders into the earth near the place he had seen in the photograph in the *Corriere della Sera*.

He finally stood up and headed back toward the winding path to the trattoria, and he was covered, his hair matted, his eyes crusted, his face splotched, with the reddish soil of Orvieto.

By the time he got to the path, the air had cleared, opening to a high piercing blue sky, the scrubby taupe landscape articulate as far as he could see.

He heard voices ahead, perhaps around the next bend, where a broad-faced Italian replica of the Virgin painted on wood was hammered to an olive tree, or below, where the ground leveled and the walking on cobblestones was particularly difficult. Sam suddenly wondered how he might appear to a stranger. He reached out his arms to check, pleased to see the dust he had rolled in had mixed with his sweat from the terrific morning heat and was adhering to his skin like clay, baking there to a thin protective coating, glossed ceramic, burnt umber, the color of the Renaissance.

Sam could hear their high-spirited conversation, not actual words, but the tone of them, and as the words clarified in the bone-dry air, the language he heard was not Italian.

HE STOPPED, absolutely still, held his breath so he wouldn't have to hear his own breathing, wrapped his arms around himself, and listened, above the harmonica sounds of the light wind, the crabby bird talk in the brush.

What he heard coming toward him on the footpath were words spoken in his own language.

ON THE TRAIN TO ROME, they sat in facing seats. Julia pressed against Sam's shoulder could not stop weeping. An elderly Italian woman seated across the aisle from them leaned over, dropping a linen handkerchief in Julia's lap.

"Keep, keep," she said.

THEY HAD BEEN WITH THE DANESIS for three days, eating and drinking and talking, sleeping together in the same large room in which they had slept when they were little, stretched out on mattresses on the tile floor, talking into the night.

"How did you know where I was?" Sam asked from his cot, lying in darkness lit by a sky scattered with stars, a slender moon dipping into the corner of the window, a brushstroke of pale silver.

On the day Rebecca Frankel had called, the day her postcard had arrived with Miriam's address in Boston, they knew how to find him. But that night William had had a stroke, so they went first to Grand Rapids.

"His memory is completely gone," Charlotte said.

"I know," Sam said. "I spoke with him."

"Except for Noli," Julia said. "He remembers her."

THEY HAD STAYED almost a week to settle their grandfather, and then Oliver had called Miriam Frankel, whose number they got on the postcard. Miriam had suggested Orvieto.

Detective Howell, checking the passenger lists from Boston to Milan, found Sam's name on a Delta Airlines flight August 12.

THE DANESI HOUSE was full of food, lunch stretching into supper, the brilliant sun giving way to dusk, shimmering candles on the long table, all the places taken by people from the village, and the Danesi family coming to take a look at the McWilliamses in the spirit of a funeral or a wedding, a celebration without the ceremony.

On the first night, with maybe thirty people in the house drinking red wine, Gió asked Sam to do a scene from *Plum & Jaggers*.

"Just to show how you make laughing in America," he said.

"In English?" Sam asked.

"What difference?" Gió said. "Laughing is laughing, yes?"

"I don't think we can," Sam said, and he grabbed Gió around the shoulders, kissed his cheek. "We are already laughing here."

ON FRIDAY, August 21, the Danesi family walked down the hill with the McWilliamses from their house to the station at Orvieto to meet the noon train to Rome. They arrived just as the sandy-haired conductor stepped off the train—the same one who had been on Sam's train from Milan. Susanna gripped the conductor's hand, speaking in rapid Italian, her arms spread, circling the McWilliamses.

"Mamma's telling him about you," Gió said.

The conductor reached over and took both of Sam's hands in his. And then Charlotte's and Oliver's and Julia's.

"He grew up in the next village," Gió translated for them. "He remembers."

AS THE TRAIN PULLED OUT of the station, the Danesis lined the platform, an army of them in the bright noon sun, waving and waving, their eyes following the moving train, their mouths like so many sparrows open in song, calling "*Ciao, ciao, ciao.*"

THE TRAIN TO ROME stopped at every small town, winding through the arid farmland, the groves of olive trees, almost prehistoric, black branches like craggy arms reaching to sky, rolling brown hills, splashed with small clusters of terra cotta houses. During the trip, as frames of Italian villages whipped by too quickly for definition, the McWilliamses were silent, staring out the window as if words between them could be lost in translation.

The city of Rome began long before the train pulled into Termini station as the farmland sprinkled with cottages gave way at the northern edge of the city to rows of houses and then apartment blocks, the shutters closed, the flowers in the window boxes drooping, laundry strung over the open spaces flapping in a light wind.

"Roma," the conductor shouted from the other end of the car. "Roma, Roma," his voice swinging to a high note.

THE MCWILLIAMSES STOOD then, opening the top section of the window beside their seats, sticking their heads out.

A sudden burst of hot air took their breath. A shaft of brilliant light obliterated the view, and for a single moment, they seemed to be spun out of sunlight, woven with the same shimmering threads.

"Roma, Roma," the conductor was saying as he made his way through the train. And passing the McWilliamses, washed in glorious light, their arms flung around one another, he lowered his voice, and speaking in their direction, he called out, "Station stop, Rome."